19
LOVE
SONGS

Also by David Levithan

19
LOVE
SONGS

DAVID
LEVITHAN

Alfred A. Knopf
New York

To Mayling and Lynda,
there at the start

and

To my parents,
there long before the start

THIS IS A BORZOI BOOK PUBLISHED BY ALFRED A. KNOPF

Text copyright © 2020 by David Levithan
Jacket art copyright © 2020 by Darren Booth

All rights reserved. Published in the United States by Alfred A. Knopf,
an imprint of Random House Children's Books, a division of
Penguin Random House LLC, New York.

Knopf, Borzoi Books, and the colophon are registered trademarks of
Penguin Random House LLC.

Visit us on the Web! GetUnderlined.com

Educators and librarians, for a variety of teaching tools, visit us at
RHTeachersLibrarians.com

Library of Congress Cataloging-in-Publication Data is available upon request.
ISBN 978-1-9848-4863-5 (trade) — ISBN 978-1-9848-4864-2 (lib. bdg.) —
ISBN 978-1-9848-4865-9 (ebook)

Printed in the United States of America
January 2020
10 9 8 7 6 5 4 3 2 1

First Edition

Track List

TRACK ONE

Quiz Bowl Antichrist

I am haunted at times by Sung Kim's varsity jacket.

He had to lobby hard to get it. Nobody denied that he had talent—in fact, he was the star of our team. But for a member of our team to get a jacket was unprecedented. Our coach backed him completely, while the other coaches in the school nearly choked on their whistles when they first heard the plan. The principal had to be called in, and it wasn't until our team made Nationals that Sung's request was finally heeded. Four weeks before we left for Indianapolis, he became the first person in our school's history to have a varsity jacket for quiz bowl.

I, for one, was mortified.

This mortification was a complete betrayal of our team, but if anyone was going to betray the quiz bowl team from the inside, it was going to be me. I was the alternate.

I had been drafted by the coach, who also happened to be my physics teacher, because while the five other members of the team could tell you the square root of the circumference of Saturn's orbit around the sun in the year 2033, not a single one of them could tell you how many Brontë sisters there'd been. In fact, the only British writer they seemed familiar with was Monty Python—and there weren't many quiz bowl questions about Monty Python. There was a gaping hole

1

in their knowledge, and I was the best lit-boy plug the school had to offer. While I hadn't read that many of the classics, I was extraordinarily aware of them. I was a walking Cliffs-Notes version of the CliffsNotes versions; even if I'd never touched *Remembrance of Things Past* or *Cry, the Beloved Country* or *Middlemarch*, I knew what they were about and who had written them. I could only name about ten elements on the periodic table, but that hardly mattered—my teammates had the whole thing memorized. They told jokes where "her neutrino!" was the punch line.

Sung was our fearless leader—fearless, that is, within the context of our practices and competitions. Put him back into the general population and he became just another math geek, too bland to be teased, too awkward to be resented. As soon as he got the varsity jacket, there was little question that it would never leave his back. All the varsity jackets in our school looked the same on the fronts—burgundy body, white sleeves, white R. But the backs were different—a picture of two guys wrestling for the wrestlers, a football for the football players, a breaststroker for the swimmers. For quiz bowl, they initially chose a faceless white kid at a podium, probably a leftover design from another school's speech and debate team. It looked as if the symbol from the men's room door was giving an inaugural address. Sung didn't feel this conveyed the team aspect of quiz bowl, so he made them add four other faceless white kids at podiums. I was, presumably, one of those five. Because even though I was an alternate, they always rotated me in.

I had agreed to join the quiz bowl team for four reasons:
(1) I needed it for my college applications.
(2) I needed a good grade in Mr. Phillips's physics class for my college applications, and I wasn't going to get it from ordinary studying.

(3) I derived a perverse pleasure from being the only person in a competitive situation who knew that Jane Eyre was a character while Jane Austen was a writer.

(4) I had an unarticulated crush on Damien Bloom.

An unarticulated crush is very different from an unrequited one, because at least with an unrequited crush you know what the hell you're doing, even if the other person isn't doing it back. An unarticulated crush is harder to grapple with, because it's a crush that you haven't even admitted to yourself. The romantic forces are all there—you want to see him, you always notice him, you treat every word from him as if it weighs more than anyone else's. But you don't know why. You don't know that you're doing it. You'd follow him to the end of the earth without ever admitting that your feet were moving.

Damien was track-team popular and hung with the cross-country crowd. If he didn't have any problem with Sung's varsity jacket, it was probably because none of the other kids in our school defined him as a quiz bowl geek. If anything, his membership on the team was seen as a fluke. Whereas I, presumably, belonged there, along with Sung and Frances Oh (perfect SAT, tragic skin) and Wes Ward (250 IQ, 250 lbs) and Gordon White (calculator watch, matching glasses). My social status was about the same as that of a water fountain in the hall—people were happy enough I was there when they needed me, but they didn't particularly want to talk to me. I wish I could say I was fine with this, and that I found what I needed in books or food or drugs or quiz bowl or other water fountain kids. But it sucked. I didn't have the disposition to be slavishly devoted to popularity and the popular kids, but at the same time, I was pretty sure my friends were losers, and barely even friends.

When we won at States, Sung, Damien, Frances, Wes, and

Gordon celebrated like they'd just gotten full scholarships to MIT. Mr. Phillips was in tears when he called his wife to tell her. A photographer from the local paper came to school to take our picture a few days later, and I tried to hide behind the others as much as possible. Sung had his jacket by that time, its white sleeves glistening like they'd been made from unicorn horns. After the article appeared, a couple of people congratulated me in the hall. But most kids snickered or didn't care. We had a crash-course candy sale to pay for our trip to Indianapolis, and I stole money from my parents' wallets and dipped into my savings in order to buy my whole portion outright, shoving the crap candy bars in our basement instead of having to ask my fellow students to pony up.

Sung, of course, wanted us to get matching varsity jackets to wear to Nationals. Damien already had a varsity jacket for cross-country that he never wore, so he was out. Frances, Wes, and Gordon said they were using all their money on the tickets and other things for Indianapolis. I simply said no. And when Sung asked me if I was sure, I told him, "You can't possibly expect me to wear that." Everybody got quiet for a second, but Sung didn't seem fazed. He just launched us into yet another practice.

If there were four reasons that I'd joined the quiz bowl team, there were two reasons that I stayed on:

(1) I had an unarticulated crush on Damien Bloom.

(These things don't change.)

(2) I really, really liked defeating people.

Note: I am not saying *I really, really liked winning.* Winning is a more abstract concept, and in quiz bowl, winning usually meant having to come back in the next round and do it all again. No, I liked *defeating people.* I liked seeing the look on the other team's faces when I got a question they couldn't answer. I loved their geektastic disappointment when they realized they weren't good enough to rank up. I loved using trivia to make people doubt themselves. I never, ever missed a literature question—I was a fucking juggernaut of authors and oeuvres. And I never, ever attempted to answer any of the math, science, or history questions. Nobody expected me to. Thus, I would always win.

The hardest were the scrimmages, when we would split into teams of three and take each other on. I didn't have any problem answering the questions correctly—I just had to make sure not to gloat. The only thing keeping me in check was Damien. Around him, I wanted to be a good guy.

If I had any enthusiasm for Indianapolis, it was because I assumed Damien and I would be rooming together. I imagined us talking all night, bonding to the point of knowledge. I could see us laughing together about the quiz bowl kids from other states who were surrounding us in their quiz bowl varsity jackets. We'd smuggle in some beers, watch bad TV, and become so comfortable with each other that I would finally feel the world was comfortable, too. This was strictly a separate-beds fantasy . . . but it was a separate-from-the-world fantasy, too. That was what I wanted.

The closer we got to Indianapolis, the more I found myself looking forward to it, and the more Sung became a dictator. If I'd thought he was serious about quiz bowl before, he was beyond any frame of reference now. He wanted to practice every day after school for six hours—pizza was brought in—and even when he saw us in the halls, he threw questions our way. At first I tried to ignore him, but that only made him YELL HIS QUESTIONS IN A LOUD, OVERLY ARTICULATED VOICE. Now anyone within four hallways of our own could hear the guy in the quiz bowl varsity jacket shout, "WHO

WAS THE LAST AMERICAN NOVELIST TO WIN THE NOBEL PRIZE FOR LITERATURE?"

And I'd say, much lower, "James Patterson."

Sung would blanch and whisper, "Wrong."

"Toni Morrison," I'd correct. "I'm just playing with ya."

"That's not funny," he'd say. And I'd run for class.

It did, at least, give me a reason to talk to Damien at lunch. I accidentally-on-purpose ended up behind him on the cafeteria line.

"Is Sung driving you crazy, too?" I asked. "With his pop quizzes?"

Damien smiled. "Nah. It's just Sung being Sung. You've gotta respect that."

As far as I could tell, the only reason to respect that was because Damien was respecting it. Which, at that moment, was reason enough.

The afternoon hallway quizzing wore me down, though. Sung got increasingly angry as I was increasingly unable to give him a straight answer.

"WHAT WAS JANE AUSTEN'S LAST FINISHED NOVEL?"

"Vaginas and Virginity."

"WHO IS THE LAST PERSON IAGO KILLS IN *OTHELLO?*"

"His manservant Bastardio, for forgetting to change the Brita filter!"

"WHAT IS THE ENDING OF HANS CHRISTIAN ANDERSEN'S 'THE LITTLE MERMAID'?"

"She turns into a fish and marries Nemo!"

"Fuck you!"

These were remarkable words to hear coming from Sung's mouth.

He went on.

"Are you trying to sabotage us? Do you WANT to LOSE?"

The other kids in the hall were loving this—a full-blown quiz bowl spat.

"Are you breaking up with me?" I joked.

Sung turned bright, bright red.

"I'll see you at practice!" he managed to get out. Then he turned around and I could see the five quiz bowlers on the back of his jacket, their blank faces not-quite-glaring at me as he stormed away.

When I arrived ten minutes late to our final pre-Indianapolis practice, Mr. Phillips looked concerned, Damien looked indifferent, Sung looked flustered and angry, Frances looked flustered, Gordon looked angry, and Wes looked distracted by whatever game he was playing on his phone.

"Everyone needs to take this very seriously," Mr. Phillips pronounced.

"Because there are small, defenseless koalas who will be killed if we don't make the final four!" I added.

"Do you want to stay here?" Sung asked, looking like I'd just stuck a magnet in his hard drive. "Is that what this is about?"

"No," I said calmly, "I'm just joking. If you can't joke about quiz bowl, what can you joke about? It's like mime in that respect."

"C'mon, Alec," Damien said. "Sung just wants us to win."

"No," I said. "Sung *only* wants us to win. There's a difference."

Damien and the others looked at me blankly. This was not, I remembered, a word-choice crowd.

Still, Damien had gotten the message across: *Lay off.* So I did, for the rest of the practice. And I didn't get a single question wrong. I even could name four Pearl S. Buck books besides *The Good Earth*—which is the English-geek equivalent of knowing how to make an atomic bomb, in that it's both difficult and totally uncool.

And how was I rewarded for this display of extraneous knowledge? At the end of the practice, as we were leaving, Mr. Phillips offhandedly told us our room assignments. Sung would be the one who got to room with Damien. And I would have to share a room with Wes, who liked to watch *Lord of the Rings* battle scenes to prepare for competition.

On the way out, I swear Sung was gloating.

If it had been up to Sung, we would have had the cheerleading squad seeing us off at the airport. I could see it now:

Two-four-six-eight, how do mollusks procreate?

One-two-three-four, name the birthplace of Niels Bohr!

Then, before we left, as a special treat, Sung would calculate the mass and volume of their pom-poms. Each of the girls would dream of being the one to wear Sung's letter jacket when he came back home, because that would make her the most popular girl in the entire sch—

"Alec, we're boarding." Damien interrupted my sarcastic reverie. The karma gods had at least seated us next to each other on the plane. Unfortunately, they then swung around (as karma gods tend to do, the jerks) and made him fall asleep the moment after takeoff. It wasn't until we were well into our descent that he opened his eyes and looked at me.

"Nervous?" he asked.

"It hasn't even occurred to me to be nervous," I answered honestly. "I mean, we don't have to win for it to look good on our transcripts. I'm already concocting this story where I overcome a bad case of consumption, the disapproval of my parents, a terrifying history of crashing in small planes, and a twenty-four-hour speech impediment in order to com-

8

pete in this tournament. As long as you overcome adversity, they don't really care if you win. Unless it's, like, a real sport."

"Dude," he said, "you read way too much."

"But clearly you don't know your science enough to move across the aisle the minute I reveal my consumptive state."

"Oh," he said, leaning a little closer, "I can catch consumption just from sitting next to you?"

"Again," I said, not leaning away, "medicine is your area of expertise. In novels, you damn well can catch consumption from sitting next to someone. You were doomed from the moment you met me."

"I'll say."

I wasn't quick enough to keep the conversation going. Damien bent down to take an issue of *Men's Health* out of his bag. And he wasn't even reading it for the pictures.

I pretended to have a hacking cough for the remaining ten minutes of the flight. The other people around me were annoyed, but I could tell that Damien was amused. It was our joke now.

We were staying at the Westin in Indianapolis, home to the Heavenly™ Bed and the Heavenly™ Bath.

"How the hell can you trademark the word *heavenly*?" I asked Wes as we dumped out our stuff. We were only staying two nights, so it hardly seemed necessary to hang anything up.

"I dunno," he answered.

"And what's up with the Heavenly™ Bath? Am I really going to have to take showers in heaven? It hardly seems worth the trouble of being good now if you're going to have to wear deodorant in the afterlife."

"I wouldn't know," Wes said, making an even stack on the bedside table of all the comics he'd brought.

"What, you've never been dead?"

He sighed.

"It's time to meet the team," he said.

Before we left, he made sure every single light in the room was off.

He even unplugged the clock.

The competition didn't start until the next morning, so the evening was devoted to the Quiz Bowl Social.

"Having a social at a quiz bowl tournament is like having all-you-can-eat ribs and inviting a bunch of vegetarians over," I told Damien as the rest of us waited for Sung and Mr. Phillips to come down to the lobby.

"I'm sure there are some cool kids here," he said.

"Yeah. And they're all back in their rooms, drinking."

Some people had dressed up for the social—meaning that some girls had worn dresses and some boys had worn ties, although none of them could muster enough strength to also wear jackets. Unless, of course, it was a varsity quiz bowl jacket. I saw at least five of them in the lobby.

"Hey, Sung, you're not so unique anymore," I pointed out when he finally showed up, his own jacket looking newly polished.

"I don't need to be unique," he scoffed. "I just need to win."

I pretended to wave a tiny flag. "Go, team."

"Alright, guys," Gordon said. "Are we ready to rumble?"

I thought he was kidding, but I wasn't entirely sure. I looked at our group—Sung's hair was plastered into perfect place, Frances had put on some makeup, Gordon was wearing bright red socks that had nothing to do with anything else he was wearing, Damien looked casually handsome, and Wes looked like he wanted to be back in our room, reading *Y: The Last Man*.

"Let's rumble!" Mr. Phillips chimed in, a little too enthusiastically for someone over the age of eleven.

"Our first match is against the team from North Dakota," Sung reminded us. "If you meet them, scope out their intelligences."

"If we see them on the dance floor, I'll be sure to mosey over and ask them to quote Virginia Woolf," I assured him. "That should strike fear into their hearts."

The social was in one of the Westin's ballrooms. There was a semi-big dance floor at the center, which nobody was coming close to. The punch was as unspiked as the haircuts, the lights dim to hide everyone's embarrassment.

"Wow," I said to Damien as we walked in and scoped it out. "This is *hot*."

Damien had such a look of social distress on his face, I almost laughed. I could imagine him reassuring himself that none of his other friends from home were ever going to see this.

"The adults are worse than the kids," Wes observed from over my shoulder.

"You're right," I said. Because while the quiz bowlers were mawkish and awkward, the faculty advisors were downright weird, wearing their best suits from 1980 and beaming like they'd finally gone from zeros to heroes in their own massively revised high school years.

Out of either cruelty or obliviousness (probably the former), the DJ decided to unpack Gwen Stefani's "Hollaback Girl." A lot of the quiz bowlers looked like they were hearing it for the first time. From the moment the beat started, it was only a question of whose resolve would dissolve first. Would the team captain from Montana start break dancing? Would the alternate from Connecticut let down her hair and flail it around?

In the end, it was a whole squad that took the floor. As a group, they started to bust out the moves—something I could never imagine our team doing. They laughed at themselves while they danced, and it was clear they were having a good time. Other kids started to join them. Even Sung, Frances, and Gordon plunged in.

"Check it out," Wes mumbled.

Gordon was doing a strut that looked like something he'd practiced at home; I had no doubt it went over better in his bedroom mirror than it did in public. Frances did a slight sway, which was in keeping with her personality. And Sung—well, Sung looked like someone's grandfather trying to dance to "Hollaback Girl."

"This shit really *is* bananas," I said to Damien. "B-A-N-A-N-A-S. Look at that varsity jacket go!"

"Enough with the jacket," Damien replied. "Let him have his fun. He's stressed enough as it is. I want a drink. You want to get a drink?"

At first I thought he meant breaking into the nearest minibar. But no, he just wanted to head over to the punch bowl. The punch was übersweet—Kool-Aid that had been cut with Sprite—and as I drank glass after glass, it almost gave me a Robitussin high.

"Do you see anyone who looks like they're from North Dakota?" I asked. "Tall hats? Presence of cattle? If so, we can go spy. If you distract them, I'll steal the laminated copies of their SAT scores from their fanny packs."

But he wasn't into it. He kept checking texts on his phone.

"Who's texting?" I finally asked.

"Just Julie," he said. "I wish she'd stop."

I assumed Just Julie was Julie Swain, who was also on cross-country. I didn't think they'd been going out. Maybe she'd wanted to and he hadn't. That would explain why he wasn't texting back.

Clearly, Damien and I weren't ever going to get into the social part of the social. He had something on his mind and I had nothing but him on my own. We'd lost Wes, and Sung, Frances, and Gordon were still on the dance floor. Sung looked like it was a job to be there, while Gordon was in his own little world. It was Frances who fascinated me the most.

"She almost looks happy," I said. "I don't know if I've ever seen her happy."

Damien nodded and drank some more punch. "She's always so serious," he agreed.

The punch was turning our lips cherry red.

"Let's get out of here," I said.

"Okay."

We were alone together in an unknown hotel in an unknown city. So we did the natural thing.

We went to his room.

And we watched TV.

It was his room, so he got to choose. We ended up watching *The Departed* on basic cable. It was, I realized, the most time we had ever spent alone together. He lay back on his bed and I sat on Sung's, making sure my angle was such that I could watch Damien as much as I watched the TV.

During the first commercial break, I asked, "Is something wrong?"

He looked at me strangely. "No. Does it seem like something's wrong?"

I shook my head. "No. Just asking."

During the second commercial break, I asked, "Were you and Julie going out?"

He put his head back on his pillow and closed his eyes.

"No." And then, about a minute later, right before the movie started again, "It wasn't anything, really."

During the third commercial break, I asked, "Does she know that?"

"What?"

"Does Julie know it wasn't anything?"

"No," he said. "It looks like she doesn't know that."

This was it, I was sure—the point where he'd ask for my advice. I could help him. I could prove myself worthy of his company.

But he let it drop. He didn't want to talk about it. He wanted to watch the movie.

I realized he needed to reveal himself to me in his own time. I couldn't rush it. I had to be patient. For the remaining commercial breaks, I made North Dakota jokes. He laughed at some of them, and even threw in a few of his own.

Sung came back when there were about fifteen minutes left in the movie. I could tell he wasn't thrilled about me sitting on his bed, but I wasn't about to move.

"Sung," I told him, "if this whole quiz bowl thing doesn't work out for you, I think you have a future in disco."

"Shut up," he grumbled, taking off the famous jacket and hanging it in the closet.

We watched the rest of the movie in silence, with Sung sitting on the edge of Damien's bed. As soon as the credits were rolling, Sung announced it was time to go to sleep.

14

"But where are you sleeping?" I asked, spreading out on his sheets.

"That's my bed," he said.

I wanted to offer Sung a swap—he could stay with Wes and talk about polynomials all night, while I could stay with Damien. But clearly that wasn't a real option.

Damien walked me to the door.

"Lay off the minibar," he said. "We need you sober tomorrow."

"I'll try," I replied. "But those little bottles are just so pretty. Every time I drink from them, I can pretend I'm a doll."

He chuckled and hit me lightly on the shoulder.

"Resist," he commanded.

Again, I told him I'd try.

Wes was in bed and the lights were off when I got to my room, so I very quietly changed into my pajamas and brushed my teeth.

I was about to nod off when Wes's voice asked, "Did you have fun?"

"Yeah," I said. "Damien and I went to his room and watched *The Departed*. It was a good time. We looked for you, but you were already gone."

"That social sucked."

"It most certainly did."

I closed my eyes.

"Goodnight," Wes said softly, making it sound like a true wish. Nobody besides my parents had ever said it to me like that before.

"Goodnight," I said back. Then I made sure he'd plugged the clock back in, and went to sleep.

The next morning, we kicked North Dakota's ass. Then, for good measure, we erased Maryland from the boards and made Oklahoma cry.

It felt good.

"Don't get too cocky," Sung warned us, which was pretty precious, since Sung was the cockiest of us all. I half expected "We Are the Champions" to come blaring out of his ears every time we won a round.

Our fourth and last match of the day—in the quarterfinals— was against the team from Clearwater, Florida, which had made it to the finals for each of the past ten years, winning four of those times. They were legendary, insofar as people like Sung had heard about them and had studied their strategies, with some tapes Mr. Phillips had managed to get off Clearwater local access.

Even though I was the alternate, I was put in the starting lineup. Clearwater was known for treating the canon like a cannon to demolish the other team.

"Bring it on," I said.

It soon became clear who my counterpart on the Clearwater team was—a wispy girl with straight brown hair who could barely bother to put down her Muriel Spark in order to start playing. The first time she opened her mouth, she revealed their secret weapon:

She was British.

Frances looked momentarily frightened by this, but I took it in stride. When the girl lunged with Byron, I parried with Asimov. When she volleyed with Burgess, I pounced with Roth. Neither of us missed a question, so it became a test of buzzer willpower. I started to ring in a split second before I knew the answer. And I always knew the answer.

Until I did the unthinkable.

I buzzed in for a science question.

Which Nobel Prize winner later went on to write The Double Helix *and* Avoid Boring People?

I realized immediately it wasn't Saul Bellow or Kenzaburo Oe.

As the judge said, "Do you have an answer?" the phrase *The Double Helix* hit in my head.

"Crick!" I exclaimed.

The judge looked at me for a moment, then down at his card. "That is incorrect. Clearwater, which Nobel Prize winner later went on to write *The Double Helix* and *Avoid Boring People?*"

It was not the lit girl who buzzed in.

"James *D.* Watson," one of the math boys answered snottily, the *D* sent as a particular *fuck you* to me.

"Sorry," I whispered to my team.

"It's okay," Damien said.

"No worries," Wes said.

Sung, I knew, wouldn't be as forgiving.

I was now off my game and more cautious with the buzzer, so Brit girl got the best of me on Caliban and Vivienne Haigh-Wood. I managed to stick *One Hundred Years of Solitude* in edgewise, but that was scant comfort. I mean, who *didn't* know *One Hundred Years of Solitude?*

Clearwater had a one-question lead with three questions left, and the last questions were about math, history, and geography. So I sat back while Sung rocked the relative areas of a rhombus and a circle, Wes sent a little love General Omar Bradley's way, and Frances wrapped it up with Tashkent, which I had not known was the capital of Uzbekistan, its name translating as "stone village."

Usually we burst out of our chairs when we won, but this

match had been so exhausting that we could only feel relieved. We shook hands with the other team—Brit girl's hand felt like it was made of paper, which I found weird.

After Clearwater had left the room, Sung called an emergency team meeting.

"That was too close," he said. Not *congratulations* or *nice work.*

No, Sung was pissed.

He talked about the need to be more aggressive on the buzzer, but also to exercise care. He said we should always *play to our strengths.* To make a blunder was to *destroy the fabric of our entire team.*

"I get it, I get it," I said.

"No," Sung told me, "I don't think you do."

"Sung," Mr. Phillips cautioned.

"I think he needs to hear this," Sung insisted. "From the very start of the year, he has refused to be a team player. And what we saw today was nothing short of an insurrection. He broke the unwritten rules."

"*He* is standing right here," I pointed out. "Just come right out and say it."

"YOU ARE NOT TO ANSWER SCIENCE QUESTIONS!" Sung yelled. "WHAT WERE YOU THINKING?"

"Hey—" Damien started to interrupt.

I held up my hand. "No, it's okay. Sung needs to get this out of his system."

"You are the *alternate,*" Sung went on.

"You don't seem to mind it when I'm answering questions, Sung."

"We only have you here because we have to!"

"That's enough," Mr. Phillips said decisively.

"No, it's not enough," I said. "I'm sick of you all acting like I'm this English freak raining on your little math-science parade. Sung seems to think my contribution to this team is a little less than everyone else's."

"Anyone can memorize book titles!" Sung shouted.

"Oh, please. Like I care what you think? You don't even know the difference between Keats and Byron."

"The difference between Keats and Byron doesn't matter!"

"None of this matters!" I shouted back. "Don't you get it, Sung? NONE OF THIS MATTERS. Yes, you have knowledge—but you're not doing anything with it. You're *reciting* it. You're not out curing cancer—you're *listing the names of the people who've tried to cure cancer.* This whole thing is a joke, Captain. It's *trivial.* Which is why everyone laughs at us."

"You think we're all trivial?" Sung challenged.

"No," I said. "I think *you're* trivial with your quiz bowl obsession. The rest of us have other things going on. We have lives."

"You're the one who's not a part of our team! You're the outcast!"

"If that's so true, Sung, then why are you the only one of us wearing a fucking varsity jacket? Why do you think nobody else wanted to be seen in one? It's not just me, Sung. It's all of us."

"*Enough!*" Mr. Phillips yelled.

Sung looked like he wanted to kill me. And I knew at the same time that he'd never look at that damn jacket the same way again.

"Why don't we all take a break over dinner," Mr. Phillips went on, "then regroup in my room at eight for a scrimmage before the semifinals tomorrow morning? I don't know who we're facing, but we're going to need to be a team to face them."

What we did next wasn't very teamlike: Mr. Phillips, a

brooding Sung, Frances, and Gordon went one way for dinner, while Wes, Damien, and I went another way.

"There's a Steak 'n Shake a few blocks away," Wes told us.

"Sounds good," Damien said.

I, brooding as well, followed.

"It was a question about books," I said, once we'd left the hotel. "I didn't realize it was a science question."

"Crick wasn't that far off," Wes pointed out.

"Yeah, but I still fucked it up."

"And we still won," Damien said.

Yeah, I knew that.

But I wasn't feeling it.

Damien and Wes tried to cheer me up. Not just by getting my burger and shake for me, but by sitting across from me and treating me like a friend.

"So how does it feel to be the Quiz Bowl Antichrist?" Damien asked in a mock-sportscaster voice, holding an invisible microphone out for my reply.

"Well, as James D. Watson said, I'm the motherfuckin' princess. All other quiz bowlers shall bow down to me. Because you know what?"

"What?" Damien and Wes both asked.

"One of these days, I'm going to be the *goddamn answer* to a quiz bowl question."

"Yeah," Wes said. "'What quiz bowl alternate murdered his team captain in the semifinals and later wrote a book, *Among Boring People?*'"

Damien shook his head. "Not funny. There will be no murder tonight or tomorrow."

"Do you realize, if we win this thing, it's going to come up on Google Search for the rest of our lives?" I said.

"Let's wear masks in the photo," Wes suggested.

"I'll be Michelangelo. You can be Donatello."

And it went on like this for a while. Damien stopped talking and watched me and Wes going back and forth. I was talking, but mostly I was watching him back. The green-blue of his eyes. The side of his neck. The curl of hair that dangled over the left corner of his forehead. No matter where I looked, there was something to see.

I didn't have any control over it. Something inside of me was shifting. Everything I'd refused to articulate was starting to spell itself out. Not as knowledge, but as the impulse beneath the knowledge. I knew I wanted to be with him, and I was also starting to feel why. He was a reason I was here. He was a reason it mattered.

I was talking to Wes, but really I was talking to Damien through what I was saying to Wes. I wanted him to find me entertaining. I wanted him to find me interesting. I wanted him to find me.

We were done pretty quickly, and before I knew it, we were walking back to the Westin. Once we got to the lobby, Wes magically decided to head back to our room until the "scrimmage" at eight. That left Damien and me with two hours and nothing to do.

"Why don't we go to my room?" Damien suggested.

I didn't argue. I started to feel nervous—unreasonably nervous. We were just two friends going to a room. There wasn't anything else to it. And yet . . . he hadn't mentioned watching TV, and last time he'd said, "Why don't we go to my room to watch TV?"

"I'm glad it's just the two of us," I ventured.

"Yeah, me too," Damien said.

We rode the elevator in silence and walked down the hallway in silence. When we got to his door, he swiped his electronic key in the lock and got a green light on the first try. I could never manage to do that.

"After you," he said, opening the door and gesturing me in.

I walked forward, down the small hallway, turning toward the beds. And that's when I realized—there was someone in the room. And it was Sung. And he was on his bed. And he wasn't wearing his jacket. Or a shirt. And he was moaning a little.

I thought we'd caught him jerking off. I couldn't help it— I burst out laughing. And that's what made him notice we were in the room. He jumped and turned around, and I realized Frances was in the bed with him, shirt also off, but bra still on.

It was all so messed up that I couldn't stop laughing. Tears were coming to my eyes.

"Get out!" Sung yelled.

"I'm sorry, Frances," I said between laughing fits. "I'm so sorry."

"GET OUT!" Sung screamed again, standing up now. Thank God he still had his pants on. "YOU ARE THE DEVIL. THE DEVIL!"

"I prefer *Antichrist*," I told him.

"THE DEVIL!"

"*THE DEVIL!*" I mimicked back.

I felt Damien's hand on my shoulder. "Let's go," he whispered.

"This is so pathetic," I said. "Sung, man, you're *pathetic*."

Sung lunged forward then, and Damien stepped in between us.

"Go," Damien told me. "*Now.*"

I was laughing again, so I apologized to Frances again, then I pulled myself into the hallway.

Damien came out a few seconds later and closed the door behind us.

"Holy shit!" I said.

"Stop it," Damien said. "Enough."

"Enough?" I laughed again. "I haven't even started."

Damien shook his head. "You're cold, man," he said. "I can't believe how cold you are."

"What?" I asked. "You don't find this funny?"

"You have no heart."

This sobered me up pretty quickly. "How can you say that?" I asked. "How can you, of all people, say that?"

"What does that mean? Me, of all people?"

He'd gotten me.

"Alec?"

"I don't know!" I shouted. "Okay? *I don't know.*"

This sounded like the truth, but it was feeling less than that. I knew. Or I was starting to know.

"I do have a heart," I said. But I stopped there.

I could feel it all coming apart. The collapse of all those invisible plans, the appearance of all those hidden thoughts.

I bolted. I left him right there in the hallway. I didn't wait for the elevator—I hit the emergency stairs. I ran like I was the one on the cross-country team, even when I heard him following me.

"Don't!" I yelled back at him.

I got to my floor and ran to my room. The card wouldn't work the first time, and I nervously looked at the stairway exit, waiting for him to show up. But he must've stopped. He must've heard. I got the key through the second time.

Wes was on his bed, reading a comic.

"You're back early," he said, not looking up.

I couldn't say a thing. There was a knock on the door. Damien calling out my name.

"Don't answer it," I said. "Please, don't answer it."

I locked myself in the bathroom. I stared at the mirror.

I heard Wes murmur something to Damien through the door without opening it. Then he was at the bathroom door.

"Alec? Are you okay?"

"I'm fine," I said, but my voice was soggy coming out of my throat.

"Open up."

I couldn't. I sat on the lip of the tub, breathing in, breathing out. I remembered the look on Sung's face and started to laugh. Then I thought of Frances lying there and felt sad. I wondered if I really didn't have a heart.

"Alec," Wes said again, gently. "Come on."

I waited until he walked off. Then I opened the door and went into the bedroom. He was back on his bed, but he hadn't picked up the comic. He was sitting at the edge, waiting for me.

I told him what had happened. Not the part about Damien, at first, but the part about Sung and Frances. He didn't laugh, and neither did I. Then I told him Damien's reaction to my reaction, without going into what was underneath.

"Do you think I'm cold?" I asked him. "Really—am I?"

"You're not cold," he said. "You're just so angry."

I must've looked surprised by this. He went on.

"You can be a total prick, Alec. There's nothing wrong with that—all of us can be total pricks. We like to think that just because we're geeks, we can't be assholes. But we can be. Most of the time, though, it's not coming from meanness or coldness. It's coming from anger. Or sadness. I mean, I see people like me and I just want to rip them apart."

"But why do I want to rip Sung apart?"

"I don't know. Because he's a prick, too. And maybe you

feel if you rip apart the quiz bowl geek, no one will think of you as a quiz bowl geek."

"But I'm not a quiz bowl geek!"

"Haven't you figured it out yet?" Wes asked. "Nobody's a quiz bowl geek. We're all just people. And you're right—what we do here has no redeeming social value whatsoever. But it can be an interesting way to pass the time."

I sat down on my bed, facing Wes so that our knees almost touched.

"I'm not a very happy person," I told him. "But sometimes I can trick myself into thinking I am."

"And where does Damien fit into all this, if I may ask?"

I shook my head. "I really have no idea. I'm still figuring it out."

"You know he likes girls?"

"I said, I'm still figuring it out."

"Fair enough."

I paused, realizing what had just been said.

"Is it that obvious?" I asked Wes.

"Only to me," he said.

It would take me another three months to understand why.

"Meanwhile," he went on, *Sung and Frances.*"

"Holy shit, right?"

"Yeah, holy shit. And you know the worst part?"

"I can't imagine what's worse than seeing it with my own eyes."

"Gordon is totally in love with Frances."

"No!"

"Yup. I wouldn't miss practice tonight for all the money in the world."

• • •

We all showed up. Mr. Phillips could sense there was some tension in the room, but he truly had no idea.

Frances was wearing Sung's varsity jacket. And suddenly I didn't mind it so much.

Gordon glared at Sung.

Sung glared at me.

I avoided Damien's eyes.

When I looked at Wes, he made me feel like I might be worth saving.

Amazingly enough, during practice we were back in fighting form, as if nothing had happened. I felt like I could admit to myself how much I wanted to win. And not just that, how much I wanted our team to win. More for Wes and Frances and Gordon and Damien than anything else.

After we were done, Damien asked me if we could talk for a minute. Everyone else headed back to their rooms and we went down to the lobby. Other quiz bowl groups were swarming around; those that hadn't made the semifinals were taking the night for what it was—a time when, for a brief pause in their high school lives, they were free from any pressure or care.

"I'm sorry," Damien said to me. "I was completely off base."

"It's okay. I shouldn't have been so mean to Sung and Frances. I should've just left."

We sat there next to each other on a lime-green couch in a hotel lobby that meant nothing to us. He wouldn't look at me. I wouldn't look at him.

"I don't know why I did that," he said. "Reacted that way."

It would take him another four months to figure it out. It would be a little too late, but he'd figure it out anyway.

. . .

We lost in the semifinals to Iowa. I knew from the look Sung gave me afterward that he would blame me for this loss for the rest of his life. Not because I missed the questions—and I did get two wrong. But for destroying his own invisible plans.

Looking back, I don't think I've ever hated any piece of clothing as much as I hated Sung's varsity jacket for those few weeks. You can't hate something that much unless you hate yourself equally as much. Not in that kind of way.

It was, I guess, Wes who taught me that. Later, when we were back home and trying to articulate ourselves better, I'd ask him how he'd known so much more than I had.

"Because I read, stupid" would be his answer.

We lost in the semifinals, but the local paper took our picture anyway. Sung looks serious and aggrieved. Gordon looks awkward. Frances looks calm. Damien looks oblivious. And Wes and me?

We look like we're in on our own joke.

In other words, happy.

TRACK TWO

Day 2934

When I am eight, Valentine's Day is a Sunday. There is no certain minute I have to wake up, no bus to catch, no homework that needs to be handed in. Sleeping can blur itself into waking, and that is exactly what it does.

I wake up with my face against Yoda's, my arm gently across Obi-Wan Kenobi. I take in the Star Wars sheets, the Star Wars blanket, the lightsaber lamp beside my bed. I have never seen any of the Star Wars movies, so this is all very strange to me. As I sit up in bed against a robot I will later learn to call a droid, I do my mental morning exercise, figuring out that my name is Jason today and that this is my bedroom. My mother's room is on the other side of the wall; from the silence, I assume she's still sleeping.

I know it's Valentine's Day because yesterday was the day before Valentine's Day. I watched yesterday's sister decorating her cards, putting extra glitter on the one belonging to her crush. She let me put stickers on the cards she cared less about, hearts I laid out in haphazard trails. I tried to imagine each kid opening his or her envelope, knowing full well I would be gone by the time they were delivered.

Now I get up and walk to the mirror. I don't really pay attention to what I look like, but I do stare for a good long time at the pattern on my pajamas. If you've never seen Wookiees dancing before, it's a very confusing sight.

On my desk, I find a dozen sealed white envelopes, each the size of a playing card. They are all addressed to MOM, the Os shaped into hearts.

It's as if Jason has left me an assignment. I gather the stack in my hand and leave the room.

Holidays were important to me when I was young, because they were the only days almost everyone could agree upon. In school, there would always be a lead-up, the anticipation gathering into a frenzy as the day grew closer and closer. With Valentine's Day, the world grew progressively red and pink as February began. It was a bright spot in a cold time, a holiday that didn't ask much more of me than to eat candy and think about love.

Because of this, I liked it a lot.

Jason's room is clearly his home base—the rest of the apartment holds fewer representatives from outside our universe. It isn't a large place—just the two bedrooms wedged together with a kitchen and a den. Big enough for two people, but I feel it's meant for at least one more.

I try to stay quiet—over the years, I've learned to wake a parent only if it's really, really important. Back before I realized I was waking into a different life each morning, I stormed carelessly into my various parents' bedrooms, no matter what time it was. Most told me to go back to bed. Some used it as an excuse to get up. And enough lashed out at me that I stopped doing it, terrified that I'd landed in the wrong kind of life, and that my excitement at being awake would be used against me.

On tiptoe steps, I enter the kitchen and find a valentine wonderland awaiting me. The room is aswarm with hearts—dropping from the ceiling, constellated across the cabinets, blooming from the countertop. There have to be hundreds of them, and to my eight-year-old eye, it looks like thousands. They peek out from drawers, scale the refrigerator, conga across the floor. In the silence of my sleeping, my mother has constructed this for me. There are hearts popping out of the toaster. Hearts running away with the spoons. Hearts swimming above napkins and hopscotching the paper towels.

I can't help but pick one up, feel the red paper between my fingers. Already, the heart in my hand is forming a personality in my head. This heart—a little squat, a little heavier on the left side—is a bit slower than the rest, but he tells good jokes. I name him Bruno. (I don't know where the name comes from; it's probably the dog or cat from a house I once lived in, the name all that remains in my memory.) Immediately, Bruno makes two friends, Sally and Lucy. They talk a valentine language, but luckily I can translate it into English.

This is how my mother finds me nearly an hour later: at the kitchen table, building a jungle gym for my new friends. Celery for a slide. Broccoli to climb. Carrot sticks at fort-making angles. Bruno still has center stage, but the cast of characters has grown to at least a dozen. I believe I know them well.

"Happy Valentine's Day!" my mother says.

Years later, I will remember her voice. I will remember the way she said it. With chime-like clarity, announcing that this is indeed a special day, and that even though I have done nothing to deserve it but be myself, it all belongs to me.

In my haste to get lost in the heart-world I've conjured, I've forgotten to put out the envelopes Jason left. I've stashed them in a corner, by the gremlin-grumbling base of the refrigerator. Now I scoot down from my chair to retrieve them. I have not touched the larger pink envelope I found with my name on it on the kitchen table. I knew to wait until Mom woke up before opening it.

My mother goes to the cupboard and reaches for something on a shelf I can't imagine ever being able to reach. A few hearts fall as the door swings, but they make a soft landing. Two red-wrapped boxes emerge in her hands. I wonder how long they've been up there, and at the same time I could just as easily believe they've appeared at this very moment.

It is just the two of us, giants in the world of hearts. It is just the two of us, together in a small kitchen on a Sunday morning. It is just the two of us, and now I am handing over my twelve envelopes and she is handing over the red-wrapped boxes, accompanied by the pink-clad card.

It is a trick I've learned, to feel as if a card is for me even if it's really addressed to the person I am that day. This is the only way I stop myself from falling through the fabric of everyday life. When I was a child, I could make myself believe that the words and the love behind them were always meant for me. Especially if I saw the expression of love in the eyes of the person who was giving the card to me.

As my mother opens her envelopes, I can see I've given her a whole pack of Star Wars valentines, providing each character with his or her own elaborate autograph. The card for me, meanwhile, has a pack of walruses on it, making the shape of a heart on an ice floe. (I have to look closely to make sure they're not Wookiees.) In the first red box my mother has given me, I find a red scarf. In the second red box, I find a pair of red mittens.

When you get older, red becomes more complicated, just as hearts become more complicated. But back then, the world was far from a bloody, angry, embarrassing thing. Red had one meaning, and that meaning was love. There in the kitchen, I wrap myself in it, I clothe myself in it, and I'm sure that my smile is just as red as the mittens, and the heart in my chest is just as red as the scarf.

My mother holds up a card with a masked figure on it. The caption reads, *May you HUNT up a BOUNTY of HEARTS.*

"I think this is my favorite," she tells me. "Boba Fett's a real romantic, isn't he?"

I have no idea what she's talking about, but I nod earnestly, which only makes her smile more.

"So what shall we do with our Valentine's Day? Maybe some valentine waffles to start?"

She has a heart-shaped cookie cutter at the ready, and uses it to force some Eggos into the holiday spirit. As she does, she hums a song I don't know. I want to sing along, but I can't. Most of the songs I've learned in school involve grand old flags and amber waves of grain. None seem to apply to this moment.

She tries to shape the butter into hearts, but it doesn't quite work. The syrup, however, allows itself a heart-shaped pour. I almost don't want to eat the waffles, they seem so loving.

I think my mother senses I'm on the verge of giving the waffles names. "Go ahead," she says, now making two for herself. "Before they get cold."

She turns on the radio, and we're serenaded by commercials and forecasts. Sitting at the kitchen table, I am reminded how households with only two people have a different kind of gravity than others. We need the background noise, because otherwise the burden is entirely on us. And at the same time, there isn't that much of a burden, because we are used to the two-person rhythm of things, the constant awareness of one another without much needing to be said. We are the only objects exerting any gravitational pull on our attentions. The pull has some slack to it, some give.

After the waffles are gone, I head back to my room and play some more with the hearts, letting them explore the *Millennium Falcon* and some sketches Jason has made of the Death Star.

As I do this, my mother washes the dishes, then goes to her room to do other things I don't notice. When she emerges again in my doorway, she has a bottle of pink liquid in her hands.

"How about a strawberry bubble bath?" she asks.

I am not going to argue with that. I watch, hearts in hand, as she draws the bath, checking to make sure the water isn't too cold and isn't too hot. When it's just right, she pours the pink in, and I watch the bubbles race to the surface. She leaves me alone to submerge myself into strawberry-scented oblivion. My thoughts wander, but not to a place where I can follow them. I turn the bubbles into peaks, into clouds that I toss into the air. It doesn't occur to me to wash myself. It's as if I believe the steam will evaporate me into being clean.

From the bathtub, I can hear my mother walking around the apartment. Every now and then, she asks if everything is okay, and I let her know I'm good. Finally she suggests it might be time for me to get out of the tub. I have already used the tap to add more hot water, and the bubbles are starting to wear thin. So I rise from the tub, a foamy tempest, and then towel myself off and get dressed in a red shirt and green jeans. I wish I had red socks and sneakers, too.

I remember this. I remember all of this.

• • •

The next thing I remember, we are walking in the zoo. I know we must have talked about going there. I know we must have driven. But those were everyday acts, and I'm sure I didn't even hold on to them at the time they were happening. The zoo, however, is different. I have been here before, with other parents, on a field trip. And I'm sure Jason has been here before, too, since his mother doesn't offer much in the way of tour guidance. Instead she brings Valentine's Day with her. I remember her pink scarf. I remember my red mittens. I remember us making our way to the mother panda and the baby panda, and I remember the story my mother tells me about how they're going to spend Valentine's Day. After everyone's gone—after even the guards go off to do other things, like check the giraffes—the pandas are going to have a party, just the two of them. They are going to sip pink lemonade through bamboo straws and share heart-shaped chocolates they've ordered all the way from China. I listen to her tell me all this, rapt, and then ask her wonder-filled questions: Will they play music at this party? Do they give each other cards? Are the chocolates the kind with fillings, or are they chocolate through and through? Do pandas like the peanut butter ones the best, like I do? My mother has an answer for each and every question.

I watch the pandas and smile. Even though they're chewing bamboo, even though they aren't really paying attention to us, I know their secret plans. Even though I know they're bears, just like the bears you have to be afraid of in the woods, when I look at them, all I can see is softness. I want to give them valentines. I want to buy them red licorice for their party, even if it ends up being from CVS, not China.

• • •

At eight, I still let myself believe, because it's more fun and welcoming to believe. The older I get, the more I will feel I have to assert my logic, the more I'll feel I have to prove that stories are lies. Or at least until I reach the point when I appreciate stories again, until I reach the point when I realize how they help me live my life. At eight, I am on the cusp. I am sure there are so many things about Jason, about Jason's mother, about the pandas in their pen, that I'm not seeing. But his mother's love is strong enough that I don't care about what I'm not seeing. Instead I want to live in the story of what is there.

The pandas don't get the red licorice, but I do. When we leave the zoo, we go on a hunt for pink lemonade, and when we find it, I use my licorice as a straw, pretending it's bamboo. When we go for lunch, I don't notice any of the couples around us. I don't measure our day against theirs. In due time, I will see the day as a conspiracy to milk romantics of their rose money. But that's not how I learned it. That isn't how any of us learn it. Our first valentines are never from someone we're dating or have a crush on. Our first valentines are always like this.

My mother convinces the amused waitress to convince the chef to make our pizza so the red will be on top, the cheese underneath. When it arrives at our table, the chef has even added red peppers, shaped in a heart. I am delighted. (A wonderful word for a wonder-filled feeling, *delighted*.)

I can coast on my excitement for a while, but by the time we get home, I'm tired. I don't remember napping, but I must nap, because I remember waking up. I remember it being light out, but just barely. I play for a few minutes with Bruno, Sally, and Lucy, and introduce them to Chewbacca, Han Solo, and

C-3PO—although, not knowing these guys' true names, I call them Rex, Harry, and Goldie, respectively. They are planning a valentine party of their own. Chewbacca Rex is a little in love with Sally, but Sally has no idea. Bruno is secretly jealous. Goldie C-3PO consoles him.

When the story has played out for as long as my attention span will allow, I decide to leave my bedroom. Quietly, I venture toward the kitchen, probably to retrieve more of Bruno, Sally, and Lucy's heart-shaped friends. When I get to the doorway, I see my mom inside, but she doesn't see me.

Here my memory takes hold. Here I contradict my earlier statement, because isn't this an everyday moment, too? Why do I end up remembering it so many years later—why do I remember this woman, who I only know for one day? She is sitting at the kitchen table. A pink-frosted cake sits in front of her, the container of frosting still on the table beside it. She has a bag of candy hearts open, and she has been putting them onto the cake. I have caught her pausing in the middle of this task. A small green candy heart is held between her thumb and finger. The bag is right by her wrist. But she isn't looking at the bag, or at the cake, or at me in the hall. She is looking at something that isn't there. She is looking at nothing at all. She is seeing something without looking. She is in the room and she isn't in the room. She is lost in her own private universe, a vast and small place that I can only see as it's reflected in her body. It is not sadness I see. I would understand sadness. I see, instead, what an adult looks like when she is unmoored from gravity. When she forgets what gravity is like. When the pull of other universes is so faint that there is only the private universe left.

I remember this so well because one day I will understand it. What's important isn't what I notice—it's this recognition beneath, and what comes next. Because the minute she sees me, gravity returns. The minute she sees me, the private universe expands. The minute she sees me, she comes back. And I think: *love*. I know then, without being able to articulate it, that love is the gravity.

She asks me if I want to finish decorating the cake. I ask her who it's for. She tells me it's for us . . . and Boba Fett, if he drops by.

I don't want Boba Fett to drop by.

We eat two slices of the cake, and I'm sure we eat dinner, too. Afterwards, I help with the dishes and steal fingerfuls of icing from the cake that remains. Pink frosting is, to me, toothpaste's super fun cousin. My mother, however, will not allow me to brush with what's left.

Instead I am asked to use the less fun cousin before I change back into my Wookiee wear and jump into bed. I am not tired, not tired at all, but then my mother comes in and says she'll read to me for a little while. I don't remember what book it was—it almost doesn't matter, because the sensation of being read to is so much more powerful than any individual story. Easing myself into her words allows me to loosen my grip on the fierce wakefulness I'd proclaimed when she entered the room. When she finishes, I am nearly in a dream state. But not quite, because I still remember her turning out the light, and then, by the glow of an R2-D2-shaped night-light, singing me off to sleep.

I could have panicked. I could have mourned ahead of time that I was going to lose this all the next day. I was old enough to know what was going on.

But I didn't do any of that. I let myself take it as mine. I let myself enjoy it.

I let myself believe.

. . .

We give each other gifts. Red scarves, red mittens. Cards and
licorice. Upside-down pizza. We give each other gifts, but
really we give each other details. When days are gone, whether
they be holidays or ordinary days, when you are nowhere near
where you once were, the details have a way of staying. Trips
to the zoo. The decorations on a cake. We keep them. They
keep us. Bedtime melodies. Constellations of construction-
paper hearts. I have added them up, and in my memory, I
see love.

TRACK THREE

The Good Girls

In high school, I was one of the good girls.

My parents didn't know what to think. Every night, there'd be the parade of phone calls for their son. I'd slip out of the room, behind closed doors, to talk about friends and homework and relationships (rarely my own) and, every now and then, the meaning of life. They didn't know all these girls' voices like I did, so they were never really certain who was calling, or why. Either I had dozens of girlfriends or I didn't have any at all.

The truth was most of my friends were girls. Mayling, Elana, Joanna, Carolyn, Lauren, and Marcie were the good girls. Lynda, Dvora, Rebecca, Susannah, Dina, Meg, and Jinny were the good girls who hit on the boy thing when we hit high school. Eliza, Jodi, Jordana, Jeannie, and Maryam were the good girls one grade below us. Jennifer, Sami, and Tracey were the good girls who didn't do the group thing with us as much. There were boys, too . . . but there weren't that many of them. The girls were the nucleus of my social life.

We didn't talk about sex; we talked about love. We never, ever used *party* as a verb. Awkwardly mixed drinks and the occasional beer or wine cooler were as alcoholic as we got. Pot was a big step. Cocaine was unimaginable. We were the kids for whom VCRs had been invented. We watched *When*

Harry Met Sally . . . over and over again and pondered its lessons like it had been filmed in Aramaic. The central question, of course, was: Can guys and girls really be friends? I liked to think I was the proof positive, because even though I fell for one of my female friends every now and then, friendship always managed to win out in the end.

It hadn't yet occurred to me to like boys.

We good girls coveted our phrasings like they were SAT flash cards. We honed our wits like Dorothy Parker at an Algonquin lunch table. We were smart, and we knew it. We were dorks, and we knew it. But instead of hiding both things, we embraced them. We created our own form of popularity. In our town of Millburn, New Jersey, where the football team never won, this was surprisingly easy to do.

Many of the girls were in the Millburnettes, the girls' singing group. If any of them dated, odds were that she'd date one of the Millburnaires. I myself failed my Millburnaire audition because I tried to make every song sound like "Bring Him Home" from *Les Misérables*. Mr. Deal, the fussy, testy diva of a chorus director, was half-appalled and half-amused. He gave me another chance, and I decided not to take it. I hadn't wanted to wear the ultra-blue polyester Millburnaire outfit anyway.

Instead I became a Millburnette groupie. And a school musical groupie (memorably playing the one-lined doorman in *Kiss Me, Kate*). I joined the fencing team—because all my friends were there, because I needed a sport for my college applications, and because at practices, some of the girls and I talked much more than we parried.

I have learned over the years that it's decidedly uncool to say I enjoyed high school—many people are lucky to have survived it, and others who didn't have as bad a time like to say they did. Since I was one of the good girls, I found life in high school to be . . . good. It wasn't always easy, and it wasn't always nice. But through it all, I felt a passive happiness that would break out sometimes into an intensely active happiness. This would usually happen in the most random ways: Mayling pulling her long sleeve to her nose and proclaiming "I am an elephant!" with the rest of us following suit; me and Lynda holding up signs to each other in the middle of the Metropolitan Opera House, since I was in the balcony and she was in the orchestra, and we couldn't go the length of an opera without passing some word to each other; me and Jennifer leaving lunch early and sitting on the fenced-off stairway that led to the auditorium, remarking on the people who passed us and, when the hallway traffic was slow, talking about books. If we never felt the full swoon of romance, we often felt the giddy buoyancy of friendship. It was a counterbalance against all the tests we faced—tests in the classrooms, tests in the hallways, tests in what we wore and what we said and who we were.

It was a sisterhood, and I was the brother. There were some conversations I wasn't a part of—you would think that hanging out with so many girls would open my eyes to their side of the sex thing, but with a few exceptions, this rarely came up. Instead I was exposed to the girls' emotional landscapes, and even more important, I was allowed to have one of my own. We wore our feelings so openly—whether it was annoyance or distress or delight or anger or affection we felt. In that time and place, I wouldn't have learned such openness from the boys. There were certainly times when everything seemed like a big traumedy . . . but I learned to deal with that. By talking it through. By talking it out. And if none of those things worked, Lynda always advised a haircut. When you wanted to change your life, she said, a haircut was often the easiest way to start.

We good girls didn't date much, for the same reason that I didn't clue in to my own boy thing as fast as I might have. In our somewhat small high school (with 160 or so students in our class), there weren't that many bookish, articulate, cute, sensitive, clever, crush-worthy boys. In retrospect, I can see a couple of crushes I had without labeling them as such—tangential boys, nobody that close to me. They were usually a year or two older than I was and talked about philosophers and writers like other boys talked about sports or computers. It's not like I dreamed of kissing them, or dating—I was just *fascinated* by them, mostly from afar, with occasional glimpses up close.

I also had friendship crushes—on boys and girls—but those were different; those friends I liked because of what I knew about them, not because of their mystery. I didn't want to be their boyfriend. I wanted to be their best friend. I learned early, and learned well, that the person you talk to about the crush is much more important than the crush itself.

Instead of dating, the good girls and I were one big date-substitute. We played a lot of Pictionary. Sober Pictionary. We ruled the school newspaper and the lit mag. The B. Dalton bookstore was our favorite store in the mall, although we were never above dancing around the aisles of Kay-Bee Toys. We went into the city on weekends and waited in the half-price ticket line for Broadway shows, or went into the Village to shop for secondhand clothes. We went to museums. We rotated between Bennigan's, T.G.I. Fridays, Chili's, and La Strada, the local pizzeria. When we weren't at the Morristown multiplex, we were at the Lost Picture Show in Union, which showed art films and had a roof that leaked. We read Margaret Atwood and J. D. Salinger and Kurt Vonnegut. (Some even read Ayn Rand, but I could never get into

it.) We talked about art without realizing we could treat it as Art. A few of us signed our yearbooks with Sondheim lyrics.

So many gay boys—whether they know they're gay yet or not—go through high school feeling like they're the only ones. They think they're the only ones who will never find love, the only ones who don't really fit in, the only ones who aren't coupled off. With the good girls, I was never the only one. Not in that way. I was sometimes the only boy. And I'm sure there were times when I thought it was ridiculous that the "dates" I had were fleeting at best. But because so many of my female friends were in the same boat, I didn't really feel alone. There were no long, dark nights of the soul, because my soul was keeping pretty good company.

The girls and I flirted and bantered. Nonstop. We passed notes. Lord, we passed notes. String these notes together and you'd get the full symphony of my high school years, an almost minute-by-minute re-creation. Constant observation, reflection, honing life into prose.

Everything remained peaceable until our senior prom came along. It wasn't a particularly big deal to me—I had already gone my junior year, the date of a girl I barely knew, who clearly had gotten to the bottom of her draft list before asking me. I'd had fun, but I'd also figured that it wasn't actually a night that would change my life forever. Going into prom season, I was (as always) unattached, and while the question of who I would ask was hotly debated when I wasn't in the room, when I returned to the room, I was left to my own obliviousness.

I decided to ask Jordana, a member of the junior posse of good girls. Bizarrely, I made this decision while watching her play the Mother Abbess in our high school's production of *The Sound of Music*. Seriously. While she was busy exhorting Maria to climb ev'ry mountain, I was thinking, *It would be fun*

to go to the prom with Jordana. Not as a date-date. But in lieu of a date-date.

I knew another boy, Josh, probably wanted to ask her, too. But I figured, hey, I'd give Jordana the option and see what she wanted to do. We went on a nondate to Bennigan's, and I stalled. I pondered. I worked myself up into an existential crisis while I ate mozzarella sticks and debated whether or not to ask her.

Which is when Roxette comes into the picture.

I almost didn't ask Jordana to be my prom date. But then a Roxette song came wafting down from the Bennigan's speakers, and it told me to listen to my heart. I figured this was a sign. My heart said go for it, so I did. I even told her I wouldn't mind if she wanted to go with Josh. She said she wanted to go with me.

I was so relieved to have it over with.

I was, however, unprepared for the fact that I had just created more traumedy than I'd ever intended to create. By choosing a prom date, I was the one who stopped the music and sent all of my female friends flying toward the musical chairs. Many, it seemed, had thought it at least a possibility that I would ask them. I had, to put it indelicately, fucked everything up. Now the good girls had to grab hold of the nearest boys and hope it would work out. By and large, it didn't work out well—even for me, since Jordana ended up wanting to go with Josh after all, causing awkwardness all around. Still, we look happy enough in the prom photos— the front row of good-girl friends, and then the back-row assortment of random boys tuxed up to squire them for the evening. All dressed up, we thought we looked so old. Now, of course, I look at the picture and see how young we actually were. We get younger every year.

Our friendships existed on the cusp of a different era; the

way we communicated and what we knew were much closer to what our parents experienced in high school than what high schoolers now know. Within five years after we graduated, everything was different. We lived in a time when we had cords on our phones—if not connecting the handset to the base, then definitely connecting the base to the wall. We lived in a time when "chatting" was something that didn't involve typing, and *text* and *page* were words that applied to books, not phones. If we wanted to see naked pictures, we had to sneak peeks in magazine stores, or rely upon drawings in *The Joy of Sex*, spreads in *National Geographic*, or carefully paused moments in R-rated videotapes. The only kids we knew in towns outside of our own were the ones we had gone to camp with. The only bands we knew were the ones played on the radio or on MTV. For me, it was a time before all the small pop-cultural things that might have tipped me off to my own identity before I hit college. Because I was happy, I didn't really question who I was.

I don't know whether the good girls were as ignorant as I was to my gayness, or if they figured it out before I did and waited for me to piece it together. One of them definitely got it—during my freshman year of college, Rebecca sent me a letter saying, basically, that it was totally cool if I was gay, and that I didn't have to hide it anymore. I was hurt—not that she thought I was gay, but that she thought I was hiding something so big from my friends. I assured her that I would tell people if I were gay—and as of that writing, I was correct. Later on, in my own time, I'd figure it out. And as soon as I did, I didn't really hide it. It seemed as natural as anything else, and I didn't go through any of the anxiety, fear, or denial that I would have no doubt experienced had I figured it out in high school. It was a gradual realization that I was completely okay with, and everyone else was completely okay with. The good girls would have been much more shocked if I'd told them I was going premed.

Because I've grown up to have a writing life that brings me into contact with a lot of teens, I see all these possibilities open now that weren't open then. I see all the fun trouble we could've gotten into. I see how late I bloomed into being gay. I see how being a good girl means missing out on some things, closing yourself off to certain experimentations and risks. It was a sheltered life, but I'm grateful I had the shelter. I needed the shelter. I bloomed late in some things, but I bloomed well in so many others. I know some good things I missed, but I also know a lot of bad things I missed, too.

Now most of the good girls—from high school, from college, from after—have found good guys or good girls to be with. And I have found the other boys who were once surrounded by good girls. Together we boys form our own good-girl circles, doing all the things we used to do exclusively with the good girls: confide, support, chatter, have fun. I don't think many of us would have imagined in high school that we would one day have such circles, that we would one day find so many guys we liked, so many guys like us.

High school does seem a long way back now. But I will say this: I'm really glad I was raised by the good girls. I wouldn't have become the guy I am without them.

TRACK FOUR

The Quarterback and the Cheerleader

Infinite Darlene is preparing for a date.

She puts on a layer of makeup, topping it off with a dash of lipstick. Her makeup is the kind that's meant to look natural—if she does a good job (and she always does a good job), nobody can tell it's there. Except for the lipstick. That's meant to be seen.

While Infinite Darlene has many, many friends, she hasn't had many, many dates. She doesn't entirely know why this is. Maybe it's because she's so busy being both the home-coming queen and the star quarterback at her school. Maybe it's because guys are intimidated by a six-foot-four trans-gender superstar. Maybe it's because the guys at her school are lame, except for her friends, who she'd never want to date. Or maybe, she reflects, it's because some people are just meant to have many, many friends and not have many, many dates.

If forced to choose, she'd take the friendships over the dates. But nobody ever forces her to do anything. When she became Infinite Darlene, she vowed that her life was her own now, nobody else's. She could give herself willingly to her friends—but it had to be her call.

One of the reasons she's so nervous about this date— uncharacteristically nervous—is that she went ahead and told all of her friends about it. They were thrilled for her—

characteristically thrilled. Now she wants it to go well, if only because they want so badly for it to go well. "You deserve this," they keep telling her, as if deserving has ever been the key to love. Paul and Noah and Joni and the rest of them don't mean to add pressure, but there it is. She feels it.

It is, by and large, an unexpected date. There hadn't been any lead-up to it, no forewarnings of flirtation, no falling into friendship and having it blossom into romance. No, instead, Cory Whitman, the head cheerleader for the Rumson Devils, had come up to her after her team had whupped Rumson, 24–10, and had asked her if she wanted to go out sometime. Of course she'd noticed him during the game, somersaulting his heart out—everybody knew that cute male cheerleaders were often used to distract the opposing team, and Infinite Darlene had let herself succumb, after she'd released her pass and her job as quarterback was done. He had a certain sly sureness with the megaphone, and a raptastic way with a rhyme. Most important, he led his squad so that they were cheering *for* the home team, not *against* the visiting team. No trash-talking. Just sportsmanship. And Infinite Darlene valued sportsmanship greatly.

She didn't say yes to his question, not right away. She wasn't that kind of girl. Instead she gave him her number and told him to give her a call—throwing up an easy roadblock that would prevent a lazy or an insincere boy from getting through. He didn't balk at this, and called later that evening. Plans were made for the following Friday night.

Of the people in Infinite Darlene's orbit, only Chuck, her number one rival on the football team, was skeptical.

"It's a trap," he said. "Rumson's always trying to mess with us."

"But we've already played them!" Infinite Darlene pointed out. "It doesn't do a lick of good to mess with us now."

"Then it's revenge."

"Truly!"

"I'm just saying, it's suspicious."

"A gorgeous head cheerleader wanting to go out on a date with me is *suspicious*. Are we talking misdemeanor or felony here, Chuck? Tell me now, so I know what to wear."

If only it were as easy as that. Infinite Darlene has no idea what to wear. After all, when Cory had made his move, she'd been in her quarterback uniform, which is pretty much the opposite of cleavage. Since it's cold out, she decides to go for a sweater and jeans. A nice sweater, nice jeans. And the sweater will be cotton, just in case he's allergic to wool.

She chastises herself for even thinking this. Who's to say that he'll get anywhere near her sweater?

Still, she also chooses something nice for underneath.

He picks her up at six.

Infinite Darlene is not waiting at the window. She is at her computer, doing last-minute research. She's learned that Cory plays basketball in the winter, that he's single (and into girls), and that he has a dangerous Scrabble habit. There is also, in the archives of the Rumson paper, a photo of him trick-or-treating at age nine as Lando Calrissian. Infinite Darlene decides not to bring this up right away.

The doorbell rings.

Character, Infinite Darlene has found, resides in the way you walk. This was one of the most fundamental challenges she faced when she decided to become Infinite Darlene. She's not as aware of it now, but she was very aware of it then—the idea of measuring her steps, taking her time, walking as if she enjoys being in her body instead of wanting to run away from it. The way she walks now, every staircase becomes a grand staircase. Every sidewalk is a runway. Even standing still, she's showcasing who she is.

(The only exception is on the football field. There her body becomes something different. Sometimes she's a building, sometimes she's a bird.)

Cory grins as she opens the door. He's happy to see her, and makes no attempt to disguise it.

Infinite Darlene's guard goes up. This is too easy. She's suspicious.

As they walk to his car, he tells her he's made a dinner reservation, and checks to see that the restaurant he's chosen is okay with her. She likes that he's made a choice, and likes it even more that he's made a good one. Perhaps this is to be expected from a head cheerleader, but Infinite Darlene has never gone out with a head cheerleader before, so she doesn't know. She realizes she's never seen him out of his own uniform. Inevitably, he's more attractive without a big *R* stuck on his chest, bisected awkwardly by a megaphone. She can't see his ass as well in his jeans, but at the same time, the denim isn't as blinding as the usual polyester.

He opens the door for her, and she lets him. She has to put the seat back in order to fit inside, but that's okay. The harder part is finding something to talk about.

Infinite Darlene is not often tongue-tied. She's quick with a quip, ready with repartee. It's these quipless, reparteetotal moments that flummox her. It's not that she's holding back—she could never go on a date with a boy who made her feel like she should hold back. Instead she's waiting for the right words to appear.

When Cory turns the car on, the radio blares, and he quickly turns it down.

"Sorry about that," he says.

This is awkward. Infinite Darlene realizes that Cory is basically a stranger.

"You played a great game the other day," he says. "You were truly awesome."

"So were you," Infinite Darlene replies. "I especially liked the goat cheer. How did it go again?"

Cory looks around, as if there's a live studio audience in the back seat of the Toyota. "Here? You want me to cheer here? I'm not sure this car is big enough for a cheer like that."

Joking. Mercifully, he is joking. Infinite Darlene knows plenty of other cheerleaders who would not be joking, who believe that the pinnacle of Western civilization is the creation of a flawless ten-person pyramid.

Infinite Darlene will not abide shyness in someone who is clearly not shy. She knows the easiest way to get him to cheer is to get the cheer wrong.

"*Go, go, go for their goat,*" she prompts.

As expected, Cory shakes his head. "Here, allow me."

Then he starts to cheer.

> *Go, go, get their goat!*
> *Pull up the drawbridge*
> *and fill the moat!*
> *Strike like a vampire*
> *goin' for the throat!*
> *Activate the phone tree*
> *and get out the vote!*

"That's inspired," Infinite Darlene observes. "Inventive."

"Well," Cory says, "there isn't much that rhymes with *Rumson*. We have to get inventive. But you're no stranger to inventive, are you?"

51

Infinite Darlene freezes. What does he mean?

"On the field," Cory quickly adds. "If Joseph hailed Mary like you hail Mary, there wouldn't have been any need for an immaculate conception."

In her head, Infinite Darlene's friends (and enemy) chime in.

Ooh, he likes you, Noah says.

He's only allowed one Jesus reference a date, says Paul. *After that, it's creepy.*

I'm telling you, it's not a pass, it's an interception! Chuck insists.

Cory says some more things about the game, and Infinite Darlene talks some more about the game, too. It might be the only thing they have in common. They want to stay on safe ground, if only for now. But they can't stay here forever.

Even though the song is on low, Cory is tapping along on the steering wheel. He has the air of a genuinely happy person—not in a moonbeams-and-rainbows way, but more that he appreciates that life is basically a good thing. Just from looking at him for twenty seconds, Infinite Darlene can sense there's always a song in his heart. Sometimes it might be a sad one. But there's always music.

"Do you know what I love?" he asks.

"No," Infinite Darlene replies. "What?"

"Stupid bumper stickers."

It takes her a moment to see it, in the lane to the right.

USA: Always strong, never wrong.

"It's like they're written by a cabal of bad cheerleaders," Cory scoffs.

"We should come up with something better," Infinite Darlene suggests.

Cory thinks about it for a moment, then offers, " 'Always *Pong*, never *Kong*'?"

52

"'Always sarong, never thong'?"

"Ooh, I like that. Let's go into the bumper sticker business."

Infinite Darlene agrees. "Let's."

It is within the lightness of this moment that Infinite Darlene closes her eyes. She likes to do this sometimes. It's similar to that memory game she played as a kid, being shown objects and then having to recount them, eyes closed, a minute later. Only this time she's taking in the whole scene. She is pausing to let the moment sink in a little deeper, and to let her other senses take on the burden of sight. There's a hint of cologne in the air, a tincture of scent that, were she asked, Infinite Darlene would say smells a lot like the color blue. There's the song on the radio and the song in his fingers, as well as the feel of the road beneath them.

It is over before Cory can notice it. For a brief moment, she was gone. But now she knows for certain that she wants to be here.

They've made it to the restaurant. Black Thai Affair—the name is nearly unforgivable, but the food is supposed to be good.

People look. They look when Infinite Darlene walks in. They look when she and Cory are seated. Infinite Darlene is used to this. The question of her body's original gender aside, there's the simple fact of her being a very, very tall woman. She is at least six inches taller than Cory. He doesn't seem to mind. Nor does he seem to realize that other people are looking. As the old song goes, he only has eyes for her.

Once Infinite Darlene and Cory get their menus, they

are faced with the essential, elemental decision that comes with going to a Thai restaurant—namely, they have to decide whether to order pad thai or not. Infinite Darlene can't resist. Cory orders a basil dish, although he does admit that pad thai had been his other choice.

They ask polite questions, and discover that Rumson isn't a bad school, but Infinite Darlene's is probably better. Cory has three sisters; Infinite Darlene is an only child. Cory loves basketball, but Infinite Darlene has resisted it all these years, because it is too obvious an option for a girl as tall as herself.

"You'd be such a natural!" Cory says.

"I used to play, but . . . ," Infinite Darlene replies, trailing off.

"But?"

But. Infinite Darlene has talked herself into a corner. She decides to get out of it by telling him the truth.

"But . . . our high school has two basketball teams, neither one of them coed. And while nobody in my town minded me playing on the girls' squad, some of the coaches from other schools had other thoughts. So I decided to stick with football and charity work, which have always been my two biggest interests."

She hates bringing up the times when her choices have hit the wall of other people's small-mindedness. Because every time she has to talk or think about it, it's like hitting the wall all over again. And she has to watch the reaction of the person she's talking to, to see if it's another wall in the making.

"That's just wrong," Cory says. "Totally wrong."

"Not as wrong as that woman's choice of footwear," Infinite Darlene says, nodding to her left, where an eavesdropping woman wears something that looks like a pump that's mated with an Ugg.

The eavesdropper, knowing she's been caught, drops away from the eaves.

"How long have you been—" Cory asks.

"So remarkable?" Infinite Darlene chimes in.

Cory smiles. "Yes. So remarkable."

It seems almost neurological, the way that his smile and his tone can alert Infinite Darlene's brain to send out the charm brigade. It's her own brand of endorphin, her own microbrew of adrenaline.

"At the risk of sounding immodest," she says, leaning in as if she's confiding, "I must declare that I have been remarkable from the very moment of my birth. The doctor took one look, and instead of saying *It's a girl* or *It's a boy*, he proclaimed, 'My heart, it's a star!'

"I was a bundle of joy. And I'll admit—over time, some of my joy fell out of the bundle, and other things got knotted up in there. I found myself forgetting to be remarkable. It stopped seeming like an option, and more like a dream. I wasn't denying the truth—I knew what the truth was—but I was denying myself the power to express it. One morning, I said, *Enough*. I didn't have to say it to anyone else, only to myself. Because I knew that once I said it to myself, I would be remarkable enough to make everyone else fall in line. And if they didn't, they weren't worth the hair on the floor of a beauty parlor."

Infinite Darlene pauses and looks at Cory, who's been following. "And you?" she asks. "How long have you been so remarkable?"

Is he blushing? Yes, Infinite Darlene thinks he blushes for a moment.

"I can remember the first time I did a perfect cartwheel," he says. "I was ten. I'd done plenty of cartwheels before—I would head out to the backyard and do cartwheel after cartwheel, to the point that there were handprints all over the grass, and my mother made me stop. But this cartwheel—every part of it worked. Everything in my body was in balance. My legs were straight in the air, then back down to earth. Heels over head, head over heels. It lasted only a few seconds, but when it was over, I knew that I had touched on something remarkable, and that I myself, for those few seconds, had been remarkable.

"That was the start of it. What's remarkable to me—what's truly remarkable—is the ability not only to find something you love doing, but to be able to share it with other people. As soon as I got on that track, things felt right."

"I want to prove things," Infinite Darlene says. "I want to prove people wrong. I want to prove myself right. But the remarkable thing was when I realized this isn't my actual reason for doing anything. If it happens, all the better. But who wants to live a life trying to prove things? I want to enjoy it, too."

This is an unusual conversation for the forty-second minute of a first date. But both Infinite Darlene and Cory are going with it. They aren't smiling at each other now—they've gotten to the point beyond that, when the twinkle in their eyes and the mischief of their grins are mere decoration for the thoughts and feelings that travel from body to body, mind to mind, heart to heart.

Because it is a Thai restaurant, the food arrives quickly.

Infinite Darlene tries to eat like a lady. Not a girl, not a woman—a lady. There is something in the challenge of it, the precision of it. It is like paying homage to a civility that has long lost its hold on the world around her.

He watches her, but not critically. He watches her, but not intrusively. There are some dates when all the other person wants to do is erase your story and write you into his. This is not one of those dates.

Infinite Darlene watches back, just as uncritically, just as widely.

When you exist as your own creation—that is, when you have worked so hard in creating yourself—it is sometimes difficult to let other people get close enough to see the seams, the flaws, the parts of you that aren't quite done yet. Infinite Darlene feels this about herself. She has yet to experience the flip side—the knowledge that by not letting the other people get too close, you also miss out on seeing their own imperfections, their own seams, their own craftsmanship.

They are two teenagers sitting at a middle table in an above-average Thai restaurant, trying to navigate their own creations in order to construct something that could contain both of them. Cory is joking and laughing and playing out some of the music from his thoughts, but he's also nervous, so deeply nervous that it's like he feels every single blood cell moving through his body, demonstrating what an ever-shifting, never-stable body he is. Infinite Darlene is tasting peanuts, tasting lime, tasting a combination of things you would never think to combine if they weren't ingredients, and she is worrying that maybe she is too tall, or not quite funny enough, or has a peanut stuck in her teeth.

Is it possible, she wonders, to have a beautiful boy in front of you without thinking, *You are surely too beautiful for me?*

Is it possible, he wonders, to be filling the air with so many words without feeling that you've hit on a single one that matches what you want to say?

Shyness, it seems, is the reason Cupid needs arrows.

Cory is too shy to tell Infinite Darlene about the moment he decided he wanted to ask her out. She had just been hiked the ball, and was scanning the field to see where to throw. The linebackers were headed her way. She had two seconds, maybe just one. And she would not let that bother her. She looked around the field with such serene concentration, and then when she found what she wanted—an open receiver, about twenty yards away—a knowing smile played across her face. Cory was mid-cheer, and he stopped cold. The syllable caught in his throat as he watched her smile and calmly release the pass. Even as the ball soared through the air, even as the linebackers blocked his view, he kept watching her. He wanted to know her. He wanted to know everything about her.

Infinite Darlene is too shy to tell him that while she has many, many friends, she hasn't had many, many dates. She is too shy to admit that while there are many moments when this doesn't bother her, there are a few moments when it does. Her friends always say they don't understand it, but deep down inside, she worries that she understands perfectly. She made her choices in order to survive, and she has indeed survived, even flourished. But she wonders if, by creating the person she wanted to be, she missed out on creating a person that someone would want to fall in love with. She knows it's possible. Truly, she does. But she also knows it isn't certain.

"How's your food?" Cory asks.

"It's good. Yours?"

"Very good. Very basil-y."

"Basilesque."

"Basilican."

"Basiltastic."

"Basilriffic."

"Basiletic."

"Basilous. My dish is rather basilous."

Infinite Darlene wraps some noodles with her chopsticks. "I'm glad we've gotten that settled."

Cory pauses. Cupid aims his arrow. Hits. Now it's up to Cory to realize that the arrow isn't meant to sit there. It's meant to be used in conversation.

"Can I ask you another adjectival question?" he ventures.

"Adjectival questions are my favorite kind!" Infinite Darlene replies.

"It's personal."

Infinite Darlene smiles. "I think I know where this is going."

"Do people ask you all the time?"

And the funny thing is that, no, they don't ask her all the time.

"Why *infinite?*" Infinite Darlene poses.

Cory nods.

"Because," she explains, "at a certain point, I realized that I was living a very finite life, and I didn't want that anymore. I know that finity is ultimately unavoidable—I mean, we all die, none of us can walk to the moon, and so forth. But I still want to live my life infinitely. I want to live as if anything's possible. Because it's just too boring, too colorless to live finitely. I know I won't go on forever, but I want to be able to go in any direction that seems right."

Maybe Cupid's arrows aren't arrows at all. Maybe, in the right hands, they're keys. Because in answering the question, Infinite Darlene realizes she's been acting finitely. She has let her insecurity lock up her desire.

"For example," she says, "a finite person would sit here and make polite conversation about the appeal of Thai food as opposed to, say, Vietnamese. A finite person would try to disguise how much she likes you, Cory, because she wouldn't challenge her own self-doubt—which can be considerably limiting, in occasions such as this. A finite person wouldn't reach over and hold your hand. But look at what I'm about to do."

He has been holding his glass of water, about to raise it to his lips. But he puts it down. He lets go. His hand is there when she reaches for it.

"You're infinite, too," Infinite Darlene says. "I can tell."
Cupid's key is in her palm, and she is slipping it to him.
"I am," he says. "I am utterly infinite."

At this moment, something shifts in Infinite Darlene. For once, it is not something she controls. In her life, there have always been two competing forces. Her friends have been the bastions of *yes*, telling her she's deserving, telling her she's a wonder, even while members of her family, members of her community, total strangers have tried to trap her with their *no*, have tried to restrict her, have tried to tear her down. It's been a constant struggle, a constant push and pull.

Now she's found the tiebreaker.

Something shifts in Cory as well. Because he's never thought of himself as infinite. And now he wonders if it's possible.

He is grateful for the thought.

When a first date really works, it works like this:

You feel the thrill of opening to the first page of a book.

And you know—instinctively, you know—it's going to be a very long book.

Just as Cory and Infinite Darlene didn't notice the stares they were getting when they sat down, they don't notice the couple now sitting in the corner. They are in their sixties, and it is the wife who is facing them who notices what is happening. She gestures to the wife whose back is to them, and the second wife turns and looks. When she turns back, the two wives smile at each other for a moment. They know exactly how that feels. They are in a later chapter of a very similar book.

"Thai food is divine," Infinite Darlene proclaims, "but Thai restaurants really drop the ball when it comes to dessert, don't they?"

Cory, in no mood for halfhearted ice cream, has to agree.

"So where do we go?" he asks.

"Where don't we go?" she replies.

There are so many places to consider. They could stop off at Spiff's Videorama and see which video they agree on the most. They could go see Infinite Darlene's friend Zeke gig at the nearby coffee shop, where every cappuccino comes with a heart on top. They could head to the new Sock 'n' Bowl and slide shoeless across the glazed floor, caring more about the joy of it than the score. They could get milkshakes and play pinball at the local diner, or wander through the cemetery and trawl for stories there. They could head to Rumson and revisit the football field, lying in the empty bleachers, searching the sky for constellations.

But those are places they've already been. They are places where their friends might be. They are the well-traveled, well-lit paths.

Neither of them wants that. There will come a time that they will introduce their friends into their story, but not now, not yet.

They get in Cory's car and drive.

• • •

Infinite Darlene has an idea. A somewhat insane idea.

She shares it with Cory. He smiles. He says it's an insane idea. But that's not going to get in their way.

It's a place neither of them has ever been.

It takes them an hour to get into the city, and will take them another half hour to get through Manhattan.

They've been talking nonstop—gossiping, joking, telling stories. As they're waiting on the helix to get into the Lincoln Tunnel, Infinite Darlene tells Cory how much she's always loved this view.

"Seeing the city like that," she says, gesturing over the traffic, toward the bright lights, "it's always taken my breath away. But once I became Infinite Darlene, it had this added element. Before, it had always been about how big it was, how grand. I've always loved shiny things, and the city was the shiniest thing of all. But after—well, it was something more than that. I know this may sound silly, but it started to feel like not only was I driving into the shiny, big city, but I was also driving into the future. I love my town, but I am much bigger than my town. The city is my future. And look, there it is."

Cory has never been as confident about his future, and says so. But he also tells her it doesn't matter.

"Sometimes the driver's along for the ride," he says.

He also appreciates shiny things. Like grace. And confidence. They offer their own beacon, often in the form of a person you come to love.

It is very easy to find the Brooklyn Bridge, but not so easy to find parking by the Brooklyn Bridge. Eventually, though,

Cory deftly squeezes into a spot a couple of blocks from the water, right on the fringes of Chinatown.

"Come on!" Infinite Darlene says. She grabs his hand and carries him forward. They are quite the couple, the quarterback and the cheerleader, but no one in New York City seems to notice. A few of the Chinatown merchants squint as Infinite Darlene glides past, but it feels like just another part of the evening, just another piece of the metropolis.

As they get closer to the pedestrian walkway, Infinite Darlene confides, "I've been curious about this ever since I was a little girl."

Cory pictures her—he actually pictures her as a little girl, perhaps in town for the Easter parade. He sees her in a dress and bonnet. And even though he knows this wasn't really what the picture was, he goes along with Infinite Darlene's construction of the past, because it's so heartfelt and so convincing.

He doesn't tell Infinite Darlene that he's afraid of heights. But when they get on the bridge—when they are standing over an actual river, with all the traffic whooshing by—his steps become a little less sure. He wasn't expecting so much wind, and neither was she. Her hair is flying everywhere . . . but she likes the feeling. She likes it when the world loosens up a little, when it moves with some freedom.

He feels a little wobbly. The traffic isn't helping. He knows the bridge has stood for over a hundred years. But he can't help but wonder if this is the night it will finally give up, say it's tired of doing this for a living.

She sees. He is putting on a brave face, but brave faces are among the easiest for a student of human nature to spot.

"Oh dear," she says. Then she amends it to: "You poor dear. What have I done to you?"

But he doesn't stop. He holds her hand and keeps going. They make it to the middle.

The web of suspension cables rises on either side of them, tracing back to the towers that look as old and immortal as anything the city has to offer. Headlights and taillights stream below them. The river undulates darkly, and the moon peeks around a cloud.

"This is not where I thought the night was heading," Cory tells Infinite Darlene.

She smiles. "Nor I, my dear. Nor I."

She is holding one of his hands. He takes her other hand. They are a ring.

He pulls down on her arms and raises up his face. She realizes what is happening and bends over slowly, so her lips will match his.

It is not Infinite Darlene's first kiss, but it's the first one that counts. Everything before has felt like an attempt. This kiss is its own creation.

She closes her eyes, but she doesn't drift very far. In fact, she doesn't drift at all. And neither does he.

Cars pass. Dozens, even hundreds, of people pass. The moon changes its position slightly. Dotted lights reflect in the water.

She opens her eyes and looks into his.

"We are the only two people in the world," she says.

"We are the only two people in the world," he agrees.

It turns out to be a very long book.

TRACK FIVE

The Mulberry Branch

1.

There must be pictures
of storytime from that time,
back when our corduroys had elastic
and our sneakers flashed red.
There has to be some record
that we were in the same room
at the same time, no possibility
of knowing that someday the girl
sitting next to me, watching
that purple crayon draw the moon,
would be the one to make me realize
I have a heart.

2.

A funny thing happened to me
on the way to Mulberry Street.
I knew you would be there
in your usual place, folded
into a chair, folded around a book,
music in your ears without you
really hearing it, because

when words and songs collide,
it's the words that get through to you,
and everything else ties for third place.
Except maybe me, except maybe
if I'm there, turning the pages
beside you, lost in my own story,
but not as lost as you are
in yours. I was picturing this
on my way to Mulberry Street
and as I did, a ragtag marching band
trumpeted their way down Prince Street,
like they'd made a wrong turn at Macy's
and were trying to horn their way back.
The Soho shoppers were stupefied,
some gleeful, others glaring.
I caught the eye of a triangle player
wearing a high square hat,
and smiled when he refused
to smile first. I wanted you
to be there, and even though
you were only a block away, it wasn't
close enough. I wanted to be close
enough to see your head lift
as the marching music infiltrated
your concentration. I wanted
to share the smile that would happen
when you figured out
what was happening.
This is what love does—
it draws these pictures
out of air that doesn't feel
thin at all. Thick air,
the undark matter

of everything I think of
when I think about you,
all these thoughts
that take up so much space
and don't take up any space
at all. When I showed up
at the library, you could see
the story written across my face,
and took off your headphones
and put down your book
so I could tell you
everything.

3.

I was at the library with friends
and you were there
with a book. I noticed
what you were reading
before I saw you were reading it.
Or at least that was my cover.
School was out, and I was
a different person out of it.
You wouldn't have liked me
in the mind-numb variation
I played during the day.
I held myself at a distance
until the last bell rang, so by the time
I hit the afternoon, I was adrenalized
from all of the things I hadn't said.
All of my friends
were like that—climbing over
the library, gossip-crazy and loud,

checking the computers every five seconds
to see how our lives
would update. If you were the
self-settled corner,
we were the self-proclaimed center.
But there was a pathway,
a tangent my eye made
when it spotted how devoted you were
to your paperback.
First I saw your glasses,
then I saw your book, then I saw
your face, and it was the face
(not the glasses, not the book)
that caused me to focus, caused me
to shake off the commotion
and dive into the silence of
myself, because it was a silence
you appeared to be sharing.
I let myself drift from the center,
first Jupiter, then Saturn, moving
a Neptune distance from my friends,
then finally Pluto cut loose
to hover at the shelf next to you,
pretending to look for something
other than the girl at my feet.
I saw you see me, saw you see
my hand reach for a book
I didn't really need, and then
put it back. Out of orbit,
I reached into the vast unknown
and said I really liked
the book you were reading—
what you would later call

my (Vonne)gut instinct—
and you said you really liked
it, too, and that was all it took
for two tangents to curve
into a new orbit, for two girls
to meet in a library.

4.

It was your mother who asked
about storytime, asked if you
remembered storytime, and
even though you couldn't,
I could. The pillows seemed
as big as cars, the carpet
ready to fly from our feet.
I was still willing to believe
that everything was true,
so I danced with the wild things,
visited the night kitchen,
said goodnight to the moon,
and all along, you were there,
too. We shared this,
long before we shared kisses
or trust or conversation.
That storyteller taught us
together, taught us how to
make soup from stone,
make way for ducklings,
make it to where the sidewalk ends,
make it through any terrible,
horrible,
no good,

very bad
day.

5.

I'd meet you in the stacks,
meet you surrounded by books,
escape from the subterranean
frustration of my day and emerge
to find you waiting for me in the
808s, my heart leaping at a Dewey
decibel, all the noise turning into something
like a song. My days had possessed
a pulse, but now they had a rhythm,
to have you there waiting for me,
even if I was the first to get there.
I knew you'd be there soon enough.
To be with you
meant not having to talk,
not having to prove myself,
not having to worry
about doing everything right,
because we were as good
in the silences as we were
in the sentences, like the balance
of the library, containing
millions of words
but creating that safe and quiet space
where they can be explored without rushing,
encountered
in our own time.
We were still tethered to school
until our homework was done,

but that felt immaterial
compared to the way our spines would touch
when we sat back to back on the floor,
the way the small kids would run
around us like we were part of a jungle gym,
how we'd find each other's loosest threads
and manage to tie them off by talking about them.
We'd exist like this until closing time,
until dinnertime, and more often than not,
we'd continue off together,
your house or mine,
it didn't really matter
because they were both stops
in the same shared world.

6.

This is what a library knows:
To read, it's not enough
to have a book.
You also need
a comfortable chair,
good light,
inabsolute quiet,
the feeling of other readers
orbiting around you.
Reading is a conversation
between you and an author,
held inside
the pages of a book.
The library allows
the conversation
to occur.

7.

To love, it's not enough
to have a girlfriend.
You also need
a comfortable heart,
good light,
inabsolute quiet,
the feeling of other friends
orbiting around you.
Love is a conversation
between you and the one you love,
held inside
the pages of a life.
For us, the library allowed
the conversation
to occur.

8.

Imagine if the storyteller
had opened her book one day
and told us the tale
of what we'd become.
What if she had seen us
on different corners
of the carpet, and had said,
'One day, such riches
shall be yours!'
We would have thought
she meant coins or candy,
the pot at the end of the rainbow,
the hoard in the dragon's lair.

But she would have told us, 'No,
there is a deeper richness
that life sometimes offers,
and you will find it
in each other.'
I would have made a face.
You would have made a face.
We would have told her to go on
with the story, get to the
adventure parts.
And she would have said,
'You will.
Mark my words,
you will.
Make soup from stone.
Make way for ducklings.
Make it to where the sidewalk ends,
make it through any terrible, horrible,
no good, very bad day,
and at the other end, you will find her
waiting for you. You will find her
again and again
and each time
you will be grateful.'

9.

The librarian lets us linger.
We can stay until
the last light is turned off,
until the carts make their way
back to the office,
empty because

all of the books are back on their shelves,
back home with their neighbors,
back where they, like we, belong.
If it were in my power,
I would keep the libraries open
all night long.
I would give the librarians
the keys to the city
so they could keep unlocking
each of us
by providing the stories
that draw us out of our shells
and into the world.

10.

You look up from the book
and your eyes are
storytelling.

11.

Nobody is writing us down
as I whisper something
that makes you laugh.
No words fall onto a page
as you take my hand
and welcome me
to a new part of the day.
We are writing ourselves,
writing each other.
I am words,
and there you are
to read them.

TRACK SIX

Your Temporary Santa

It's hard not to feel just a little bit fat when your boyfriend asks you to be Santa Claus.

"But I'm Jewish," I protest. "It would be one thing if you were asking me to be Jesus—he, at least, was a member of my tribe, and looks good in a Speedo. Plus, Santa requires you to be jolly, whereas Jesus only requires you to be born."

"I'm serious," Connor says. It is rare enough for him to be serious with me that he has to point it out. "This might be the last Christmas where Riley believes in Santa. And if I try to be Santa, she'll know. It has to be you. I don't have anyone else."

"What about Lana?" I ask, referring to the older of his younger sisters.

He shakes his head. "There's no way. There's just no way."

This does not surprise me. Lana's demeanor is more claws-out than Claus-on. She is only twelve, and I am scared of her.

"Pweeeeeeeeeeeeeease," Connor cajoles.

I tell him I can't believe he's resorting to his cute voice. As if I'm more likely to make a fool of myself if he's making a fool of himself.

"The suit won't even need to be altered!" he promises.

This is, of course, what I am afraid of.

●　●　●

Christmas Eve for me has always been about my family figuring out which movies we're going to see the next day. (The way we deliberate, I think it's easier to choose a pope.) Once that's done, we retreat to our separate corners to do our separate things.

Nobody in my family is particularly religious, but there's still no way I'm letting them see me leave the house in a Santa costume. Instead I sneak out a little before midnight and attempt to change in the back seat of my car. Because it is a two-door Accord, this requires some maneuvering on my part. Any casual passerby looking into the window would think I was either strangling Santa or making out with him. The pants and my jeans don't get along, so I have to strip down to my boxers, then become Santa below the belt. I had thought it would feel like pajamas, but instead it's like I'm wearing a discarded curtain.

And that's not even taking into account the white fur. It occurs to me now to wonder where, exactly, this fur is supposed to have come from, if Santa spends so much time at the North Pole. Perhaps it's him, not global warming, that's dooming the polar bears. It's a thought. Not much of one, but it's all I can muster at this hour, in the back seat of this car.

As I'm strapping on my belly and putting on my coat, Connor is meant to be asleep, safe in his dreams. He offered to stay up, but I thought that would be too risky—if we got caught, not only would we be in trouble, but the jig would be up with Riley. Lana and his mother are supposed to be asleep, too—I don't think they have any idea I'm coming, and only have a vague idea of who I am in the first place. It's Riley who's supposed to be awake—if not right at this moment, then when I appear in her living room. This is all for her six-year-old eyes to take in. I wouldn't be doing it otherwise.

I also have a gift of my own to deliver—a wrapped box

for Connor, which I am trying desperately not to smash as I grasp in the dark for my boots and my beard. It's the first Christmas since we started dating, and I spent way too much time thinking about what to get him. He says presents aren't important, but I think they are—not because of how much they cost, but for the opportunity they provide to say *I understand you*. Plus, there was the risk factor: When I ordered the present three weeks ago, there was always the slim chance we wouldn't make it to Christmas. But that hasn't happened. We've made it.

Once I'm dressed, I find it near impossible to slide into the front seat with any ease. I must manipulate both the seat and the steering wheel in order to lever my Santatude into the driver's seat. Suddenly I understand the appeal of an open sled.

I have only been to Connor's house a few times, and most of those were before we started dating. His mother mostly knows me as one of a group of friends, a body on the couch or a face over a bowl of chips, because Connor and I were very much part of a six before we decided to become a two. Every now and then, Riley would visit our adolescent playground, steal some of our snacks, flirt with whoever would pay attention to her. Lana, meanwhile, would stay in her room and blast her music loud enough to haunt any sound we were trying to make.

I feel strange pulling up the driveway in a Santa suit, so I park at the curb, in front of the house next door. I can only imagine what I must look like as I step out of the car—the street is eerily quiet, its own midnight mass. Instead of feeling like a roly-poly emissary of cheer and good will, I picture myself as the killer from a Z-grade horror movie—*Santa's Slay Ride!*—about to wreak havoc on some upstanding citizens and a few underintelligent, underdressed youth. Then I realize I've left Connor's key in my jeans, so I have to go back and fetch it—making myself look like an *incompetent* serial killer.

Plus, the beard itches.

Even though we're Jewish, my parents insisted at first that Santa did, in fact, exist. He just never came to our house. The way they presented it, it was a time-management issue.

"He can only go to so many houses in one night," they told me. "So he skips over the boys and girls who already had eight days of Chanukah. But you can wave to him as he flies past, if you want."

This meant that at a young age I would stay up late on Christmas Eve to wave to Santa before he visited our neighbors' house. These neighbors, who had a boy my age, were the real reason I wasn't told the truth about Santa—my parents assumed that I would share my myth-busting knowledge the minute I learned it, which was not an incorrect assumption. I had already ruined the Easter Bunny for most of my friends—while a fat man flying around the world to give presents seemed rational to me, the idea of a bunny handing out eggs just seemed stupid.

In the end, it was the neighbor boy who gave me the information I needed to expose the truth. Our conversation went something like this:

Him: "Santa's other name is Saint Nick."

Me: "Saint Nick Claus?"

Him: "No. Just Saint Nick. For Saint Nicholas."

Me: "But aren't all saints dead? Like, if Santa Claus is a saint, doesn't that mean he's *dead*?"

I could see the truth hitting him. Then he burst into tears.

• • •

I have been given very explicit instructions, as if this is some one-man production of *Ocean's Eleven*. The presents have already been placed under the tree, and the stockings have already been stuffed, and I am supposed to undo this to some degree, then jostle Riley's door frame so she wakes up, sneaks out, and sees me put everything in place. I have made Connor assure me at least a half dozen times that his mom doesn't keep a firearm under her bed. He swears that she does not, and that she will be so tranq'd up that I could ride a full co-terie of reindeer through her bedroom and she still wouldn't wake up. I fear this has implications for fire safety, but keep that fear to myself.

I want Connor to be awake. I want him to be with me in his house. It's strange to tiptoe through the kitchen without him. It's strange to be hearing the shelter-silence of the hall-way without having his breathing there as well. I know his presence would ruin the charade, but I want him whispering from the wings, my own yuletide Cyrano.

Instead I have pictures of him watching over me, pictures of him and his sisters, with an occasional cameo by their mom. A photographic growth chart as I get closer to the liv-ing room. I am waiting for one of the photos to start laughing at me—the left leg of my pants keeps getting caught beneath my boot. I fear a rip at any time.

The room is lit by the tree, and the tree is lit by strings of colored lights. There's a star at the top, and I think that, yes, this is how it's supposed to be—the point of a Christmas tree is for it to look like all the other Christmas trees, but still be a little bit your own. There aren't as many presents underneath as I imagined there would be. I have to remind myself that we aren't dealing with von Trapps here—there are only four people in this house. And there's only one day of Christmas, not eight.

I feel somewhat ridiculous moving the presents to the base of the fireplace—but if I'm going to fake this, I'm going to have to fake it authentically, and make it look like the chimney was my entryway, despite my—*Santa's*—girth. I keep my stirrings to a sub-mouse level, because the last thing I want is Riley waking up and seeing Santa pulling her presents from under the tree, which would totally bedevil our plans. When the right number of gifts have been safely stationed, I add my present for Connor into the mix—I haven't told him I'm going to leave it, and I like the idea of surprising him.

I am not usually up this late without a computer open in front of me. The heat in the room draws up into my armpits to remind me all over again of what I'm wearing. I decide not to take things out of the stockings, because I'm worried I won't remember how to put everything back in the right place.

Now I have to go jostle Riley's door and alert her to my presence. I have no idea what I'm supposed to do if she doesn't come out of her room. Am I supposed to go in and get her? Waking up to Santa leaning over your bed would probably be traumatizing. The last thing I want is for her to scream. The last thing I want is to have to explain any of this to her mother.

At least her door is easy to identify—Connor may be the gay one, but Riley's cornered the market on the Disney princesses. I wish I'd brought a bell to jingle, or a reindeer to make the appropriate hoof-roof sounds. Knocking seems wrong. From the door, Elsa gives me an icy stare, and Ariel looks at me like I'm drowning. Even perky Belle's smile seems to say, *The only thing worse than being Santa is being a half-assed Santa. Do your job or you're only getting five nights of Chanukah next year.*

Quietly, I lean into Belle so that my beard is brushing her

cheek. Then, louder with each syllable, I release a "ho . . . Ho . . . HO!" I hear a rustling on the other side of the door— Riley's clearly been waiting for this moment. Treading with the authority of a man a couple hundred pounds larger than me, I move back to the living room.

When I'm out of the hall, a doorway squeaks open. Pint-size footsteps patter behind me, trying to be silent but not quite managing it.

I have to ask myself: *What would Santa do?* I head to where I stashed the presents, and start returning them to their places under the tree. This seems a little menial for Santa—surely there are elves to do this kind of thing? But I suppose since he travels solo, this is part of the gig. I think about whistling a tune, but "Santa Claus Is Comin' to Town" seems too egotistical, and "Jingle Bells" makes me think of—

"Excuse me," a small voice interrupts.

I look down, and there's Riley in a nightgown that makes me think of Wendy from *Peter Pan*. Only it's Tinker Bell who's wearing it. Riley is a sleepy-eyed wisp of a girl at this hour. But her voice is wide awake.

Connor had told me she wouldn't interrupt. He'd sworn she'd see me and run back to bed, pleased to have her Christmas wishes confirmed.

"Yes, little girl," I say. I am very conscious that this makes me sound like the Big Bad Wolf, so I cheer it up about halfway through, which makes me sound like the Big Bad Wolf after three Red Bulls.

"Are you real?"

"Of course I'm real! I'm right here!"

This logic seems to satisfy her . . . momentarily.

"But who are you?" she asks.

Who do you want me to be? I almost ask back. But I know the answer. And it isn't me. And it isn't Santa Claus.

I am grateful for the dimness of the room, and the tenacity of my beard. I am grateful that I remembered to change out of my sneakers. And I am scared that I am going to fuck this up for her anyway. If I don't answer well, I am going to give her the amazing gracelessness of the hour she first disbelieved.

And at the same time . . . I can't bring myself to say *I am Santa Claus*. Because I know I am not Santa Claus. And I know I am not a good enough liar to make her believe it.

So I say, jolly as a jelly donut, "You know who I am. I came all the way from the North Pole to be with you tonight."

Her eyes widen. And in that moment, in that momentary loss of logic to wonder, I see the family resemblance. I see Connor and the way he is never too cool to show that something is special to him—whether it's his glee as we're watching *Harold and Maude*, or his beaming when a favorite song comes on the radio, or the simple smile he gets when I walk into the room and he's been waiting for me. There is no cynicism there. It's as if he hasn't even heard of the concept of cynicism. Which allows me to retreat from it, from time to time.

Now here's Riley, at that age when the delicate shell of childhood is starting to show its cracks. I know all of the department-store questions I could be asking her—*Have you been a good girl this year? What would you like Santa to bring you?* But that's not what I want to say.

"Don't stop believing," I tell her.

She looks at me quizzically. "Like the song?"

I chortle out a "ho ho ho!" and then say, "Yes. *Exactly* like the song."

I am bending over so I can look her in the eye as I say this. Before I can rise up, she reaches out for my beard. I flinch, expecting the yank, the unmasking. But instead she reaches past it to pat me on the shoulder.

"You're doing a very good job," she says.

I have no idea if she's talking to me or to Santa. In order for the former to continue to do a good job, I have to act as if it's the latter.

"*Ho ho ho!* Thank you, Riley!"

She's happily surprised. "You know my name!"

"Of course! How else would I know which presents to bring?"

This statement pleases her. She nods and takes a step back.

I smile.

She smiles.

I smile some more. Shuffle a little.

She smiles back. Doesn't move.

I wonder if it would be rude for Santa to glance at his watch.

She keeps looking at me.

"So . . . um . . . I'm not supposed to deliver the presents while you're in the room. It's against the Santa rules."

"But you're the only Santa. Don't you make the rules?"

I shake my head. "Nope. They're passed down from Santa to Santa."

"And who was the Santa before you?"

I think for a second before I say, "My mom."

She giggles at that.

I smile.

She smiles.

She will not leave the room.

I imagine Connor watching us, thoroughly amused.

You're so bad at goodbyes, he whispers in my ear. Which is true. There is an average of about forty-seven minutes between the time we first type *goodnight* and the moment we actually stop sending our words back and forth.

"The reindeer need me," I say. "Other kids need me. This is actually near the start of my route."

I know that six-year-olds are rarely moved by an appeal to the greater good. But Riley seems to get it. She backs up a little. Thinks about it.

Then, before I can prepare myself, she runs in for a hug. Her head snuggles against the pillow of my stomach. Her arms link behind my legs. There's no way she can't tell the pillow is a pillow. There's no way she can avoid how baggy the pants are around my legs. But that's not what she's thinking about. Right now, all she's thinking about is holding on. I feel it in the way she puts all of her six-year-old strength into it.

She wants me to be real.

"Merry Christmas, Riley," Santa says. "Merry, merry Christmas."

She pulls away, looks up at me, and says, with complete earnestness, "I'm gonna go to sleep now."

"Sweet dreams," Santa wishes her. Then I add another "Ho ho ho!" for good measure.

She returns to her room with the same careful footsteps as before. She wants to keep the secret from the rest of the house.

I watch her go, and wait until I hear the determined close of her door. Then I move more presents back under the tree. Within a minute, though, there's another noise. It sounds like . . . clapping.

"Bravo, Santa," a sarcastic voice says. "That must make you feel awesome, fooling little girls like that."

Lana is in the doorway that leads to the kitchen. She's got on a nightshirt and sweatpants, but doesn't look like she's slept yet tonight—she's vampiric even on a full night's sleep, so it's hard to tell for sure.

"Hi, Lana," I say quietly. I don't want Riley to hear us.

"Hi, *Santa*." She steps into the room and looks me over. I am not used to such scrutiny from a twelve-year-old. "I have no idea what sexual favors my brother promised you to do this, but really? You look like a dumbfuck asshat."

"It's wonderful to see you, too!" I chirp, and continue to put the presents back under the tree.

"What, no 'ho ho ho' for me? Is it because I've been a bad girl this year? It seems so entirely fair that an old white guy would get to judge that. Haven't you at least brought me my lump of coal?"

"*Shhh*. She'll hear you."

"And that would be a bad thing why? I know Connor is a big fan of maintaining illusions, but I think that's bullshit. I can't *believe* he gave you that costume. He had no right to do that."

I have not been dating Connor long enough to yell at his sister. I know this. Which is why I don't answer her, don't look at her. The presents are almost all under the tree by now. Then I can go.

"What . . . reindeer got your tongue?" Lana taunts. "Oh, I see how it is. Indulge Riley in whatever delusion you want. But you don't have to pay attention to me. None of you do."

"Lana, really. Keep your voice down, please."

"*Please!* Santa, you're so *polite*." She's coming closer now. "No wonder Connor likes you."

Normally, it would make me really happy to hear that Connor likes me. But she says it like it's an accusation.

"You know who always did this, right?" she goes on. "You know whose suit that is? You know that for years I was just as stupid as Riley, thinking that it was Santa, thinking that it would always be this way. But now I'm guessing Connor was the stupidest, if he thought he could just dress you up and make it like he wasn't abandoned like the rest of us."

I move the last present back into place.

"What? Aren't you going to defend him? Aren't you going to tell me that it makes sense? I'm dying to hear how you can justify being here. How you pretend this is normal when everything has completely fallen apart."

I look at her in the eye for the first time. But the way she's looking at me is so unfriendly that I have to look away.

"I'm here because he asked me to," I say. "That's all."

"Awwww," she says, as if I were a kitten video. "You're in *wuv*."

And this time I can't stand it. This time I have to say something. So I look her in the eye again, and this time, unwavering, I say, "Yes. I am. In love."

For a second, she is silent. For a second, I think this has placated her. For a second, I think she'll understand. But her recovery is so smooth it doesn't even seem like she's recovering.

"I hate you," she says.

Now I'm the one who's stunned.

"Why?" I ask.

"Because you can't have him. You can't just start dating him and then have him. You can't be this to him. You're not important enough to be this."

My natural inclination is to say I'm sorry. To apologize for being here. To apologize for tricking her sister into believing for one last year.

But I'm not really sorry, I find. So instead I say, "You're so angry."

"Duh! I think I have reason to be."

"But not with me."

As soon as I say it, I realize it's the wrong thing to say. Because it's not about me at all.

"It's not because you're gay," Lana says. "You know that, right? I'd be just as pissed if you were a girl."

It's a strange concession to get.

"So what do you want for Christmas, little girl?" I resume in my Santa voice.

I figure she'll give me shit for the *little girl* part. But instead she says, "I want it to not be you in that suit."

I nod. I go back to my own voice. "I get that. But you've got to tell me something Santa can actually give you."

"It's not like you brought any presents."

"I brought one."

"For Riley? Oh, for Connor."

"I hope you understand why I didn't bring one for you."

"Why?"

"Because you're always so goddamn fucking mean to me."

She laughs out in surprise, then says, "Fair enough."

We stand in silence for a moment. Then we both hear it.

A door opening. We stay silent.

Small footsteps.

"Shit," Lana whispers.

Riley reappears, and only seems a little bothered to see that Lana's with me.

"Are you getting him cookies?" the younger sister asks of the older. "I was going to sleep, but I remembered I didn't give him any cookies."

And the older sister, without missing a beat, replies, "I'll go get them."

She leaves for the kitchen. Riley, unable to help herself, stares at the presents under the tree. I remember doing the same thing with the presents around the menorah—trying to calculate which ones were for me, and what could be inside. My mother would often wrap things in boxes larger than they needed, just to throw me off.

"Where do you go next?" Riley asks me.

"Nebraska," I reply.

She nods.

Lana comes out of the kitchen with some Pepperidge Farm cookies thrown on a plate and a glass of milk.

"Here you go," she says.

I take a cookie. It's a little stale.

"Best cookie I've had all night!" I proclaim for Riley's benefit.

I can see Lana wants to cry bullshit. But she keeps it to herself.

"Well, then," she says, "I guess it's time for you to go."

"To Nebraska!" Riley chimes in.

The weird thing is, I want to stay. Now that we've gotten here, now that at least one of them knows who I really am, I want to remain a part of this. I want Lana to offer to wake Connor up. I want the four of us to eat cookies until sunrise.

"C'mon." Lana interrupts my thoughts. "Nebraska is waiting."

"You're so right," I say, moving toward the door.

"Not that way!" Lana gestures to the chimney. "This is the only way up to the roof."

I can feel Riley's eyes on me. Although I'm sure there is one somewhere, I can't think of a rational explanation for me to use the door.

So I head over to the fireplace. It looks like it's never been used. I lean in and see the chimney isn't very wide. I lean back out and make eye contact with Riley.

"Off you go to bed!" I cry.

Riley starts to wave. Lana mostly smirks.

"Safe travels," she says.

I don't know what else to do. I crawl into the fireplace. Then I pull myself up into the chimney and count to two hundred—which is roughly the number of cobwebs I'm surrounded by. For one scary moment, I think my stomach is going to keep me wedged inside, but there is a little room to maneuver—thankfully, Santa hasn't been having cookies at all the stops. There is dust on my tongue, dust in my eyes. Surely there are better ways to enter and exit a house? Why doesn't Santa just park the goddamn sleigh in the driveway like a normal guest?

I hear Lana wish Riley goodnight. I hear both doors close. Quietly, I pull myself out of the chimney and shake as much dust as possible from my suit, causing a hoarder's snowfall on the carpet. Let Lana explain that one.

My work here is done, I think. But the thought feels hollow. I know I can't leave without seeing him. That wasn't the plan, but none of this was really the plan. I can't be in his house without letting him know I was here. It will all be unfinished, otherwise.

The house has retreated into its nighttime breathing of whirs and clicks and groans. I step carefully for a moment, then stop: There is no way that Riley will have fallen asleep by now, and the path to Connor's door leads right past hers. So I stand still, and realize how rarely I ever stand still. I have to quell any desire to be participant, and recline into the shape of a total observer. My phone, the weapon with which I usually kill time, is back in the car. Unarmed, I look around. The Christmas-lit room appears lonely in its pausing; something is missing, and I am not that something. There are books on the shelves, but I cannot read what they are. They are a row of shapes leaning. On one shelf, the books are guarded by pairs of small figurines. Salt and pepper shakers. Somebody's collection.

I let the minutes pass, but by thinking about them, I make them pass slowly. This is not my house, and I am caught in the knowledge that it never will be. I half expect Lana to come back out, to tell me to go home. *Why are you still here?* she'd ask, and the only answer I could give would be her brother's name.

I know he wanted me here, but why did it have to be like this? I want him to introduce me as his boyfriend. I want to be sitting at the dinner table, making jokes with Riley that Lana can't help but laugh at, too. I want them to see me holding his hand. I want to be holding his hand. I want him to love me when I'm naughty and when I'm nice. I want. I want. I want.

I am worried about being in love, because it involves asking so much. I am worried that my life will never fit into his. That I will never know him. That he will never know me. That we get to hear the stories, but never get to hear the full truth.

"Enough," I say to myself. I need to say it out loud, because I need to really hear it.

I listen for Riley. I listen for Lana. I hope they're not listening for Santa, or for me.

I make it down the hall. I make it past their doors. Connor's room is in sight.

It's only when I am standing in front of it, only when I am about to let myself inside, that I sense there's someone else in the hall with me. I turn around and see her standing in her doorway—Connor's mother. Her eyes are nearly closed, her hair limp. She's wearing a Tennessee Williams nightgown that makes me feel sad and awkward to see it. It hangs lifeless on her body, worn too often, too long. I should not be seeing her like this, the deep dark haze of it.

90

I want to be as much of a ghost to her as she is to me. But there can be no hiding. I am about to explain. I am about to tell her the whole thing. But she stops me by speaking first.

"Where have you been?" she asks.

I suddenly feel I could never explain enough. I could never give the right answer.

"I'm not here," I say.

She nods, understanding this. I think there will be more, but there isn't any more. She turns back to her room and closes the door behind her.

I know I should not have seen this. Even if she forgets, I will know. And for a moment, I find myself feeling sorry for Santa. I can only imagine what he sees in his trespasses. But, of course, those would all be people he doesn't really know. I have to imagine it's less sad with strangers.

I am not going to tell Connor any of this. I am just going to say hello and say goodnight. I sneak into his room and close the door with as little sound as possible. I want him to have been awake the whole time, wishing me well. I want him to greet me the moment the coast is clear. But all that welcomes me is the sound of his sleeping. There is enough light coming in from the window that the room is a blue-dark shadow. I can see him there in his bed. I can see the rise and fall of his breathing. His phone is on the floor, fallen from his hand. I know it was there in case I needed him.

I have never seen him sleeping before. I have never seen him like this, enfolded in an unthreatening somewhere else. My heart is drawn, almost involuntarily, toward him. I see him asleep and feel I could love him for a very long time.

But here I am, standing outside of it. Even as I love him, I feel self-conscious. I am the interruption. I am the piece that's not a dream. I am here because I climbed through the chimney instead of knocking on the door.

I take off my hat and unstick my beard. I take off my boots and move them aside. I unfasten my stomach and let it fall to the floor. I pull the red curtain from around my body, pull it over my head. I shed the pants, feel the cold air on my legs. I do all of this quietly. It's only as I am folding Santa's clothes into a safe red square that I hear Connor say my name.

It should be enough as I step over to him and see the welcome in his eyes. It should be enough to see his hair pointing in all different directions, and the fact that there are cowboys on his pajama pants and he is telling me he can't believe he fell asleep. It should be enough that he is beckoning me now—it should be enough to join him in the bed, blanket pulled aside. It should be enough to feel his hand on my shoulder, his lips lightly on my lips. But something is not right. I still feel that, in some way, I should not be here.

"I'm an imposter," I whisper.

"Yes," he whispers back. "But you're the right imposter."

Without my Santa suit, I am shivering. Without my Santa suit, I am just me, and I am in his house after midnight on Christmas Day. Without my Santa suit, I am real, and I want this to be reality. I want this to be the way things are, or at least how they will be.

Connor feels me shiver. Without a word, he wraps the blanket around us. Our home within his home. Our world within this world.

Outside, there may be reindeer that fly across the moon. Outside, there may be questions with the wrong answers and lies that are better to tell. Outside, it may be cold. But I am here. I am here, and he is here, and everything I need to know is that I will hold him and he will hold me until I am warm again, until I know I belong.

TRACK SEVEN

Storytime

When I was little, my parents had a routine for putting me and my sister to bed. There would be the one-hour warning, then the half-hour warning, then the five-minute warning. My sister and I had no real grasp of time—the worth of a minute was as intangible then as it is now, albeit in a considerably different way. The rhythm of our evening was set to these warnings—when to head upstairs, when to get into our pajamas, when to brush our teeth. Eventually time would be up and we'd crawl into our respective beds in our respective rooms. There we'd find the most magical thing of all: that time had not, in fact, run out. There were still a few minutes left in the evening, and that was storytime.

Our parents would alternate. My mother with my sister and my father with me, then the reverse the next night. Wherever one left off, the other would pick up. I have no idea if they compared notes, or if they just assumed (rightfully) that my sister and I would only hold them to the loose demands of dream logic.

My stories would always start with a prince.

"What is the prince's name?" my mother or father would ask.

I knew I could answer with my own name, but I never did.

Instead I would pluck words from the air—words overheard, words not really understood.

"Halogen," my answer might be.

"And what is the name of Prince Halogen's kingdom?"

"Orchestra."

My mother or father would nod, and the story would begin. The first night, Prince Halogen might be on a quest to find the Golden Volt of Arcadia. The next night, he might encounter a magical football field, and have to score a last-minute field goal that would cause all of the citizens in Orchestra to play their instruments in cheer. Then he would return to his quest for the Golden Volt, aided by an ogre with a soft spot for peanut butter, the color puce, and valiant boys named after light bulbs.

I couldn't have been more pleased if my parents had taken two empty knitting needles and knitted a new blanket to wrap around my body each night, conjuring the yarn from the thickness of the night air, dressing me for sleep in the color of words.

"Did your parents read you to sleep?" I'm often asked now, because of what I've chosen to do with my life.

"Yes," I always say. But there were no books involved. Just two people in the dark. One telling a story, the other listening raptly. This is what I remember of my childhood: each night a different chapter of a story that would never, ever end.

When it came to relationships, I had lost my imagination.

I had just broken up with Peck, after almost two years. The ending had been deeply grounded in reality, as endings often are—the intense attrition of falling apart while at the same time trying to remain together, the catalog of disappointment and regret that plays over every interaction, until finally the whole thing collapses or merely sinks. There is a certain awe afterwards, when you look at the rubble or the hole and you picture what used to be there. But that awe is not magic; it's an aftershock of failure.

In the months-long postmortem—when I persistently dissected the past, trying to figure out what went wrong—there were no flights of fancy, no stories told that weren't biased reportage of What (Might Have) Really Happened. And this didn't just apply to Peck—I went back, to my relationships with John and Cameron and Kraig, each one put under the microscope, each one subject to the false and bitter science of laying blame. I pulled everyone I could into this examination—my friends, my family, my therapist. I became a creature of documentary earnestness, as pleasant to be with as a news channel.

I was in no mood to date, but I went on dates anyway, just to prove that I could still be appealing, still desired. This was a mistake. The interactions—over coffee, over drinks, over dinner—had all the romantic current of a job interview, the tenderness of a transcript. When asked a question, I gave an answer, but it was all information, no storytelling. I thought the other guy would call me out on it, might shake me up, but the truth was that most of the guys I went on dates with were as deadened by the process as I was.

I gave up. Instead of retreating to somewhere fantastical, somewhere inspired, I settled into the pall of the day-to-day. I ceded my attention to blogs and unreal housewives on TV. I stopped writing, stopped making things up.

I was no fun to be around, even for me.

I didn't even want to go to the party. Brent was Lisa's friend, not mine.

"It's bowling," she said. "How can bowling not be fun?"

I didn't really feel I needed to answer that question.

Lisa resorted to the classic it's-Saturday-night-and-if-you-stay-home-you're-pathetic argument, which worked wonders.

So there I was, bowling. I was not a disastrous bowler, nor was I good enough to take any pride in it. We were split into teams, and that's how I met Callum. There was no machination involved here—it was entirely random, which we would later appreciate.

The first words he said to me were: "My bowling performance depends entirely on the song that's playing. I really hope they play good music here."

A Lady Gaga song was being piped in. To my gay discredit, I didn't know which one.

"How's this?" I asked.

"I prefer the Breeders," he told me. "If they play 'Cannonball,' I'm guaranteed a strike."

I smiled as if I knew who the Breeders were. We went our separate ways to select our bowling balls.

When we returned, we discovered that we'd both chosen green.

"Luck of the Irish," Callum said, tipping an imaginary hat.

I'll be honest: I didn't like him right away.

There were four of us for each lane. Callum and Rinna were both co-workers of Brent's. (I tried to remember what Brent did, and couldn't.) I made much of my inability to bowl well, and secretly wanted to wipe the floor with everyone else at the party. I was not thinking of us as a team, per se, but Callum was relentless in treating us like one. He cheered for me, he cheered for Lisa, he cheered for Rinna, and when it was his turn, he cheered for the ball. When Rinna faltered, he gave her pointers. When I faltered, he knew to keep his distance.

"I'm telling you," he said, "it's the music."

Humbled by two gutter shots in a row, I offered to get another round of drinks. As I did, I asked the guy behind the counter if it was possible to make a musical request. He pointed me in the direction of the girl disinfecting shoes.

"Do you have the Breeders?" I asked her.

She shook her head and gave me a look that made me feel old.

I tried again. "If I gave you my phone, could you hook it up? It's for the birthday boy."

"I guess," she said.

I downloaded the song and handed my phone over. When I returned to my lane with the drinks, Callum was busy bowling and Rinna and Lisa both gave me a look, having seen me give away my phone. I told them it would all make sense in the next frame.

I didn't know why I was doing it. Maybe it had been too long since I'd made anybody happy, and this seemed like a really simple way to make someone happy. It wasn't meant as flirtation, or even kindness. It was just something to do.

I told the shoe girl to start playing it when Callum next got up to bowl. She didn't want to end the previous song early, so when he picked up his Irish-lucky ball, there was still the outro of a Rihanna bondage ballad playing. But as he weighed the ball in his hand and prepared to throw, the air was filled with a very distinctive guitar riff. He nearly dropped the ball in surprise, then turned to the rest of us and *beamed*.

"Holy shit!" he cried, and then proceeded to bowl an eight.

The score didn't matter, though. When he came back to the seats, he was in a full serendipity buzz.

"This is so cool! I never in a million years thought they'd play this song. It's so random."

I wasn't going to tell him, but Lisa had other ideas.

"It's not completely random," she said. "I believe you had a little help."

And I found myself actually blushing.

He thanked me. I said it was nothing, and went to retrieve my phone. He knew well enough not to thank me again, not to stick our conversation into that loop. Instead, when the party was wrapping up, he took my phone out of my pocket and put in his number. Then he called it, so he'd have my number in his own phone.

"That way I can call you first," he said with a smile. "Otherwise, putting my number in your phone is a completely passive-aggressive move."

He called me fifteen minutes later, and I said sure.

I didn't write autobiography. I wrote to leave autobiography behind.

When I was in kindergarten and asked to draw my family, I'd conjure Spider-Man, a blue elephant, the sun (wearing pants), a banana, and something I called a ninja tree. Even then, I knew that reality wasn't nearly as interesting as the reality my mind could create. I could tell bedtime stories during the day. Sometimes this got me branded as a liar. Then I got older, and was called creative.

My fabrications seemed to be of a different fabric from the stuff of my life. When writing, I never limited myself to being me, to knowing the facts as I knew them. It's not that I wrote fantasy—I didn't think of it as fantasy. I thought of it as another person's reality, another place's reality, separate from my own. Fiction was what happened when I released words onto the keys, played unseeable movies in my head. It was not life. It was never meant to be life.

We didn't sleep together until the fifth date.

It's not that the eagerness eluded us. Even during the first date, there was a giddy physicality to our movements, that telegraphic dance of words and touches. But our calendars conspired against us—there was always something one of us needed to wake up early for, or a reason we needed to part at a certain hour. Normally, this would have built frustration within me, but with Callum, it felt like everything would happen in its own time. We knew we were attracted to each other, without having to say so. There was an energy in the air, and we knew we would harness it.

I always liked having guys come to my apartment—I liked sleeping in my own bed—but we ended up at Callum's after that fifth date, because it was in a closer part of Brooklyn. I didn't know what to expect. Some guys I dated had Star Wars sheets on their beds; others slept on futons salvaged from the street, or had apartments that were the epitome of *Architectural Digest*ion. Callum was a graphic designer for a nonprofit and dressed like the rest of Brooklyn, so I wasn't sure whether I was going to get Swedish progressive or hipster ironic. But ultimately, his apartment's aesthetic was *home*. I can't think of another word to describe it. It was lived-in without being messy, furniture chosen for comfort, not statement. On the refrigerator were drawings he and his brother had done when they were kids—"penguins taking over the world," he explained.

We drank and we talked and then, word-drunk and winehappy, we fell into kissing, fell into horizontality, fell into bed. It was comfortable there, too.

When we were done, when we were reduced to two deeply satisfied heartbeats, I leaned into him as he held on to me, the lightness of smiles in the air, in our words.

"Tell me a story," he said.

"About what?" I asked.

"You're the writer. You tell me."

I shifted so I could see him, kiss him again.

"Writing stories and telling stories are two very different things," I said. "Writing, for me, involves a copious amount of staring off into space. I'm awful at making things up on the spot."

"C'mon," he said, pulling the sheet up to our shoulders.

Even in the near dark, Callum's eyes caught the light, glimmered in my direction. I felt such a wild rush of liking for him then—the rush that comes from finding someone good, someone worthy, someone wonderful.

"I need you to name the prince," I found myself saying.

"The prince?"

"In this story. What's his name?"

"Isadora."

I smiled. "And what is the name of Prince Isadora's kingdom?"

"Euphoria."

I did not start with *Once upon a time*, although I might as well have. Because that's what it felt like—starting off at once, upon a time.

I had no desire to move quickly into a relationship. But Callum wasn't "a relationship." He was Callum.

Our days redrew themselves to bring us closer to each other. I would wake at the same time he did, just to have that hour of snooze-alarm negotiation, stumbling for coffee, dreading and cheerleading at the start of the day. Then he would head to work and I would head to my laptop, plugging into whatever world I was bringing into shape. I ended up working better at his kitchen table than I did at any spot in my own apartment, or at any café. I would leave during the day, to get lunch, to do the laundry, to run whatever errand needed running. But when he came home, he'd find me at the table, typing away or staring into space. I'd often ask him for a page's worth of time, to make a graceful exit from whatever scene I was in. Then I would shut the laptop and close that world for the night. We made dinner, and I heard about his day. Then we'd watch some television, or go see a movie. Then bedtime, which always ended with storytime. Even if we were exhausted, I would tell him something new about Prince Isadora and the land of Euphoria. Sometimes it was just a fact—"In Euphoria, the census is taken by centaurs"—and other times the story would continue. There were times he'd fall asleep as I was talking, and other times I'd fall asleep in between sentences. But most nights I got to the point when I'd say, "And the rest, we shall find out tomorrow."

"Goodnight, Prince Isadora," Callum would say.

And I'd reply, "Goodnight, Euphoria."

For five months, we had this. For five months, it was easy. We might not have labeled it as easy, because there were still small struggles along the way. The worsening of his job. My inability to make my deadline, and the fact that I wouldn't be paid until I hit it. The friend or two of his I didn't like, and the friend or three of mine he couldn't stand. The feeling that it was too soon to talk about moving in together, but also the ridiculousness of double rent when we spent every night together. There were bumps in the road, for sure. But there was no doubt as to the direction we were traveling.

Then, five months into it, things started to go wrong. Not for us, but for him.

It started with small things. He left his wallet at a restaurant, and when he got it back, his credit card and debit card were gone. His computer, without any warning, turned a sword to its own heart, taking all of his files with it. An expected tax refund morphed into an unexpected tax debt. Trying to hold open a subway door for an old lady, he jammed his finger so badly that it needed to be put in a splint, which made his work as a designer much harder. We tried to make light of it, and at night I had much worse misfortunes befall Prince Isadora—plagues of penguins that ate all the crops, an attack from a horde of bears that pummeled their prey with bad stand-up comedy, a princess in a tower who Prince Isadora thought loved him, only to find that she was auditioning for reality TV.

"Poor Prince Isadora," Callum would say.

And I'd say, "Oh, but it could be worse."

Without ever saying it, we both believed that our luck rode a sine wave, that the ups would follow the downs in time, that life could somehow recognize when it had thrown too many troughs, and adjust accordingly.

Like fools, we believed in fairness.

The phone call did not come at three in the morning. It came at three in the afternoon, and there was no way for Callum to know it was a bad phone call until he picked up. I was not there. He was at work, and I was at home in the world of my words. He thought his mother was calling to say hello. But when he picked up, she couldn't choke out any words on the other end. She had to pass the phone to her sister, Callum's aunt, who said his brother had been in an accident, and hadn't made it through.

If I'd been a different kind of writer—if I'd been the kind who checks the internet every five minutes—I might have seen it on the news. Just one line on the Yahoo home page: *Fifteen-car pile-up on icy Massachusetts highway; five dead.* Had I seen it, I might have thought briefly of Callum's family up there. But I didn't see it, so when Callum called me, I was expecting a question about dinner.

Within minutes of hanging up, I had arranged for a rent-a-car and packed our bags. Rinna walked Callum home, left him in my care. His suit was in my hand as they walked in the door, and when he saw it, he burst into a new round of tears. I went over to comfort him, but what comfort could I really offer? I felt so deeply inadequate, and so incredibly mad at the universe.

On the drive up to Boston, we listened to wordless music; Callum wasn't ready yet to hear what the singers had to offer. When he spoke, it was of concern for his parents, concern for his brother's girlfriend. I didn't force my own concern on him. The conversation was his to control.

That night, sharing his childhood bedroom, was when we moved in with each other. It didn't need to be discussed, or even openly acknowledged. We had become inseparable, and now we knew it.

As we turned off the lights on a long, awful day, I was expecting Callum to want to be alone with his thoughts, in his own space. But instead he drew close to me, and as he had on the far easier, much less broken night before, he asked me to tell him a story.

I could not bring myself to put Prince Isadora through anything else. I couldn't bear the thought of any more hardship. Yes, I realized, imagination can always show us how much worse it can be. But now I needed imagination to give me something better.

So that night, Prince Isadora went bowling for the first time, and very quickly fell in love.

Three weeks later—*three weeks*—Callum lost his job.

His boss felt awful about it. Genuinely awful. But the fiscal year was ending that week, and it needed to be done before then. Callum wasn't the only one cut—the nonprofit had to shed a dozen employees, because the donations had stopped coming in. They were sure Callum could continue doing some freelance design work. Numb, he thanked his boss for that.

This time he didn't call me. When he came home, he found me unpacking some of my books onto his shelves. I had given up my place two days before.

"Oh dear," he said. "I seem to have lost my job."

"Goodness, that's a rather big thing to lose," I said. "Do you remember where you last put it?"

He smiled. Put down his bag.

"I love you," he said.

"I love you, too," I told him.

"This is bad. Really bad."

"Let's not focus on the lost," I told him. "Let's focus on the found."

I knew he was devastated. It was so clear. But I also knew he didn't want to see the devastation reflected in my face, my posture.

He hadn't taken off his coat, so I grabbed mine, and we went to our favorite bar. Over strong martinis, he told me what had happened.

"Their timing is really impressive," I observed.

"I know," Callum said, clinking my glass.

"We'll figure something out," I said, making sure he heard the *we*.

"We will," he replied. "And in the meantime, we're not telling my parents."

"I wouldn't dream of it."

Callum looked at me softly then, tenderly.

"Thank you," he said.

"For what?" I asked.

And he replied, "For enduring everything I'm about to put you through."

We spent money we didn't really have, the money we were hypothetically saving by living together, by not drinking every night, by never smoking. I bought him a new computer and a new suit for interviews.

At first, with the two of us home during the day, it felt like an extended weekend. But then it started to feel like a weekend that had outlasted its stay. He volunteered to go elsewhere, to kill time in museums and movies. But I had no desire to exile him from his own apartment, even if it was now technically both of ours. So I took my laptop and set up shop in libraries, in cafés, and even in the apartment of a friend who needed a house sitter for a month.

Because Callum's days were now longer, mine felt longer, too, as if I could feel his restlessness, his helplessness, wherever I was. I found that his truth started to permeate my fiction. Out of love, out of concern, out of frustration, his was the story I couldn't stop telling. I wanted to wrestle control from whoever was writing his script, and take it on myself. I wanted to force the happy ending. And since I couldn't do that, I gave it to my characters instead.

The one place reality didn't interfere was in bed at night, where I'd unspool the trials and triumphs of Prince Isadora. Mountains bent to his will. Dragons scattered from his path. Bureaucrats dropped their pencils and monkeys gathered them to make yellow tree houses in his honor.

I knew Callum was unhappy, and I also knew that I was not the cause of the unhappiness. So I did the best that I could. I found the life raft and inflated it with words. Some were the usual consolations: *It will get better. Work will come. This will end. He wouldn't want you to be paralyzed with sadness. He'd want you to go on.* And others were fantastical fictions drawn in the middle of the night, the refuge of a wandering mind, infused by the collateral joy that comes from making something out of nothing. Words were my tools of creation. And love, I learned, is a constant act of creation, just as creation is almost always an act of love.

There was constant guilt. He was a much better person than I was, so I felt that he should be treated better by life. I'd love to say it was harder to go through secondhand, that witnessing misery is harder than experiencing it. But that's not true. There's pain in both, but more pain in the latter.

A bad patch, people would tell us. *What doesn't kill you makes you stronger.*

But no. What doesn't kill you can leave you weak, vulnerable, sad. There is strength in survival, yes. Profound strength. But that does not negate despair.

Callum started to talk about leaving the city, because the city was so easy to blame. He mentioned this as an escape we could both make. But my life was here. And even though I loved him, I didn't know if I loved him more than the rest of my life.

The tension built, and since neither of us could really handle tension, the argument broke out pretty quickly. Over dinner, our futures locked horns. I told him that he didn't want to leave the city, that he was just giving up. He told me I had no idea what he was going through, or how haunted he was by the way things could go so wrong.

"You didn't do anything to deserve this," I told him.

"If I stay here, I'll just keep slipping into the same hole," he said. "This is the abyss. I truly feel like it's the abyss."

What had once been a bright spark in him was now turning into a different conflagration. It wasn't that his spirit was being snuffed out. It still burned, but now it burned harmfully.

"We can figure something out," I said. "You're not as deep in the abyss as you think you are."

"I don't want to think it gets any worse than this," he said. "This whole year is a disaster." He stopped, heard what he'd said. "Except for the part where I met you."

"Yes," I couldn't help but say. "Except that minor detail."

"You know that's not what I mean."

I did know. I told him I knew. But still it hovered there.

After dinner was over, he went into the bedroom to work on his website, while I stayed at the kitchen table, ostensibly to get some writing done. But there was nothing there for me to write. The words in my head didn't correspond in any way to the words that needed to be on the screen.

What do I want to say? my character kept asking himself.

But I was the only one who could give him the answer, and I was blank.

I scattered my attention to various websites, all as a way of avoiding the next step of my conversation with Callum.

Finally, after about an hour, I headed into the bedroom. He didn't turn as I came in, focusing on the windows on his screen. I didn't want to wander back out, but I didn't want to skulk, either. So I just lay down on the bed and closed my eyes. The sound of his typing continued, then stopped. I heard him stand up from his chair, then felt the dip in the bed as he joined me there.

"Callum—" I started. I was about to apologize. For what, I wasn't sure. I just felt the need to apologize.

"Shh," he told me. "I only want a story."

This is why we love stories, and love them from an early age: Nothing bad ever lasts in stories. And this is ultimately why we love life, too—because nothing bad ever lasts in life, not with the same intensity with which it initially appears. If we pay attention, stories can teach us that.

I didn't tell Callum this. Not outright. Instead Prince Isadora traveled through twelve different kingdoms that night. Time and again, it looked like he wouldn't make it home to Euphoria. Storms raged. Sirens called. Monsters attacked. Doubt and grief dug in. But time and again, Prince Isadora made it back.

There are times when you need discussion, when you need conversation, when things need to be worked out by letting words work them out. But other times, you can stand on the bedrock, the essential nature of who you both are, and watch the words fly above you, dazzling the eye, impermanent and beautiful in the things they can conjure.

By three in the morning, we are a story in ourselves: two grown men still in our clothes, huddled comfortably in our life raft, traveling forward, forward, toward the welcoming shore.

TRACK EIGHT

A Better Writer

There's no real story here—but isn't that true for most crushes? Or maybe there is a story, but it's just not the one I thought I was living at the time. That's true for most crushes, too.

I was a freshman in college, and I got into a creative writing class. It would end up being the only creative writing class I ever took, but that's immaterial. It was my second semester, and I was proud I'd made the cut. Almost everyone else in the class was older than me. Including Jamie Walker.

Jamie Walker was from the town I lived in the first year of my life, only two towns over from the town I lived in for the rest of my life (up until college). He had dark curly hair, was about my height. I can't remember the color of his eyes, but I do remember they had a glimmer to them, the glimmer that people who are engaged by life tend to have. I am much more of a sucker for cute than hot, and he was definitely cute. Or at least in my memory he is. I could easily take my facebook down from my bookshelf (that's small-*f* *facebook*—it's a real book) and check. But I'm so much older than him now, and that two-year difference made him so much older than me then. I don't want to alter that imbalance. I want to remember him as he was, even if that memory's vague, and perhaps even wrong. Who he was to me matters so much more than who he actually was.

This was 1991; it's important to note that. This was before email, before *Ellen*, before you could turn on your computer and see the world. This was before I knew I was gay, before I knew that kissing boys wasn't just something that happened, but was something I wanted to do. This was before I felt I could call myself a writer, before I had really written anything truly good.

Our class met in the library, which would have been romantic if it hadn't been one of those modern libraries where all you feel is the concrete, not the books. Our instructor was an MFA student who later went on to publish nothing whatsoever that I can find. Her teaching methodology seemed to be: *If you can't say something nice, say nothing at all.* Which left her largely silent as we all tore each other apart.

In the absence of an instructor's heavy hand, a creative writing seminar becomes a cauldron of hurt feelings, cutthroat ambition, unbridled defensiveness, and tenuous alliances that would make any third-rate parliament proud. From the very first day, you try to find your allies, and then as the critiques come in, you reassess your allegiances. I don't remember a lot about the other people who were in our class—there was a science fiction writer who confounded us with his syntax and the way the letter z could crop up in each and every one of his characters' names. And then there was the girl who'd written a piece about a bad breakup, and then burst into tears when I pointed out that the main character wasn't very sympathetic. (I learned a very valuable lesson then: Treat all breakup stories as autobiography, just in case.) And there was one guy who spent at least five minutes harping on the fact that a character in one of my stories had tried to spot a Volkswagen as he drove a long road in Michigan. "Why a

Volkswagen?" he kept asking. I tried to tell him there was no deeper meaning to it, but he didn't believe me.

I can't remember what that guy looked like, but I can remember that as the weather got warmer and spring came, Jamie Walker wore V-neck T-shirts. I don't think I'd ever seen anyone wear an undershirt as a shirt before, especially a V-neck. If I hadn't already had a crush on him, the V-neck would have sent me spiraling. I, who never looked at necks, found myself studying his neck. I, who was never distracted by the space below the neck, was suddenly drawn there. My own chest was already hairy—a fact I had no desire to share with the world. But there were some stray hairs in the deeper part of his V, an echo of the occasional stubble on his chin. What I felt was a charged curiosity, but it was a confused curiosity. Did I want to touch that space, trace that trail, or did I simply want to be that body myself? Did I find him attractive, or did I wish to be that attractive? It was the openness that was sexy, and it was the openness that I lacked.

We liked each other's writing. That was clear early on. When all the critiques of my pages were passed back to me, his handwriting was the first I sought out. We often sat next to or near each other, and would talk on the way out of class. But we'd always go our separate ways once we reached the bottom of the library steps.

I might have forgotten about him. (A catalog of crushes is an extremely finite thing.) But our instructor surprised us one day with an assignment: We were to swap stories with another person in class, and deconstruct one another's writing. Poems could be turned into stories; stories could be turned into poems. We could choose our partners. And Jamie chose me.

The next week, we swapped stories. Not just on paper but electronically—which meant, at the time, on a disk. I waited until I was back in my room to read his. I was alone—I can remember this. My roommate was gone. I was nervous and excited—the two most applicable adjectives for a crush. I had given Jamie a story about a family whose grandfather is a tyrant, and the grandson, tired of trying to live up to him, shoots him in a hunting accident. I was proud of this story, even if it was, as most of my fiction was, entirely fictional, without many details of my own life scattered around. Jamie's stories, from what I can recall, were usually about college students doing foolish things, in friendship or romance or some tangle of both. I expected more of the same, and loved the fact that he had written it knowing that I would be its first reader.

His story started plainly enough, with two high school boys watching *L.A. Law*. One of the most popular shows on TV at the time, *L.A. Law* was about . . . well, a group of lawyers in L.A. They were vain, troubled, and comic, and they usually won their cases. The men were sexy in that corny 1980s way—hair a-poof, muscles worked out, abs not yet an indicator for beauty. Not my type. I was holding out for River Phoenix. Or, if I had to settle, Keanu Reeves.

In the story, there's a tension between the boys as they watch *L.A. Law*—romantic tension. Relationship tension. And then the scene shifts, and you're in the *L.A. Law* episode. Two of the male characters are arguing. But there's also romantic tension between them. And then, right when you think it's going to erupt into a fight, they start making out. Jimmy Smits and Corbin Bernsen. Or maybe Jimmy Smits and Blair Underwood. I can't remember which. But suddenly the clothes are coming off. The need is overpowering. Belts are undone, pants are shed. And the kisses are real. These are two men who are in love with each other, and their kisses are real.

I had read hundreds of books up to that point. I had read hundreds of stories. I had copies of Jackie Collins and Nancy

Friday and Ken Follett that opened up on their own to the sex scenes because I had consulted them so often. But nothing I had read had prepared me for this. I had never known that reading words on a page could give you the same sensation as someone breathing on your neck, running his hand over your arm, undoing the top button of your pants. I had never known that a story could convey the feeling of a hard kiss, a warm body, fingers under elastic. I had known words could capture the mechanics, but not the intensity. But here were these characters—grasping, longing, battling, letting go. I believed them. And, somewhere unacknowledged but getting louder, I knew I wanted to be them. I wanted to be like that.

I was going to fail the assignment, because I didn't want to change a thing. Sure, a word or two, here or there. I was fine editing it. But I couldn't deconstruct it. I couldn't rearrange it, alter it, make it into something else. I tried. I tried playing it backwards. I tried inverting the frame. But ultimately I couldn't change it. It had to be what it was.

Jamie, if you're out there, why did you give me this story? Did you know what I was, and know that I didn't really know it yet? Was it a flirtation, or even something more than that? Or did this just happen to be the story that was on your computer on the day the assignment was given? Did you just happen to turn on *L.A. Law* that night and decide to play with it a little, not really giving any thought as to who its first reader would be? Did you mean to tell me something, or did you simply tell me something anyway?

In the story I want to tell, I wrote a little note at the bottom of what he wrote. When he saw it, he smiled and told me we should talk about it after class. For an hour, we sat there as girls read their blood poetry and the science fiction boy told us about the time Zaffir and Zazzlow traversed the space-time continuum in order to fetch the dread mineral

Zylon out of the grasp of the cruel overlord Zartra. Our expectation bloomed into something more certain than expectation, and our nervousness solidified into something closer to intent. When the class ended, we wordlessly led each other to the back of the library, to a carrel far from any other students, and that was where he kissed me, that was where I finally got to touch that neck, that chest, that was where my hand pressed against that V and his hand lowered down my back, and that was where I cried because I had gotten what I wanted, that was when the joy of it was so much that I actually cried, because I had found what I was looking for, and it wasn't just him, it was everything, and when he saw I was crying, his kisses changed into something more comforting, something that understood, and he whispered *shh shh*, then made a joke that made it all okay, that made me kiss him again, that made me lead him back out, holding his hand, to get some dinner, to walk through the night, to stay up with each other, then sleep with each other, then greet the next morning as if it were ours together.

But I didn't write a note at the bottom of what he wrote—at least, not that note. I don't even know if I told him how much I liked the story; I might have just said how hard it was to cut down. He had taken my short story and turned it from fifteen pages to something like three, jutting phrases against each other to create a prose poem of indeterminate meaning. I think later on he told me he'd liked some of my edits on his story, but that was it.

I never ended up seeing him out of class. Toward the end of the year, the newspaper I was working at ran a two-page spread of photos from our university's LGBA Ball. There were a few photos of him there, dressed (if I am remembering correctly) in a sleeveless number that would have made Audrey Hepburn proud. I was no doubt hanging out with my dorm friends that night, swathed in flannel, watching *Twin Peaks*, enjoying myself in a different way.

I never took another writing class. But gay characters started appearing in my fiction. Sometimes they knew they were gay. Sometimes they didn't. Sometimes I knew they were gay. Sometimes I didn't. Not until later.

The difference between a crush and a love is its viability. I could try to revise the past into a world where Jamie and I could have been together. But that wasn't the world my head was living in at the time.

It is often the case that at the end of the crush, the only thing you've learned is how to better deal with the next crush that comes along. In this case, I got a little more. Whether or not he meant to—and I strongly suspect he didn't—Jamie Walker made me a better writer. Or at least he opened up something in that part of me. The rest, in time, would follow.

TRACK NINE

8-Song Memoir

What I remember most is lunging across the apartment, try-ing to get there before the end of the song.

This is not, admittedly, the part of making a mixtape that glows with nostalgia. This is not the creation of the cover (collage? watercolor? Sharpie?) or the intimacy of song selec-tion. But I guess I'm nostalgic for it, after all: —I know that I have four minutes and twelve seconds to do something else while Tori Amos sings about being silent all these years. I start to write a letter as her voice lifts from the double-cassette recorder in the kitchen. I stop to look up when she sings, *Don't look up—the sky is falling,* because I always look up when she sings those words. I am paying attention. I am listening to this song that I will soon be giving to someone else.

Only . . .

There's a hiccup in my attention span.

The song is suddenly about to end and I am at the other end of the apartment.

So I do what instinct tells me to do—I careen into the kitchen and throw myself at the pause button, trying to hit it before the next song begins. (If I fail? The price is the sloppy sound of a click, betraying the fact that I had to hit stop, not pause. I've rewound to leave a record of my mistake.)

116

Some of you know exactly what I mean. Many of you don't. And I guess *that,* more than anything else, is what makes me nostalgic.

I used my Walkman long after most people had switched over to Discmen. (iPods weren't even gleams in our eyes. They were science fiction.)

At work, we had the Tape Graveyard, the place where cassettes would go after they'd been replaced by CDs. Or sometimes they were cassettes we'd never wanted in the first place, sent to us by Columbia House. (We were too lazy to respond to the monthly missives, and then too lazy to mail back the automatic shipments.)

I loved the Tape Graveyard: It was one of the only places where Wilson Phillips could hang out with R.E.M. and Talking Heads without judgment, where Thompson Twins and 'Til Tuesday could compare haircuts, where my boss kept the Reggae Christmas Tape we always played for Holiday Card Signing. After that boss left, I inherited the Tape Graveyard, and it remained intact until a few months ago, when my office made a move to a space that is deeply unfriendly to filing cabinets. Many of the tapes got lost in the whittling, but I did insist on keeping some of them, even if there's no cassette player in sight, because there is something intrinsically valuable, at least in terms of my soul, to be found in a K-tel collection of hits from 1987.

There weren't supposed to be mixes in the Tape Graveyard. But as I was clearing things out, I found one. Its label was in my handwriting, and its name made me laugh out loud:

Dread and Yearning

There is something so amazingly adolescent about that, so touching in its sincerity. (In college, I put most of my favorite songs on a mix entitled *Beautiful Desolation*. This mix, *Dread and Yearning*, sounded like a follow-up.)

I have no true recollection of making this mix. The second side isn't labeled, so at first I don't even know how many songs are on it. But now, on a rainy Sunday night with Valentine's Day approaching, I think it's time to see what magnetized message sits inside the plastic case.

I track down some AA batteries.

I put them in my Walkman.

I don't have my fuzzy-circle headphones anymore (I broke them; I always broke them), so earbuds will have to do.

I press play.

The mix, I discover, is unfinished. There are only eight songs that the whirling of the Walkman brings back to life.

Track One: *Horses in the Room* by Everything But The Girl

I do not believe that you need one specific person
to make your life whole,
but I do believe that at any given moment,
someone could appear at your door
who will change your life.

What I've discovered over the years,
which was never a foregone conclusion, is this:
I don't want to be the person who opens the door.
I want to be the person at the door.

118

Come in, come in, whoever you are,
Tracey Thorn sings.
(I love Tracey Thorn, because if she were a character,
I would have to name her Tracey Thorn.)
Whenever I put this song at the start of a mix—
and I still do—
It is a welcome to someone I've already welcomed.
It is the warmth of the room when you step in from
    the door.
It is certain in its hope and uncertain in everything
    else

which is often how I find love.

Track Two: *Fields of Gold* by Sting

How can I love this song when
I want to laugh
every time he sings *barley?*
I cannot find anything romantic
about barley.

Or walking in fields of gold,
for that matter.
Trampling over barley,
barley stalks hitting you when the wind blows,
barley scratching at your skin,
barley getting caught in the bottom of your shoe.
No, thank you.

When it comes to love,
we remember the light,

not the crops.
I remember what it was like
to walk next to you as the day melted itself
into twilight.
We could have been walking through corn,
or wheat, or Park Avenue.
I only recall snippets of what we said,
but I remember clearly saying something to you,
and you saying something back to me.

Track Three: *Love Song for a Vampire* by Annie Lennox

Most of my favorite singers choose to present love
as a tug-of-war between bliss and derangement.
Robyn dancing on her own,
Björk and her army of me, Sia swinging on her
(I don't need to say it), or Lorde undercutting
her own swagger with the cold light of day.
It is possible that Annie Lennox is the mother
of all these singers and songs, at least
in the lineage of my listening.

This song is from *Bram Stoker's Dracula*,
dating from the brief moment in cinematic history
when Hollywood thought it was a good idea
to trap Winona Ryder in the nineteenth century.
Her breathy heaving is the only thing I remember
about the movie, so it's easy to separate the song,
and take the *vampire* metaphorically.
Annie Lennox is torn apart and so in love.
Still falls the rain, she sings, letting the listener know

that it's not so much a question of *here it comes again*
as it is a question of learning to love
even when it's raining.

Track Four: *Lead a Normal Life* by Peter Gabriel

My first concert that wasn't Billy Joel
was Peter Gabriel at Great Woods in July of '87.
I was at Wellesley for its summer program and
this was a big field trip; I remember the sky
over the amphitheater as the light show synthesized
the air. Like most high schoolers at that time, I thought
Peter Gabriel had been born with *So,*
wielding a sledgehammer and giving Lloyd Dobler
the right song with which to woo Diane.
(Columbia House would have happily sent me
Gabriel's earlier records, but I was too lazy to try.)

All of which is to say:
I found his earlier work later.
But clearly not memorably enough,
because this song comes on the mix
and I have no idea what it is.
Eventually the instrumentation clues me in
that it's Peter Gabriel
and the voice confirms it.
It's what radio (remember radio?) used to refer to as
a "deep cut"—and I am trying to figure out
what compelled me to reach for it.
We want to see you live a normal life—when I was

in my early twenties, did I hear this and think *dread* or
did I hear it and think *yearning*?
I don't think it's possible I already understood
that the answer is both at once, and that it can be
the yearning to be normal
that spurs the dread.

One last note:
As I was being driven to the airport earlier today,
the radio was playing some of my favorite songs
from some of my favorite times—
Belinda Carlisle's "Heaven Is a Place on Earth"
Cher's "Believe"
Imagine Dragons' "It's Time" (from before they
bombasted)—
Peter Gabriel might have come on next.
I looked to the dashboard, expecting some satellite
station, and instead it was 106.7 . . . Lite FM.
The announcer even said it, "You're listening to
Lite FM," and I felt a profound betrayal by time
and airways,
because Lite FM had always existed
in the domain of dentistry and department stores,
diet music to prevent any rush of feeling to the head.
I know I'm no longer Z100's target audience
but *lite* is a term I don't want to claim. Please,
give the station back to Karen Carpenter's subversions
and Barry Manilow's lack thereof.
Otherwise, hand me Peter Gabriel's sledgehammer
and let me smash the station before Nirvana joins the
playlist.

Track Five: *In Your Care* by Tasmin Archer

Much more dread than yearning here,
in another song I haven't heard in at least a decade.

How could
you let
me down
when I'm in your care?
is the question posed, and I wonder now at how
I can understand what she means even though
I've never felt the same betrayal.

Sometimes the power of the articulation
is stronger than your own experience. Or,
perhaps even more, the song links two things
I have experienced—*let me down, in your care*—
and by linking them, I get a glimpse of
what her voice is telling me
is a hard road. As I get older, I realize
we don't need the love songs that
blind us with the clichés. We need
the love songs that tell the truth,
and convey it convincingly.

Track Six: *Walking in My Shoes* by Depeche Mode

In 1995 or whenever this mix was made,
it would have been malpractice
to make a mix called *Dread and Yearning*
without at least one Depeche Mode song.

Here let me requiem for my dear friend Lynda,
as one mixtape leads me to remember another.
Toward the end of sophomore year at MHS,
a track list in Lynda's immaculate handwriting:
Depeche Mode, Erasure, The Cure, Alphaville,
People Are People, A Little Respect, Lovesong,
Forever Young.
It opened my eyes to Blasphemous Rumours,
to the power in admitting out loud that God
has a sick sense of humor.
But the one that got me was Somebody,
how straightforward it was in its longing—
what the heart wants is really quite simple,
as the surf inexplicably comes to shore
in the background of the song.

Before you come to any conclusions
try walking in my shoes
—I never wore black in high school,
and any darkness in my days or my heart
was purely the mark of melodrama, not
experience. These songs didn't confirm
my life; they expanded it, to make me ready
when the darkness needed to be wrestled,
in the name of love,
or of what love can do to us.

Track Seven: *Here. In My Head* by Tori Amos

You don't want a song with this title
to be linear.

Maybe Thomas Jefferson wasn't born in your backyard like
you have said. . . .
My mind has said so many things, some of them
as contradictory
as Thomas Jefferson.

Especially when we're in love,
we play hide-and-seek with ourselves.

I remember the first time I saw Tori Amos live
(Berklee Performance Center, *Little Earthquakes* tour)
and the astonishment of how she played piano,
the full-body experience that led to the notes.
This is the transmission
from the keys and the wires:
The music in our heads always circles back around
to itself, and we search for ourselves
somewhere in the notes.

Track Eight: *Mary* by Tori Amos

Insane enough to have two songs by the same singer,
but to have them back to back . . .
what were you thinking, younger David?
There are rules to mixtapes, although I couldn't tell you
how I learned them. The first mixtape I made
was for myself; the second was probably for my mother.
The first I received may have been the one from Lynda;
a little over a year later, my high school best friend, Cary,

gave me the first of our mixtapes, kicking off with
The The, *This Is the Day*, which is now the key song
in a movie based on a book I wrote. The soundtrack
of our lives only grows; songs may fall away, but they
can always return, sometimes when you least expect
    them.

Tori sings to us, telling us not to be afraid.
We're just waking up
and I hear help is on the way
There has never been a time when it's hurt to hear this.
There have been plenty of times when it's helped.
The singer lets us know:
Help is on the way.
Just press play.
Fast-forward to it if you have to.

The first person who gives the song
is the person who writes it.
The second is the person who sings it.
Then it's up to us
to give it to each other.

I find it interesting to hear
what's disappeared as we come
to the last song on this tape.
The dread has ebbed,
the yearning lulled.
What I'm left with,
more than twenty years later,
is that sense of *just waking up*
that a song can bring,
the spirit of understanding

that serenades us into believing
that we understand, that our lives,
even when they're silent,
always contain music.

From that, we make our mixes.

TRACK TEN

Snow Day

On the day of Avery and Ryan's fifth date, it snowed.

This was not out of the ordinary—it snowed a lot in the towns where they lived. But this was the first snowfall, and that always occasioned a certain amount of surprise. Winter was no longer deniable, even though there were still some leaves that had yet to abdicate from the trees. The days had already been shortening, a minute or two of sunlight leaking away each evening, but that wasn't as noticeable as the sudden shift to snow.

Had Avery and Ryan lived in the same town, the snow wouldn't have had much impact on their date. Their progress toward each other would have been a measure slower, a measure more thoughtful, but everything would have gone as planned. As it happened, it was Ryan's turn to drive to Avery. Had they lived somewhere else, they might have met midway, but for them there was nothing midway, nor was there anything, really, within a fifty-mile radius. A pair of movie theaters. A few diners. A mall that had seen better days. A Walmart that had stolen away those better days for something cheaper. Places where you could hang out, but you wouldn't particularly want to, at least not for a special occasion. And at this point, for Avery and Ryan, each date was a special occasion.

They had met at a dance—a gay prom—the blue-haired boy (Ryan) and the pink-haired boy (Avery) spotting one another and filling one another's minds with music and color, shyness and an inexplicable but powerful urge to overcome this shyness. On their first date, they'd gone rowing on a stream by Avery's aunt's house. Talking to each other as they'd never talked to anyone else before, especially not on a date, they had summoned the ghosts of their former selves and the promise of their future selves—and it hadn't been nearly as scary as each of them had feared.

On their second date, in Ryan's town, they'd gone imaginary golfing at a mini-golf range that had fallen into disrepair. Their relationship had also threatened to fall into disrepair there, too, but romance had managed to triumph over rage, as Ryan narrowly avoided the trap of allowing bullies to bully him into doing something stupid. The third and fourth dates were more straightforward—movies watched on Avery's couch (date three) and at Ryan's local movie theater (date four). Ryan had now met Avery's parents; Avery had yet to meet Ryan's parents, but at least he knew the reason had nothing to do with him and everything to do with Ryan's parents, who weren't quite ready for their blue-haired son to bring home a pink-haired boyfriend (or a boyfriend with any other hair color, for that matter).

Avery's parents had always been understanding—even before he'd realized he was meant to be a boy. When that had come up, they hadn't dismissed it or tried to persuade Avery otherwise. And when Ryan had appeared in Avery's life, and Avery had let him appear in his parents' lives as well, they had been nothing short of welcoming. Avery wasn't particularly surprised by this, even if it still felt like he was sharing a new chapter of his story with them, and he was a little nervous about how they'd read it. Ryan, meanwhile, was unfamiliar with this level of acceptance. He didn't know how to act around anyone's parents, because his own were so negating. It made him sad, how weirded out he was by how friendly Avery's parents were. He hoped this second time would go smoother.

Ryan did not check the weather forecast as he grabbed his keys and left his house. There might have been murmurs about snow at school, but Ryan had learned to tune out all murmuring when he was there; most of the murmurs were nastier and less important than the weather report. When the first flakes hit his windshield, it was so gradual that it looked as if small, translucent spiders were dropping from the sky, leaving filaments in their wake. It was only when he was ten minutes from Avery's house that the wipers needed to be turned on and the car needed to slow. The snowflakes had begun to crowd the sky, and Ryan could not help but smile at the snow's sudden presence, the way something solid could materialize from air. *Accio snowfall.*

He felt he knew the route by heart . . . but sometimes the heart makes wrong turns. It was just a matter of finding the right way back on course. He could have called Avery to ask for directions, but he chose to rely on his phone's navigational skills instead, since he wanted Avery to believe he could find his way from memory. (On the fifth date, you are always looking for ways to prove the path to the sixth, seventh, and eighth.)

Avery was waiting by his window, so he was aware of the snow, too. It wasn't so dense that his delight needed to skid and swerve into worry. No, as he watched the downward drift, he wasn't picturing Ryan in any wreck, or even imagining Ryan forced to turn back home. Instead he felt that elemental wonder that comes from seeing the world so casually altered, the transfixing sensation of watching something so intricately patternless fall.

When Ryan's car appeared within the snowfall, Avery's heart became the opposite of snowfall—that strange, wind-blown moment when you look and see the snow is actually drifting upward. Snowrise. When Avery saw Ryan pulling into his driveway, his heart was snowrise.

He was trying to guard this heart of his, but the guards were distracted. He was trying to cage his excitement, but he kept leaving the door unlatched. He knew it was dangerous to like someone so much.

There was nervousness, too. Ryan had been to the house before, but it had been a short visit, spent mostly in the family room. This time they were sure to explore further. Avery had control of his room, but he didn't have control over the whole house. His mother liked to hang up family pictures, and as a result there were lots of photos of Avery as a kid, Avery before everything was noticed, Avery before everything was understood. His mother had been very clear about this: It would hurt more to erase the past. Better, she said, to come to peace with it. There was no reason to hide it, no reason to disown the child Avery had been. Avery thought it was much more complicated than this, but at the same time, his parents had been so cool with everything else that he didn't think it would be fair to tell them to take down all the photographs of the time before. In some of the photographs, Avery looked very happy. On some of those days, he was. On others, not as much. Only Avery had access to the feelings that had gone on underneath. Even when he was just a kid.

He certainly couldn't ask his parents to take down the photos now, just because Ryan was coming over. He knew it wasn't worth it to try to curate his past, to try to present it to Ryan as if it had been otherwise. One of the most exciting and intimidating things about Ryan was the fact that Avery wanted to tell him the truth. This was what they'd recognized in each other. No pretending. They would talk to each other undisguised.

This made Ryan anxious, too, but it was an anxiety he was willing to navigate, the same way he was willing to step out in the snow and walk through the wind in order to get inside. He could see Avery in the window as he pulled into the driveway, could see his pink hair and could notice the lamp right next to him, the way it shone out on such a dimming day. Ryan had once heard the phrase *leave a light on for me* and thought it was one of the most romantic expressions he'd ever heard. He liked the idea that when you fall in love with someone, the other person becomes your lighthouse keeper, even if it means staying up all night, even if it means staring out into the darkness until the darkness assumes the shape of your love and comes back to you.

Ryan turned off the car and almost immediately the windshield was covered. He turned off the headlights and for a moment there was the sincere silence of an entirely natural world. Even though his lighthouse keeper waited, he sat for a few seconds and listened to the music of the snow, to the slight tintinnabulation of snowflakes conversing with glass. He opened the door and let his sneaker sink into the sparse accumulation that covered the driveway. The cold immediately attached itself to his ears, his fingers. He raced up the steps, inaugural footprints in his wake. When he got to the door, it was already open. When he got to the door, he found Avery let loose from the window, Avery in a blue sweater, Avery smiling as if Ryan's arrival was the greatest gift a boy could ever want.

There was a moment when they stopped and looked at

each other. A little more snow fell on Ryan's shoulder and dusted his hair. He didn't notice. Not until he was inside and Avery was brushing it off, using it as an excuse for an immediate touch, a welcome that started at the top of his head and worked its way to the side of his face and down his neck.

"I'm so glad you're here," Avery said.

"And I'm so glad to be here," Ryan answered. Partly because it was true and partly to be complementary.

Avery, having been inside the past couple of hours, had no idea how warm his house was, how it felt to Ryan as if cookies were being baked a few feet away. It was the kind of warmth you wanted to nestle into.

There were footsteps from another room, Avery's mother calling out, "Is he here?" Ryan stomped his shoes on the mat, took off his coat, and handed it to Avery, who hung it on a doorknob, where it would dangle until it was dry enough for the closet. Avery's mother appeared from her home office, welcoming Ryan and asking him about his drive. Ryan wasn't used to this kind of chitchat from a parent—maybe his father would have given him an *Is the car driving okay?* but he wouldn't have wanted to know anything beyond that. For Avery's mother, it seemed like the chitchat was meant as an entryway into more conversations, more topics.

Avery's mother asked Ryan to leave his sneakers by the door, but she made it feel like a favor rather than a command. Ryan complied, then felt like he was broadcasting the hole in the heel of his left sock. If Avery's mother noticed, she didn't say anything.

(Ryan's mother would have said something, and it wouldn't have been very nice.)

"Well, I won't get in your way," Avery's mother said, getting in their way a little bit longer. "If you need anything, you know where I'll be. There should be muffins in the kitchen—I think we have blueberry, maybe some carrot—or that might be bran. I'm not sure how you feel about bran, Ryan. Or about raisins—I think those have rai—"

"We've got it, Mom," Avery interrupted. Ryan was amused to see him so exasperated by prolonged muffin talk.

Avery's mother laughed, held up her hand in surrender.

"As I said, I'll be in my office if you need anything."

She shot Avery one last look—*I love you even when you're rude to me in front of your friend*—and skedaddled.

Ryan could feel the wood floor through the hole in his sock. When Avery's mother left the room, it was just the two of them and the sound of the snow outside. Ryan stepped away from the door and took up Avery's old position at the window. The snow was now blowing in gusts that looked like clouds dissolving in the midst of a fight. The branches of the trees were beginning to bow and sway, as if beckoning the snow to fall even faster.

I'm lucky to have made it, Ryan thought.

Avery walked up behind him, and for a moment didn't know where to put his hands. To have Ryan so close after spending so much time imagining him close . . . Gently, he moved his arm under Ryan's arm, moved his hand across Ryan's chest. Then he pressed his own chest against Ryan's back, his chin peeking over Ryan's shoulder so they could both look at the snow together.

Neither one of them said out loud how beautiful it was, but both of them thought it was quite beautiful.

Avery felt Ryan tense for a second, then realized why. Mrs. Parker from across the street was coming out of her house, as she had every twenty minutes for the past two hours, to spread salt on her path. It was the same motion she used to scatter bread crumbs for birds in the summertime.

She was not looking up, but Ryan was tensing at the idea of her looking up. Seeing them. Taking this moment that was theirs and making it into something else in her head.

Avery knew she wouldn't care, might even find it sweet, to see the blue-haired boy and pink-haired boy entwined like journal and clasp. But there was no way for Ryan to know that. He was projecting his own neighbors onto her.

Instead of explaining this, Ryan turned. Avery loosened his grip, to allow another hold to form. Now they were face to face, moving back into the hallway, blocked from the outside by the door.

"I've missed you," Ryan said.

Avery leaned in and kissed him. Once, but lingeringly.

"I've missed you, too."

Ryan and Avery talked every day, and texted nearly every hour they were awake. They chatted for long spells each evening, a running commentary that rippled often into digression. But none of that could cure the missingness they felt; if anything, it made the missingness more acute. As Avery had put it to Ryan late one night, far after they were supposed to have gone to sleep: *What we're doing right now is watermelon-flavored. When we're together, it's watermelon.* This had made sense to Ryan then, and it made even more sense to him now. Kissing Avery was watermelon. Having his arms around him was watermelon. Being able to see the look on his face as he talked was watermelon.

"What do you want to do?" Avery asked.

And Ryan thought, *This. Watermelon.*

Here, on the fifth date, another precious inkling of a truth about love: that there is a point you reach when it doesn't really matter what you do, that the question of what to do becomes beside the point for long stretches. The answer reduces to the smallest, most important words:

You.

Here.

Us.

This.

All so easy to fit into the equally small word *Now*, and the slightly longer word *Love*.

But Ryan was sixteen. He didn't realize that any of these small words were worthy answers, just as Avery didn't know that it was alright to not have a plan for what to do next.

Not knowing what the answer should be, Ryan replied, "It's your house. You lead the way."

Had it been up to Avery, he would have stayed right there, kissing Ryan for a few minutes more. But there was always the risk that his mother would remember another flavor of muffin in the kitchen, and would return to tell them about it.

"How about my bedroom?" he proposed. Then, blushing, he felt compelled to add, "Not because it has a bed, but because it's, uh, my room."

Ryan smiled. "Sounds good."

This is the geography of a house, at five in the afternoon on a fifth date:

In one room, a mother types. Every now and then, she stops to think about what she's typing, but her thoughts rarely stray farther than that. In the kitchen, the refrigerator and the clock have a barely audible conversation. The garage waits like a sleeping whale; when a father comes home in an hour, it will open its mouth with a bellow that everyone else in the house will notice. For its part, the family room gently offers some spilled lamplight out into the growing night. The front hall is damp with footprints; a pair of sneakers waits by the door. In the hallway, two boys walk one after the other, both in socks, both looking at one another far more than they are looking at the walls, or their steps, or at anything lining the walls. Ahead of them, a bedroom waits for the flick of a switch to bring it to life. Beyond that, there's another bedroom, currently resting. In the bathroom, a faucet drips, as if trying to imitate the precipitation outside. A toilet seat has been left up. Three toothbrushes stand at attention; since they aren't speaking, we must assume they are listening to everything else that goes on in the house.

All of this is surrounded by snow. The roof is now covered. The car in the driveway is as white as the driveway. Were you looking from above, you would have to look closely to see a house at all.

But you are not looking from above.

Ryan had glimpsed Avery's room the last time he'd been over, but now he had a chance to study it. The posters on the wall were of artists, not bands. The bookshelves had been arranged in stripes of color—blue then red then blue then red then green then red then green then yellow then green, and so on. The bed was in the corner, the room's single window at its head.

Ryan walked over there and looked out. In a few minutes, it would be too dark to see the snow, but now it could still be traced and tracked. Avery joined him, and together they watched the snowflakes traveling like raindrops, punctuation marks to let them know where the gravity belonged.

Avery sat down on the floor, his back against the bed. Ryan followed, sat right next to him so their legs touched and their arms overlapped. It was weird, Avery thought, how this worked. When someone stared at you, you could feel so much like a body, with all your flaws blaring like bad advertisements. But when someone was next to you, when someone was as much of a body to you as you were to them, it became more comfortable, more valuable. Feeling Ryan's skin and knowing that at the very same time Ryan was feeling his skin. Knowing they were different, but maybe the sensation of it was the same, just like breathing was the same, like a heartbeat was the same. Avery leaned into that. Felt.

"So how was your day?" Ryan asked, and for the next few minutes, they talked about school, about friends, about the snow first appearing in the sky. This was part of what they needed, too—to be like everyone else, to have the time to lean like this and recount the time since they'd last spoken. There were no revelations here, nothing out of the ordinary. There was just the ordinary being spelled out, the truth left between the letters. The most exciting part of their day had been anticipating this, being excited about this very thing.

"Is that a yearbook?" Ryan asked, looking at the bottom of Avery's bookshelf. He moved to pull it over.

"No!" Avery said. "No you don't!"

Ryan made an exaggerated grab for it. Avery made an exaggerated tackle. Conceding with a playful lack of resistance, Ryan stretched out on the ground. Avery pinned him anyway.

This is where it can turn from playfulness. This is where heat can subsume warmth. But neither Ryan nor Avery wanted that—not now, not yet, not this early in the date. So instead they kept it playful—Avery leaning down for a kiss, then pulling back right at the moment their lips should have met. Laughing. Then going down for a real kiss, Ryan arching up to meet it.

Avery loosened his grip. They kissed some more. Ryan reached out, as if he were about to rustle Avery's pink hair or trace the curve of his shoulder. But it was another fake-out—

Ryan's arm extended just long enough to get to the yearbook, to take it from the shelf.

Avery groaned, but did not fight it. Not even when Ryan sat up and started to thumb through. It was last year's yearbook, and since Avery had been a sophomore, he hadn't made much of an impression in its pages.

As Ryan thumbed through, Avery watched him do it, noticed small things he hadn't noticed before—the places where Ryan's blue hair was starting to revert to bleach, the Little Dipper of birthmarks on his arm. Ryan asked a few questions about a few of the people in the photos, and Avery answered when he could—his school was too big for him to know everyone, and he wasn't attitudinally inclined to know everyone, anyway. He had his small pod of friends, and that was where he spent most of his time.

Ryan finally came to the page where Avery's sophomore picture resided, part of the mosaic of stamp-sized malcontents forced by the class photographer into their frames. The photo was too small for Avery to really hate it, although the person in it already felt like a skin he'd shed.

"Nice haircut," Ryan said, with no real meanness in the tease.

"I was experimenting!"

"With what?"

"Bad haircuts!"

It was a black-and-white photo (only upperclassmen got color), so you couldn't really see the pathetic orange that Avery had occasioned for photo day—it was something that looked like marmalade when he'd been aiming for jack-o'-lantern. Pink had soon followed, and had stayed for longer than it usually did on a high school boy.

"I used to wear mine down to my shoulders," Ryan confessed. "I was twelve or thirteen, and I thought it made me *tough*. Like, if I could have grown a beard then, I would've done that, too. I look back now and know it was camouflage—and not even good camouflage. My mother caught me flicking it back one day and asked me point-blank, 'Why are you doing that?' And I thought, *Oh, right*. The next time we went to the barber, she didn't have to say a thing. I told him to cut it off, and he called out to the rest of the guys in the barbershop for a round of applause."

"Do you miss it?" Avery asked.

Ryan snorted. "Not at all. Do you want to know what's a bad combination? Long hair and a twelve-year-old boy. I probably could have wrung the grease out and bottled it, it was getting so gross."

Avery instinctively itched his hair as Ryan talked about this. Ryan noticed and smiled.

"Sorry," Ryan continued. "Gross. I know. But it's my way of saying we've all got bad haircuts in our past. Or bad lack-of-haircuts."

The garage opened its mouth at this point, filling the house with its call. Avery looked at the clock—it was a little early for his father to be home.

"They must've closed his office because of the snow," he said to Ryan, acknowledging the noise. "It must be getting pretty bad out."

They left the implications of this unsaid. If it was bad enough for Avery's dad to leave early, it probably meant Ryan should be making an emergency exit. But Ryan decided he had no intention of doing that.

(It didn't even occur to Avery that Ryan might have to leave early.)

"Boys!" Avery's mother called out. "Dinner in a half hour!"

Avery hadn't intended for them to have dinner with his

parents. He'd thought they'd go out, even if it was just for Burger King. He stood up to look back out the window and saw that, yes, it would have to be an eating-in night. Their road was not on the priority list to be plowed, and by now it was hard to tell where the curb stopped and the road began. Ryan's car was starting to look like an igloo; you couldn't really tell if it was a car or a really big turtle underneath.

It still didn't occur to Avery that Ryan might have to leave early. Or already lost his chance to leave early. Neither of them had listened to the forecast. For all they knew, the snow was about to stop.

"A half hour." Ryan came over and whispered in Avery's ear. "What can we do with a half hour?"

The answer?

His hands were on Avery's hips.

The answer?

Kisses. Variations of kisses. Repetitions of kisses. Learning each other through kisses.

The answer?

Clothes staying on, because there were parents walking in the hall, because this wasn't that, not yet. But just because clothes stayed on, it didn't mean there weren't bodies to be felt through fabric, skin to feel the pressure, feel the touch.

The answer?

It didn't really matter what they did.

While Avery and Ryan had been oblivious to the coming snowstorm, Avery's mother had prepared. There was food in the pantry, food in the refrigerator, and even candles and matches waiting on the kitchen counter, just in case the power went out. There was also the constant narration of the Weather Channel from the television in the family room, the entire storm looking like a single cloud marauding over a quarter of the country.

Ryan and Avery acted as one another's mirrors, making sure all their clothing looked settled before heading to the kitchen. If Avery's parents noticed anything was off, they didn't say a word. Plus, Avery's mother was busy with dinner and Avery's father was busy with the weather. Since it was now dark out, the television acted as his window.

"There you are," Avery's mother said when they walked into the room, as if she hadn't known where they were all along. "I think we need to have a talk. First off, I realized I didn't ask you if you have any allergies or food restrictions, Ryan."

"I'm good with whatever," Ryan replied. There were about a hundred foods he hated, but he figured this wasn't what she was asking. His position here was untested enough that he'd eat anything she made.

"Great. We're having chicken, potatoes, and broccoli—I figured that wouldn't be very controversial. The bigger issue is the snow. They're saying the highways are a complete mess, and the storm's not going to slow down until midnight at the earliest. So it's looking like you're going to have to spend the night here, Ryan. There's no way I'm letting you drive home in this. I'd like to talk to your mother, if that's okay. Explain what's going on. I can't imagine there's going to be school tomorrow."

Avery tried unsuccessfully to suppress a yip of joy, afraid that if the universe knew how pleased he was by this turn of events, it would send a sudden heat wave. Then he realized this was silly, and allowed his mom to take some satisfaction in the way he buzzed and beamed.

Ryan's spirits, in the meantime, couldn't bounce quite as high as Avery's. He was sure that Avery's mother was right, and that there was no feasible, safe way for him to get home. He even knew his parents would concede that. But there would still be the matter of why he'd come here in the first place, why he hadn't turned back at the first glimmer of trouble. There wouldn't be hell to pay so much as he'd get a much bigger weekly allowance of hell.

"I can just call her," he told Avery's mom. "Explain the situation."

"Trust me," came the reply, "I'm a mother. She's going to want to talk to me."

Sure enough, after Ryan called and told his mother what was up, and that what was supposed to be a date (he didn't use the word *date*) had turned into a sleepover (he went nowhere near the word *sleepover*), she immediately asked to talk to Avery's mother. As if the blizzard were some moon landing he was shooting on a soundstage, just to trick his parents so he could have a night of unrelenting sin.

Ryan had no idea what, if anything, Avery had told his mom about Ryan's parents, but Avery's mom upped the cheer factor in her voice by at least three whorls when she said, "Hi, there!" at the start of their conversation. Then there was a serious "Yes" and an empathetic "Oh, believe me, I understand." After that—Ryan had no idea, because Avery's mom walked out of the kitchen, and stayed out of the kitchen for another five minutes.

"Clearly, they're arranging our marriage," Avery commented in the interim.

"If I weren't so terrified, I'd find that funny," Ryan replied.

Avery's father came into the kitchen, plucked a grape from the refrigerator, and popped it into his mouth.

"Smells good," he said.

"We'll be sure to pass that on to Mom," Avery replied.

Avery's father looked around. "Oh. Where is she?"

143

"Talking to Ryan's mom. He's staying tonight."

"Good deal," Avery's father said. Then he turned to Ryan. "You don't mind sleeping in the backyard, do you? We've got a great sleeping bag somewhere in the basement. I think it's *insulated*."

"Dad. Not cool."

"Dad not trying to be cool."

Avery's mother returned to the kitchen. Avery thought she looked a little less carefree than she'd looked before. Ryan thought she looked like she'd just talked to his mother.

"Well—that's all sorted out. Apparently, Ryan, your father wanted to drive over here to pick you up—but I convinced your mother that would be a bad idea. I don't think they understood how far away we live. But no matter—they're now on board. I promised to take care of you, so please, no knife juggling or putting your head in any plastic bags." (She did not mean this as a sexual reference. Ryan and Avery totally heard it as a sexual reference.)

"And," she continued, "I also promised that you'll stay in the guest room. Which in this house means the couch. The good news for you is that it opens up."

Avery knew better than to challenge this decision, but was already strategizing ways around it. The idea of sharing sleep with Ryan was undeniably appealing.

Ryan wondered if he should call his parents back, apologize. What would make it better?

Nothing, his instincts told him. *Just be happy you're not there. Be happy you're here.*

Avery touched him on the back and he startled. He couldn't appreciate Avery's affection as much with Avery's parents watching. It felt . . . wrong. Not bad—just something that had to be worked up to.

Sensing this, Avery put his hand down. His mom, meanwhile, cursed loudly and made a lunge for the oven, sighing with relief when no smoke billowed out as she opened it.

"Dinner," she said, "will soon be served."

During dinner, Ryan observed the way that family shorthand could be used not for accusation but for humor. There were things they were saying that were perfectly understandable on their own—*Where's the avocado?*—but didn't make much sense for an outsider within the context of the conversation.

During dinner, Avery observed how shy Ryan became, how reactive. Avery was keenly aware of how ridiculous his family was, and he made sure to fill Ryan in whenever what they were saying made no sense. ("There was this deeply unfortunate period when I was eight that I wanted avocado on everything. Since avocados are not cheap, and are not something you just pick up at 7-Eleven, this was a royal pain for Mom and Dad. They'd give me a steak and I'd say, 'Where's the avocado?' Or spaghetti. Or, I don't know, a hot dog.")

During dinner, Avery's mother also observed how shy Ryan became, although she had much less to compare it to.

During dinner, Avery's father tried to wrap his mind around the fact that Avery had brought a boyfriend home for them to meet. It felt like a big step, but since Avery wasn't acting as if it were a big step, his father tried to keep his feelings to himself.

Outside, it continued to snow.

When dinner was over, Ryan stood to clear the table. Everyone else told him he didn't have to, that he was the guest. But he refused their refusal, unable to explain to them that he felt he had to contribute in some way. Avery and his parents relented, working Ryan into their routine of clearing and scraping and rinsing and drying. There were some hiccups, but for the most part, Ryan worked in well. And in this way, he stopped feeling like such a guest. In this way, he started to feel like he belonged in this kitchen, with these people. They talked to each other instead of watching TV as they did the dishes. He answered questions when he was asked, but didn't have any questions to ask of them.

This changed when it was back to him and Avery, back to them alone. Avery's mother and father beat their retreat—even though it wasn't even eight o'clock, they said they were going to turn in. Probably watch a movie. Go to sleep early. Avery's father joked that he'd be waking them up at dawn to help dig out the driveway. Ryan was going to say that was alright with him—it only seemed fair to reciprocate the hospitality—but Avery, sensing this voluntary spirit, said, loudly, "No, I don't think that's going to happen."

Ryan never would have talked to his father like that.

Avery's father laughed.

"Alright, alright," Avery's mother said, shooing him out of the room. Then she turned to Avery and said, "I've put out towels for Ryan in the bathroom and sheets for the sofa in the family room—I mean, *guest room.*" Then she got more thoughtful, and looked at them both in turn. "I'm right to trust you two, correct? Keep it PG. Maybe PG-13. You're just getting to know each other and—"

"We know," Avery interrupted, mortified. "PG-13."

(For his part, Ryan wanted to sink through the floor.)

"Okay," Avery's mother said. "We have an understanding." She looked squarely at Ryan, who somehow managed to match her eye. "Here's the thing—I promised your mother that you would sleep in the guest room. So you have to sleep in the guest room." Then she turned to Avery. "I did not, however, make any promises about where *you* would sleep. Because I trust you both to . . . take it slow."

"Mom! We get it!"

Avery's mother smiled. "Good. And if you go outside, for heaven's sake, wear boots."

They did not go outside at first. Instead they went to the family room, as if that was expected of them. They sat on the couch and watched the Weather Channel on mute, face to face with the satellites' rendering of the storm. Avery picked up the remote control and was about to ask Ryan what he wanted to watch . . . but Ryan was already watching something: a photograph of Avery and his family at Disneyland, the summer before third grade. Avery was wearing Mickey Mouse ears and his expression was, frankly, goofy. He had no idea who'd taken the photo, who'd allowed their molecular family to retain its formation—Avery the middle smile, bookended by his parents.

"It's so corny," he said now. "I begged them to take it down, but they like to taunt me."

"I like it," Ryan said quietly. "It looks fun."

We learn each other by listening, and in this moment, Avery learned volumes from just six words. He learned that Ryan had never been to Disneyland, and probably not any-place like Disneyland. He learned that this wasn't an option, this wasn't the way Ryan's life worked. He learned that the things that might be embarrassing to him might not be embarrassing to Ryan. He learned that while he didn't have to be careful with Ryan, he also had to try to avoid being careless.

"It was fun," he admitted. "I kept correcting people—they wanted me to be Minnie and I was like, no, do you see any bow on this head? I'm *Mickey*."

147

Ryan reached for his hand. Held it.

"But you're so much *cuter* than Mickey."

Avery laughed. "Oh, thanks!"

The photograph no longer had their attention. Now it was their hands, their fingers. The epicenter of their calm, the point of most connection.

Each in his own way felt a small shock of surprise within the comfort of their pleasure. When you have to fight for your identity and win your identity, there is always a part of you that thinks there has to be a trade-off, that by stepping away from the norm you have been prescribed, you risk stepping away from the normal happinesses as well. You feel you will have to fight harder for someone to love you. You feel you will have to bear the risk of more loneliness in order to be who you need to be.

And yet.

Much more often than not, with that small shock of surprise, the fight will come loose, and the risk will fall aside like a broken cocoon, and you will find yourself completely un-alone, not only seen by someone else, but felt. This was part of what you were trying to get to, and now it is here.

Avery closed his eyes and leaned into Ryan. Ryan closed his eyes and leaned into Avery. For a few minutes, they let that be their lives. From the parents' bedroom, there was the indistinct sound of some TV show. Outside, there were the fairy footsteps of snow. Avery could feel Ryan breathing. Ryan's eyes were closed, but in his mind, he was seeing them on the couch, was imagining what it looked like with Avery's head on his shoulder.

Then: A squeeze on Ryan's hand. Avery sitting up. Ryan opened his eyes, turned to him, and saw him smiling.

"Outside," Avery said. "We need to go outside."

• • •

There was no way Avery's old boots would fit Ryan, so Ryan borrowed Avery's father's from the bottom of the closet. (Avery swore it was okay.) They bundled one another as best as they could—Avery wrapping the scarf around Ryan so fervently that his neck was temporarily mummified; Ryan insisting on zipping Avery up, on putting the hat on his head. Just so his hands could linger on Avery's cheeks. Just so it could lead to a kiss.

All the paths—even the driveway—had disappeared with the hours. When they stepped outside, it was into a crystalline silence, a white darkness. The snow still fell, but almost as an afterthought now, a gentle patter.

Avery took Ryan's mitten in his own mitten and led him into the yard. Ryan thought for a moment of the neighbor across the street, of any neighbor . . . but then he chose to put those thoughts aside. He focused on the way his boots sank into the surface with every step. He focused on the frosty filaments that landed on his cheek. He focused on mittens, and Avery, and on the depth of the quiet around them. This was a world without cars, a world without an alarm set for the next morning.

Avery let go. He couldn't help himself—the snow was just too perfect to be ignored. Ryan didn't understand until too late what he was doing. By the time Avery had formed the snowball, Ryan was only just reaching for his own scoop of ammunition. Avery took aim. Fired.

Bull's-eye.

Ryan retaliated, but Avery dodged, then fired again and hit. Ryan assembled a snow boulder and moved in at close range to pounce. Avery tried to wriggle away, but was only half-successful. More shots were fired. More footsteps covered the yard.

Finally Ryan couldn't take it any longer, and tackled Avery to the ground. Their coats were so thick, it was almost like a pillow fight, only with the boys acting as the pillows. It was a soft landing, a soft tackle. Avery tried to wriggle out of Ryan's grip, and then he stopped trying. He lay there in the snow and Ryan lay there next to him, and then they were kissing again, snowflake eyelashes and cold-flush cheeks.

Ryan rolled onto his back and they both faced the sky, watching the snowflakes fall. Like stargazing, only with the stars coming when they were called. Ryan's head was next to Avery's head, his hip next to Avery's hip. Avery put his legs together, in the shape of one leg. And Ryan, knowing what Avery was doing, did the same. His left mitten found Avery's right mitten and they held. Then, on the count of three, they extended their other arms, lifted their way to wings. A single snow angel, larger than either of them could be on his own.

"This is not what I thought I'd be doing right now," Ryan said. Had it been a regular night, he probably would have been driving back at this hour.

"I know," Avery whispered.

Ryan could feel the damp cold seeping into his jeans. He could tell his nose was unpleased and runny. The line between the bottom of his hat and the collar of his coat was allowing an unkind chill to set in at the back of his neck, despite the scarf. Still, he had no desire to move.

Avery blinked away the snow that gathered around his eyes. He listened hard and couldn't hear anything but snow language (faint), tree language (fainter), and the tiny rustle of Ryan's jacket against his.

"We are the only people in the world," he said.

"We are," Ryan agreed.

They moved their legs. They pulled in their wings. They turned in to each other. And as they did, they lightly altered the surface of the ground, the shape of the world. They didn't realize this, not in these terms. But they felt it nonetheless.

Strands of pink hair peeked out from underneath Avery's hat. Damp pieces of blue hair clung to the side of Ryan's face, curving around his right eye. Ryan wanted to kiss Avery again, but his nose was too runny. Avery was happy to listen to the quiet, to look at this boy in front of him.

They held there.

Snow absorbed into their jeans. Snow gathered on their coats and their hats. Ryan wiped his nose with his mitten, then wiped his mitten off in the snow.

"If I'm not mistaken," Avery said, "I think this is how people die of hypothermia."

He sounded exactly like his mother. He did not notice this. Ryan did, in a good way.

"Time to return to the real world," Ryan said.

"No," Avery corrected. "This is the real world, too."

Is it? Ryan asked himself, not entirely free from doubt.

"It is," he answered aloud.

Avery stood up, then extended a mitten to help Ryan up. Ryan didn't really need the boost, but took it anyway.

He also used it as a decoy to take Avery's attention away from the snowball he'd formed in his other hand.

Coming in from the snow outside: At no other time does home seem so much like hearth. Avery and Ryan didn't appreciate how wet and bedraggled they were until the door was closed and they were shucking off their coats and slicking off their boots. Their shirts were fine—maybe even a little sweaty—but their jeans and socks were soaked through.

"Let's get those pants off of you," Avery purred, and they both laughed, because neither of them had aspirations to turn this moment into porn. Eventually, yes. But not right now.

It's not that Avery wasn't curious. It's not that he hadn't scrutinized every bare moment of skin that Ryan had ever shown.

It's not that Ryan wasn't tempted. He was so far away from his parents, so far away from any restriction. But he was also wearing an embarrassingly shoddy pair of briefs. And it was so quiet that he felt if he undid his fly, the sound of the zipper would fly throughout the house and cause Avery's parents to come running.

"I'll be right back," Avery said. He ran to the small laundry room off the garage, and was relieved to find the dryer had been run, not yet emptied. He pulled out a pair of his father's sweatpants and a dry pair of his own jeans. Quickly, he changed into this new pair of jeans, then emptied out the dryer and put the old pair inside, along with his socks. Then, barefoot, he returned to Ryan, offering the sweatpants and pointing him in the direction of the bathroom, where a dry towel waited. Now it was Ryan's turn to say, "I'll be right back," as he tiptoed off to change.

They weren't separated for longer than five minutes, but each of them felt the separation, felt the other one in another part of the house, waiting. In the bathroom, after bunching up the ankles of the sweats so they wouldn't drag on the floor, Ryan looked at his watch and was amazed to see it was ten-thirty. But he couldn't figure out if he was amazed that it was so early or already so late. They seemed to be the same thing in the snowbound night.

When Ryan returned to the family room, he found Avery had transformed the sofa into a bed, and was be-sheeting it. For a second, he stood in the doorway and watched as Avery threw his body over the bed to try to make the fourth corner of the fitted sheet stretch. Ryan put his wet clothes on the floor and went over to help.

"Here," he said.

Avery unfolded the top sheet and threw half of it over to Ryan. The truth was, he never, ever made his bed if he could get away with not making it—but since this was where Ryan would be sleeping, he felt he should make it right. So there they were, smoothing the surface, making parallel movements to tuck in, make it even.

Next, the blanket. The same teamwork of two.

This blanket only came out for relatives, rare guests. Avery had never noticed it so much before.

Pillows were put in place, and the job was done. Avery looked across the bed at Ryan and he wanted to crawl right over, pull Ryan right down, mess up everything they'd just made.

But Ryan didn't catch the signal. He felt bad about his wet clothes sitting on the carpet. So he moved and picked them up again, asked Avery where they should go.

"I got it," Avery said.

"No, no, it's fine—just tell me where they go."

"In the dryer. Here."

Avery walked Ryan to the laundry room and opened the dryer for him, as if he were its doorman. Ryan bowed his thanks and threw his jeans and socks on top of Avery's. With the press of a few buttons, they began to tumble.

"So what now?" Avery asked, hoping the answer would be a return to the bed they'd created.

"I want to see your room," Ryan replied. His way of saying *I want to know your room*, which was another way of saying *I want to know you*.

"Okay." If there was any disappointment in Avery's voice,

Ryan didn't hear it. Which was good, because if Ryan had heard it, he wouldn't have understood that the disappointment was a compliment to him, too.

Once they were in the room, Avery expected Ryan to sit down, stay awhile. But instead he remained standing, looking around at everything.

"What's the most embarrassing thing that you're proud of here?" Ryan asked. As soon as he said it, he didn't think he'd made any sense. But Avery knew what he meant.

"Over here," he said. He walked over to his bookshelf, where a pink plush unicorn was guarding the collected works of Beverly Cleary. "This is Gloria. And she was, without question, my best friend for a very long time. We were never apart for long. She used to be much brighter, but she's mellowed. I guess we both have. My parents did not know what to make of my deep affection for her. They thought I should aim higher in the best-friend department. There was no way for them to understand that I'd made her into the part of me that I needed to hear . . . even if it was in unicorn form. But hey, my parents had to unlearn a lot of things. Which is just another way of saying they had to learn a lot of things. We all did. We all still do. You do. I do. We're all really new at this."

Ryan walked over to Avery, stood right in front of him. "I'm definitely new at this," he said. He wasn't talking about what Avery was talking about. Instead he was saying that all of those things could be unlearned and learned, but the really hard part, the really awkward and scary and wonderful part, was being in a room with someone you liked and trying to find the right things to say, the right things to do with your body, the clearest signal to send to say that this meant a lot, that this really meant a lot.

Avery raised the unicorn so her horn touched Ryan's nose. Ryan laughed.

"She approves," Avery assured him.

We find someone to love, and in finding that person, we find our own capability to love them.

Most of the time—no, all of the time—we have had no idea what we were capable of.

Two boys kissing in a room.

One boy pausing to tell the story of the time he brought a unicorn to school.

The other boy talking about his own brush with unicorns, this one on a folder he had to keep hidden under his bed. When his parents found it, he told them it belonged to a girl from school, that she had used it to give him her part of a joint assignment. Which was true, but not the reason he'd kept it long after the assignment was done.

Both boys talking about unicorns and parents, teachers and erasers shaped like stars. Both boys debating whether there was really anything guilty about guilty pleasures. Both boys taking pleasure in deciding there was not.

Everyone here has forgotten about laundry, about bed-time, about snow.

Midnight is just another minute, when you're not looking at the clock.

• • •

It was Avery who yawned first, and the moment he started, something was set off in Ryan, and he started yawning, too.

They were leaning against Avery's bed when this happened, but they knew this was not the bed where they would end up. They'd promised. Plus, the bed in the family room was bigger.

Avery's mother had put out a new toothbrush for Ryan, from her dentist-visit stash. So they could stand side by side at the bathroom sink, brushing and spitting together. This was a first time for both of them, and they each felt the intimacy of it, the significance of such a quotidian joy. It was no big deal, and that was why it was a big deal.

They did not talk about the sleeping arrangement; they simply went to the bed and arranged themselves for sleep. Ryan hadn't been sure this would happen; Avery hadn't been sure Ryan would want it. Their uncertainty showed, but so did their want, their almost existential want. They lay beside each other, but it wasn't like it had been in the snow. There were layers between them, but the layers were thin. They leaned in and kissed, and the longer they kissed, the more feverish it became. Kissing with their lips, yes, but also kissing with their hands, with their skin, with their breathing and their heat. Ryan reached around Avery, pulled his body close, and Avery reached around Ryan's back and pulled his body close, too, and together they felt like they were fusing, felt like they were both two and one. No clothes needed to be shed. No lines had to be crossed. This was everything, this closeness. This sensation of one another. This sense that touch could generate such feeling.

Then the slowdown. The lighter touches. The lying there and breathing one another in. Wondering how the heartbeat could spread through so much of the body. Feeling the heat subside, but not entirely.

The drifting of voices and the approach of sleep. Avery

watching Ryan fight it, blinking out and blinking back, and then coming unmoored again. Avery wished him a goodnight. Ryan smiled, cuddled in. Wished him a goodnight back. Then fell—the gentlest kind of fall.

Avery could not fall asleep as easily. Avery needed to think about this as it was happening. Avery needed to understand it in order to enjoy it. So he watched Ryan through the blue-black darkness, watched as his chest rose and subsided, extraordinary machine. *How did this happen?* Avery asked himself. *How is this possible?* Because this was a room he knew well. His parents were asleep in another room, allowing this. The snow kept falling outside, the reason Ryan was still here. All of it. This. You watch this person you are just getting to know, this person you want to tie notions onto, and suddenly the world is no longer a conspiracy of forces against you, but instead you understand that there are good conspiracies, too, there are forces that will help you, that want you to find this remarkable form of personal peace, this four-letter universe of a word.

In Avery's head, this all translated into *I really like you* and *I want this to work* and *I don't believe this* and *I want to believe this* and *This is real. This is real. This is real.*

It's hard to fall asleep to such thoughts. You have to wait for them to slow. You have to wait for them to cool.

While you do, you watch the person across from you. And somehow, you watch yourself, too.

There is no way of knowing this, and no way of proving this, and there will certainly be no way of remembering this, but the moment Avery fell asleep, the snowfall stopped.

• • •

Just before dawn, Ryan heard tanks scraping through the streets. His first instinct was to think the alien invasion had begun . . . but then he heard the sound further and realized it wasn't tanks, it was a snowplow.

Go away, he thought. *Stop doing that.*

Later, Ryan was the first in the house to wake for real. Disoriented by the house, by the room, by the bed—but then grounded by the pink hair just a few inches from his eyes, the soft truth of the sleeping body at his side. And not just at his side—sometime in the night, Avery's arm had reached for Ryan's arm and stayed there, once again overlapping.

The room was lit only by the light filtering in from outside, tinting the air the color of snow. Ryan stood up and walked to the window, bent back the shade and looked at the blanketed landscape, the igloo of his car. Icicles, some the length of swords, dangled from the roof.

"Is it still snowing?" Avery asked from behind him.

"No," Ryan answered, turning. Watching as Avery slowly sat up, impulsively stretched—those early-morning infant movements, when we see if everything is still working, and if we remember how it all works. Even though Avery's hair was a pink nest and his eyes were scrunched up and his cheek bore the imprint of a pillowcase's seam, in this light, this pale morning filter, Ryan felt such a remarkable attraction toward him—desire, yes, but also a profound fondness for this moment, a deep cherishing of whatever this was.

"Let's build a snow dragon," Avery mumbled, eyes closing.

Ryan didn't think he'd heard this right. "What?" he asked—gently, just in case Avery was going back to sleep.

"A snow dragon," Avery repeated more emphatically, eyes

158

still closed. "Surely they have snow dragons where you come from?"

"Nope," Ryan confessed.

"Well then." Avery opened his eyes. "I guess I'll just have to show you."

They didn't bother changing out of their sleep clothes. Instead they went back to the dryer and Ryan pulled his jeans on over the sweats he was wearing. Socks returned to feet. Boots returned to socks. Mittens returned to hands.

It was so bright outside, and no longer quiet—the morning being scored by the sound of dripping, the sound of shovels being used a few houses over. If he looked closely, Avery could see shallow commemorations of last night's footprints. Even the snow angel remained as a shadow of its former self—still there, but partly lifted.

Snow was gathered, but never so deeply that the grass would begin to show, spoiling the illusion of white. What started as a mound slowly became a shape. What seemed at first a shape evolved into a body. And from the body, a neck was grown, a head. Wings on the ground. A tail. A bystander might not have been able to decipher it. But when Avery's mother looked out the window, she turned to her husband and said, "Oh, look, they're building a snow dragon!"

We all know that nothing built with snow will last.

But we all remember what it's like to have snow in our hands, to make something soft less soft so we can build with it. We all remember the sensation of being outside, of making a shape, of building.

So something of it must last.

• • •

159

Later, Ryan would find the texts from his father, telling him the roads were fine now, so he should come home. And after Ryan replied by turning off his phone, Avery's mother would receive a call from his mother, saying just about the same thing. Later, Ryan, Avery, and Avery's parents would take turns with their two shovels, digging out Ryan's car, making a path for him to leave. But not before lunch. Not before a last round of kissing in Avery's bedroom. Not before photographs were taken with their creation.

As they built the snow dragon, they talked, but not about the snow dragon. Avery didn't tell Ryan what shapes to make; Ryan didn't make suggestions about the pattern of the scales that they traced with their bare fingers into the dragon's skin. It didn't matter that Avery had done this before. It didn't matter that Ryan hadn't. The end result was nothing like what it would have been if Avery had built it alone, or if Ryan had. You would never be able to entirely tell who did what. Whatever resulted was unique to the two of them.

It was, they would say later, the first thing they built together.

It would be the first of many things that would be entirely theirs.

TRACK ELEVEN

The Woods

It is not my intention to surprise him. I just happen to bump
into his housemate on her way in, and forget to text him that
I'm in the building. The door to his room isn't all-the-way
closed, so I push it open without feeling the need to knock. I
say "hello" as soon as I step inside—it's not like I'm sneaking
in. He's at his desk, and the moment my voice registers, he
slams his laptop shut. Then he turns around, thinking he's
removed all traces of guilt from his face. But I can still see
them there.

I have never, in over a year of us being together, seen him
slam his laptop shut. So I'm figuring this has to be pretty bad.

"What are you doing?" I ask. And even as I'm asking, I'm
coming up with answers. An obvious one, harkening back
to the times I've slammed my own laptop shut, is porn. But
we're far enough along in our own sex life that it seems ridiculous for him to fear me catching him in an ogle or a wank. I
think I've made it perfectly clear that I believe all kinds of
sex acts are fine, as long as they're consensual. And I've also
made it clear that there are certain things I will never consent
to. Which means, as I play this out in my head, that whatever
porn he's been watching has to involve something so despi-
cable that he's afraid it will pervert our relationship to an ir-
reparable degree.

Or—other option—he's been cheating on me, and I've just caught him in the act.

"Seriously," I say, "you need to tell me why you just did that."

I can see him snagged on the horns of the dilemma, trying to squeeze his way off, but only making the wounds worse.

"If I tell you something," he says, "do you promise not to judge?"

"I can't promise that," I reply. "I'm already judging." I feel it behooves the situation for one of us to be telling the truth. And anyone who answers yes to a question like *Do you promise not to judge?* is unquestionably a liar. Judgment is not something one can control—only the expression of judgment can be tamed.

Not that I'm in any mood to tame my judgment.

"Tell me anyway," I say.

He sighs. "There's something I've been hiding from you, because I just don't know how to have this conversation."

Now I'm the one snagged on the horns. This strengthens my anger—my *outrage!*—at whatever he's done, whatever he's about to tell me. And it also makes me immeasurably sad, because, yes, this is going to hurt. At this point, we're supposed to know each other's major secrets—the secrets we don't know yet are supposed to be the minor ones, the forgettable ones, the ones that were buried so long ago that no one remembers where the graves are. But this—I can feel what's coming is a major secret, a present-day secret that's going to reveal that I am, in fact, the buried one.

Who is it? I want to ask. But I don't say the words out loud, because saying them out loud will make this scene real. And I'm afraid of that. I was really enjoying our life together, until a minute ago.

"Okay." He looks down at the laptop in a way that I

162

imagine a murderer looks at his gun, after the deed is done. Then he looks back at me. "It started three years ago. Before I ever met you."

So it's an ex-boyfriend. A non-ex ex-boyfriend. A hex-boyfriend.

"And . . . I don't know. There was never any way to tell you. I thought that if you never knew, it didn't matter. At least, not in terms of you."

So everyone knows about it except me. Everyone.

"I don't expect you to get it. I know it's not your thing."

Infidelity? Damn right, that's not my thing.

"But—I'm just going to say it, okay?"

I nod.

"For the past few years, I've spent a lot of my time writing Taylor Swift fan fiction. Like, *a lot* of it. And I guess I've become . . . popular at it."

I stare at him. This is not the kind of joke he'd make. It's either the worst cover story ever fabricated to hide infidelity with an ex or . . . he's serious.

He opens up the laptop, gestures me to come look.

It's a blog; I've caught him in the middle of an entry. The banner at the top trumpets:

The Triumphs and Travails of the Fearless Miss S

Someone has drawn a picture of Taylor Swift beneath it. She looks like a stylish swashbuckler. Or maybe a fashion ninja.

Under that are the stats.

My boyfriend has 394,039 followers.

For the next three hours, I catch up. I sit there in his room, on his laptop, and learn what he's been doing when I haven't been around. Or when I've been in the very same room, thinking he was writing emails or watching videos.

Owen can't bear to be around as I read it, so he heads out to run errands. I'm so engrossed I barely notice when he leaves.

It's not what I thought it would be. I was expecting, for lack of a better term, extreme kissyface. I don't know very much about Taylor Swift circa the year of our Lord(e) 2015, but I do know she falls in love a lot. And breaks up a lot. And writes a lot of songs about it. So I'm expecting stories along those lines. Maybe with some shopping thrown in, because Taylor Swift has always reminded me of one of those girls in the mall who really seems to be *enjoying* her shopping.

But that's not the way Owen's written it. Instead, The Fearless Miss S is this dashing, daring superhero whose biggest superpower seems to be, of all things, empathy. In episodes that span the globe, she fights off dastardly bastards and fair-weather friends, usually on behalf of a girl or gay boy who didn't know any better. Her archnemesis is Justin Bieber, the most duplicitous rogue within The Secret Society of Insincere Canadians, a nefarious organization that almost managed to take over the world during the chart reign of "My Heart Will Go On." Mostly, Bieber and The Fearless Miss S fight over the misbegotten heart of a girl named Selena. (A quick Google search informs me that this is Selena Gomez, an actual person—or at least as much as a celebrity can be called an actual person.) The action jumps from past to present, and incorporates song lyrics in unexpected ways. There's even an origin story that the reader has to piece together over time, involving a mysterious experiment that goes awry when three radioactive tears hit an acoustic guitar. The Fearless Miss S is plunged into what's called The Jonas Vortex—then fights her way out with strength and song.

I can't say I particularly see the appeal. It's fun, for sure. But I wouldn't read more than one installment if I didn't know my boyfriend had written it.

Other people, though, are clearly hooked. There are hundreds—sometimes thousands—of comments for each entry. There are, I see, fan blogs for Owen's fan blog. The Fearless Miss S's Facebook page shows people from all over the world (particularly the Netherlands) dressed as her, or dressed in T-shirts emblazoned with what I can only imagine are her more popular catchphrases. Like: *Banality Belongs With Bieber, But You Belong With Me.* Or: *I Knew You Were Trouble, Which Is Why I Kicked Your Ass.* Or (and I'll admit I don't understand this one): *You Don't Have 2 B 22 2 B 22.*

I stop reading when Owen shuffles back in. He holds a bag of donuts—a transparent form of bribery that I unconditionally accept.

"So, yeah," he says, passing the bag over. "That's that."

"I like it," I tell him. "It's fun."

He stands more rigid. "Fun."

"I really enjoyed it."

"*Enjoyed.*"

"Yes, enjoyed." I don't understand why he's acting like this isn't a compliment.

But clearly Owen doesn't see it that way. "You're not saying it's good. You're dancing around it. I knew I shouldn't have shown you."

"No! It's good! I mean, for what it is."

"What do you mean, *for what it is?*"

"I mean, I'm not supposed to compare it to Alice Munro, am I? If I am, you certainly win on the action/adventure/pop-culture front, but she *might* win when it comes to the beauty of her sentences. Anyway—I don't think Munro's fans are your target audience, right? You'd be nicer to Canadians if that were true."

"And who do you think my target audience is?"

This is feeling like a trick question.

"I don't know," I say. "Who's your target audience?"

He's disappointed in me. I can see it. I have not earned my donut.

"Me," he says. "I'm my target audience. I started writing it for me. Then it just . . . spread."

"To almost four hundred thousand people."

"I guess. Yeah."

"That's awesome," I say, standing up and offering the bag of donuts back to him, letting him take first pick. "Really. It's amazing."

"Okay," he says, reaching in for a chocolate-glazed.

I don't ask him why he didn't tell me. And he doesn't say that he's happy I finally know. We just let it sit there, open on the laptop, until we've let it sit for long enough that the screen saver rises, and we move on to something else.

The next day at work, I dip back in.

It's Gabriela's fault. We're swapping the usual how-was-your-night pleasantries and I figure I'll interject a hey-I-found-out-my-boyfriend-writes-stories-about-Taylor-Swift-that-a-lot-of-people-read.

"What's his blog called?" she asks.

"The Triumphs and Something of The Fearless Miss S."

Gabriela laughs. "No way."

"You know it?"

"Are you kidding? I spend more time on that than Kim Kardashian spends talking about her butt."

Gabriela is a fifty-six-year-old lesbian from Park Slope

who drags me to see Toshi Reagon every time she plays the Bandshell. I had not pegged her as a Taylor Swift fan.

"Yeah," I say. "It's pretty cool."

"That must be hard for you, dating a writer. There must be moments when you think, *God, I hope I'm not the Bieber in this scenario.*"

"Well, it's not *autobiography,*" I point out. "It's not like I'm married to David Sedaris or Cheryl Strayed. I mean, he's writing about Taylor Swift."

"Whatever you say, Clark. All I know is that if I can think The Fearless Miss S is a lot like me, then Owen probably feels she's a lot like him, too."

"Oh, sure, sure," I say. But really what I'm thinking is, *Why did you immediately assume I was the Bieber in the scenario?*

Which is why I dip back in. To see what I can find.

The problem is, I'm Canadian.

I've never been a pop singer, but I'm from Ottawa. I don't listen to much Canadian pop—nothing since the heyday of Alanis Morissette, which doesn't really count as pop, in my opinion. Nor does Arcade Fire or Feist or Owen Pallett—so nothing on my playlist should qualify me for The Secret Society of Insincere Canadians.

Unless, of course, I've been enrolled for membership without knowing it.

I know I'm being paranoid. Owen knows plenty of Canadians here in New York. Although, when I think about it, I realize that all of them are my friends.

The point is: I am not Justin Bieber.

For the first time, my buzz cut comes as an advantage, because there's a lot of talk in the stories about Bieber's bangs. There are also secret messages encoded in his tattoos, whereas the only marks on my arms are those that came with birth. He also calls people *baby* a lot. I don't think I've ever called anyone *baby*. Not even a baby.

Still, the anti-Canadian undercurrent can't be ignored. Things take a terrible twist in a flashback to the summer of '13, when it's revealed that the big jefe of the Insincere Canadian cadre is not, as had been expected, Céline Dion. No, in a shocker that (unbelievably) leaves me reeling, the woman pulling the strings is none other than *Joni Mitchell*. Apparently she is so terrified by the notion that Miss S will play her in a biopic that she hires a young Kennedy to court Miss S and spark her into oblivion. It almost works—with her faithful sidekick Abigail sidelined outside the gates at Hyannis Port, Miss S has her own Canadian missile crisis. But before the young Kennedy can banish her maidenhood to Camelot, Miss S rallies, discovering Joni Mitchell's plan and turning the tables. The craven Kennedy is contained with the kiss-off "I drank a case of you, asshole, and I'm still on my feet." I laugh at this, but I'm also a little disturbed, since that's a theft from my favorite Joni Mitchell song, one I've crooned in much nicer tones to Owen as we've made dinner and driven down highways.

I shake my head and tell myself I'm being ridiculous. Since I feel compelled to tell myself this *out loud*, it doesn't entirely inspire confidence. Back in my head, I determine there are dozens of reasons for Owen to have kept the blog a secret . . . and that an autobiographical nature does *not* have to be one of them. Also, it started before I came onto the scene. When he chose Bieber as a malevolent force, Owen wasn't dating a Canadian. Unless there's another Canadian in his past that I don't know about.

It's about Taylor Swift, I remind myself. *Taylor. Swift.*

I want to shake it off, but I can't. I find myself meandering back to Gabriela's office toward the end of the day. She's finishing a report on one of our clients' back taxes; I'm going to owe her a cursory proofread shortly.

"Do you have a sec?" I ask.

She nods, but doesn't look up.

"What's the appeal? I mean, of Taylor Swift. Why would you read about her?"

Gabriela looks up at me now, surprisingly serious.

"For one, the girl writes good songs. And she goes through all the drama that the rest of us go through—only when she goes through it, everyone is watching. It's very relatable."

"But how is it relatable? I mean, she's an attractive, thin, rich blond girl who hasn't had a normal life since she was, like, twelve. What's relatable about that?"

Gabriela shakes her head. "You're not listening. It's the songs. She gets it in her songs. And anyway, The Fearless Miss S isn't really Taylor Swift. She's like this riff on Taylor Swift. She's her own woman. And I like reading what she's up to."

"But why Taylor Swift? Why not Tegan and Sara? They're much more interesting." (*And*, I don't add, *Canadian*.)

"Are you asking about me, or are you asking about why your boyfriend chose Taylor Swift?"

"I guess I'm asking about Owen."

"Then maybe you should be sending the question his way."

The way she says this, I feel chastised.

The way she says this, I feel like I've been acting like Justin Bieber.

I go over to Owen's place and find him on his computer—openly on his computer. Usually he gets home only a few minutes before me, from his job at a FedEx office, but he looks plenty settled in right now.

"Am I interrupting?" I ask.

"Yeah," he says, not looking away from the screen. "But that's okay. Let me just finish this paragraph and we can grab dinner."

I'm not used to our pauses being measured in paragraphs instead of minutes, but I figure there isn't really that much of a difference. I look over his shoulder to see what The Fearless Miss S is up to.

"Can you not do that?" Owen says. "I mean, you're literally breathing down my neck."

I mutter an apology and pull out my phone to check my email while I wait.

I wonder if I should have gotten us a table for four. Because it's like they're here with us at the table.

Miss S.

Bieber.

It's not like Owen doesn't notice. He asks me about my day, asks me about what I'm ordering, but I can sense him waiting for me to bring them up.

"So it ends up that Gabriela's a fan of yours," I offer. "When I told her about the blog, she was really excited."

I figure this will please Owen; he's always liked Gabriela, and now she's liking him back in two ways.

But instead he puts down his Diet Coke without taking a sip.

"Clark." His voice is therapy-strained in its earnestness. "You can't tell anyone. No one can know."

"You didn't say that. You never said that."

"I thought it was understood."

"Why would it be understood?"

"Because if I wasn't even telling you, I obviously don't want other people to know. It has to be a secret."

"Why? Are you afraid Bieber will track you down and—I don't know, make you listen to his early albums? Throw a little light white-boy Canadian rap your way?"

"I just like to keep it separate."

"Are there legal implications? Taylor Swift can't sue your ass, can she?"

"No! I just—it's where I go to when I'm not me, if that makes any sense. And when people talk to Miss S, they're talking to her, not me. That's important."

"And when you say people talk to her . . ."

"They send messages. They want advice. Mostly they want me to tell them what they already know they need to do. Dump the guy. Stand up for themselves. Get rid of the friend who isn't treating them like a friend."

"They tell you about all that stuff?"

"Yes and no. They tell Miss S about that stuff. And she answers."

"But Miss S isn't you? And she isn't Taylor Swift?"

"Correct."

"Don't the girls think they're writing to Taylor Swift?"

"It's not always girls. And no—I think they understand the difference. Although obviously they wouldn't be bonding with Miss S in the first place if it weren't for what Taylor does."

I can't help myself. "So you're on a first-name basis with her now?"

He blushes, and resents it. "Shut up. You call Florence by her first name."

"Because that's her band. Florence and the Machine."

"I guess Taylor's just a first-name type of person. I don't know."

"So what's the appeal? I mean, to you."

"Of Taylor?"

"Yes."

"I think I'm like most people—when I see her, I see this gawky, unpopular girl who's made good. I can relate to that."

"How can you call her unpopular? She's, like, the most popular girl in the world right now!"

"But she's not like Madonna or Beyoncé, who give you this sense that they don't really give a shit about people. Taylor really cares. That comes through."

"Yes, that comes through her teams of publicists! Look, Owen—you haven't met the girl. You don't *know* her. You only know what she wants you to know about her."

This is the moment the food arrives. I've scored my point. I'm ready to talk about something else.

"That looks good," I say, gesturing to Owen's burrito.

But he doesn't bite.

"This is why I didn't want to tell you. This is exactly the conversation I didn't want to have with you. I knew you'd make me feel stupid. But you know what? I refuse to let you make me feel stupid. I *refuse*."

I resent this accusation deeply. "Good for you, Miss S," I reply. "I'm glad that whenever I have an opinion you don't agree with, it gets filed under *condescension*. And I'm glad that the reason you didn't tell me about this huge thing in your life was because you thought I would be a jerk about it. I'm glad that's what you *assumed*. That paints an extraordinarily generous portrait of me. And it doesn't even take into account any, I don't know, *embarrassment* you might feel about this thing that you don't even put your name on."

"How much of it have you actually read?"

"I've read *all of it*. So at least grant me that my opinion is an *informed* one."

Owen throws his napkin on the table. "No," he says, standing up. "I can't do this. I've had this nightmare before, and I have no desire to have it again while I'm awake."

"Sit down," I say, trying to take the edge out of my voice. "Seriously. We are *not* going to have our first major fight be over Taylor Swift. Let's at least wait until we're trying to figure out which neighborhood to move into together."

He doesn't sit down. "It's too late," he says. "I'm going."

"You're being melodramatic."

"No, I'm being *real*."

He says it like it's in quotes, so I figure it's from a Taylor Swift song. Then I make the mistake of asking, "Is that from a Taylor Swift song?"

"No," he tells me. "But this is: *Why you gotta be so mean?*"

"Seriously?" I ask.

The answer comes from his leaving.

I tell the waiter to bag up the burrito. On the way to Owen's apartment, I buy another Diet Coke. His housemate lets me in and I leave the meal outside his closed bedroom door. Taylor Swift is blaring from inside, nearly drowning out the sound of typing.

I wait until I'm out of the building before I text him and tell him where his dinner is waiting. I wait for the *thank you* that will let me know everything's moving back toward okay. But I don't hear from him for the rest of the night.

"Being boyfriend or girlfriend with someone doesn't mean loving every single thing they love, right?" I ask Gabriela the next morning over break-room coffee.

"No," she says. "But it sure as hell helps when you do."

173

. . .

As soon as I get to my computer, I conjure Miss S onto my screen. I'm afraid to read what she did last night, but I can't avoid it, either.

It isn't pretty.

The Fearless Miss S is about to perform at the Grammys. This should be a triumphant moment for her—she might not have won Best New Artist the year she was nominated, but now she's the favorite to win everything else. She's going to debut a new single, and her fans are tuning in by the millions. At least seven of her exes are in the audience, and she's made sure they all have aisle seats. As soon as she takes the stage, cameras will be set up right at their sides, to catch every moment of their reactions as she performs. If they so much as grimace or sneer, the whole world is going to see what she had to deal with when she was trying to love them.

Only—there are some things even The Fearless Miss S can't control. As she's finishing her vocal exercises in her dressing room backstage, an ex named Johnny Guitar comes sauntering in. Her best friend, Abigail, has run off to get her a Diet Coke from Target, so Miss S is trapped alone with him.

"I told you not to talk to me again," she protests.

Johnny Guitar smiles, but doesn't say a word. He just takes the guitar from his back and starts to play.

Miss S is suddenly not so fearless.

"No," she tells him. "Don't do this."

He continues to play. He's a master at the guitar, a master at sounds that aren't words. She still hears them as conversation. And she knows what they're saying: As adored as she is, she's still not an artist. She needs producers and stylists and (every now and then) a little overdubbing or Auto-Tune. She's not *authentic*. She can play the guitar, sure. But she can't do anything particularly new with it.

She knows she needs to leave the room. She knows it's almost time for her to go out there and perform.

His guitar catches that thought. *Perform*, it says over and over. Diminishing her into a show pony. A hack. A TV contestant.

He doesn't have to say a word to make her feel small. He knows this.

The smile doesn't leave his face as he pulls chords from the air and mangles them into brilliance.

She puts down her own guitar. Why bother holding it? She's not going to make it to the stage. . . .

I stop reading. Not because I want to stop, but because there isn't anything else to read.

I want him to be here. I want to ask him: *Is that really how you see me? Is that really what you think I do?*

It's not fair. I wasn't smiling last night. I'm not smiling now.

I text him. *I'm not smiling. I'm upset.*

I know he's at work. I know I can't go there, can't have the conversation right this moment. I also know there's something else I have to do right away.

I go into Gabriela's office. I don't even bother to close the door.

"I think I need to go home and listen to a lot of Taylor Swift," I tell her.

She gives me the nod. Says she can cover things.

If people ask, she'll tell them I'm having a family emergency.

It doesn't feel so far from the truth.

•   •   •

175

I get home and acquire every song Taylor Swift has ever released. I even pay for them, just in case Owen checks.

I decide to go in chronological order, which requires some fortitude. The cover of her first album isn't promising—she looks like she's auditioning for the role of a sultry mermaid in a low-budget shampoo commercial. The songs themselves don't do much more for me. It's like there's no difference between the sweetness and the sorrow—they're all sung in the same tone. I can only take so much adolescent sincerity. After listening to the first album, I need to blast Fiona Apple's "Criminal" just to find my bearings.

I get more into the groove with the second album. I know some of these songs, and most of them aren't bad. Even the ones that were massively overplayed back in 2008 have moments of awesomeness within them, more noticeable now that they're not being massively overplayed.

I keep going. By the time I'm at 1989, I'm in something of a fugue state. When I hit "Out of the Woods," something inside of me latches on. It doesn't matter that it's basically a Bleachers song sung by someone else. It doesn't matter that there are only about three lines' worth of lyrics. It doesn't matter that my dating history is hardly the same as Taylor Swift's romantic roller coaster. I'm drawn in and hooked. I listen to the song three times in a row. Then I listen to the rest of the album, and go straight back to "Out of the Woods." Repeat it.

Dinnertime passes. Night falls. I am caught in the loop of my headphones.

I find myself wondering: What makes a great song great? It can't be the message. There are thousands of other songs out there that say the exact same thing. What is it about the way this particular song is saying it that makes it last longer in my ears, so long that it makes a home in my mind?

176

I text Owen:

The funny thing about pop music is that it doesn't actually pop. The bubble holds.

Normally, this would elicit a ☺. Instead, after a minute, I get:

Correct.

I am not, it seems, either out of the woods or in the clear.

I turn off iTunes, but the tunes still play inside of I. I'm brushing my teeth to a blank space. I've got a James Dean look in my eye as I get out of the day's clothes. And when I'm in bed, phone at my side, waiting for another word from him, I go back into the out-of-the-woods-out-of-the-woods-out-of-the-woods.

Tomorrow? I text him.

Right before I fall asleep, he texts back, *Okay.*

I don't have to search out Gabriela when I get to the office. She's waiting for me.

"Here are the things you need to deal with first," she says, handing me a stack of invoices that need to be coded. "Then check your inbox."

I put the paperwork aside and go straight for her email. There's a link to StubHub showing me tickets to a Taylor Swift concert at the United Palace next Thursday.

The tickets cost roughly the price of an engagement ring. Or at least they cost more than I have ever spent at Target in my life. Or a lifetime's supply of Diet Coke.

Of course, Owen might already have tickets, as part of his Secret Life. From what I can tell, they're very hard to come by—but I figure I should check.

Can I see you tonight? I text. *And are you free next Thursday or Friday?*

The rolling ellipsis appears immediately on my screen.

Yes on all three counts, he replies.

I have to stop myself from calculating all the things we could do with the money I'm about to spend. Fly to London. Buy a nice couch, or three crappy couches. See *Hedwig* on Broadway a dozen times.

But this. This is what he wants, more than any of those other things.

I buy the tickets.

"You just cost me a lot of money," I tell Gabriela, poking my head into her office.

"Good man," she replies.

Back at my desk, I check in on Miss S. I'm not expecting anything new—Owen usually takes a few days between posts. This time, though, he's kept going. There's a new entry, time-stamped three a.m. EST.

We pick up exactly where we left off, with The Fearless Miss S paralyzed in the face of Johnny Guitar and his axiomatic wizardry. Outside, the crowd has begun to cheer for her, waiting for her to come onto the stage. But she can't hear any of it. She is overwhelmed by Johnny Guitar's precision, drenched in his virtuosity. Tears start to form in the corners of her eyes—

Until she blinks them away.

Even as her ex-boyfriend jimmies all the locks guarding her self-esteem, she reaches down for her own guitar. She knows she doesn't play anywhere near as well as he does. She knows he's mastered the blues while she's stayed in shades of pink and red. She knows no one will ever take her seriously as a musician. But she plays anyway. As he slides and struts and wails with his strings, she strums a simple melody. He ratchets up his tempo, stops smiling, and starts to break a sweat. She hums along with her song, ignores all the other sounds in the room, all the voices in her head telling her she will never be good enough, never be strong enough, never be *respected*. She is the recorder who took on the orchestra. Johnny Guitar is grimacing, his fingertips so calloused that he no longer feels—not even when they crack and bleed. The Fearless Miss S stays inside her song, finds peace in her song, will continue to play her song even though she's the only one hearing it. Because that's the most important thing, that you hear it yourself.

Johnny Guitar roars and lurches into feedback, falling at her feet in a fireball, dying for his art, which isn't worth dying for. The Fearless Miss S steps over him and walks out of the dressing room, strumming her guitar the whole time. She passes roadies and members of other bands; they all nod as she passes, not wanting to interrupt as she plays. She should be heading to makeup for one last pass before she meets the public, but she walks right by her Mistress of Disguise, then right past Abigail, who at least has the sense to follow and plug in her guitar just before she hits the stage. Without missing a beat, The Fearless Miss S begins to sing. The crowd jumps to its feet, an instrument itself, donating its own sounds.

Abigail smiles and picks up the case of Diet Coke she'd been carrying. When she gets back to the Fearless Miss S's dressing room, she doesn't find Johnny Guitar—only his leather jacket and his guitar, both smoking, embers at their edges.

Over the speakers in the dressing room, Abigail can hear

the Fearless Miss S triumph on the stage. When the song is done, Miss S has only one thing to say to the adoring crowd:

"The funny thing about pop music is that it doesn't actually pop. The bubble holds. . . ."

We meet for dinner at an Italian place near his apartment. It's only been two days, but I feel like it's been much longer since I've seen him. When you love someone, the emotional distance you travel can feel very much like time itself.

I know I should start by telling him I'm sorry, but instead I start by telling him how much I missed him.

He doesn't point out it's only been two days. So I know he's feeling it, too.

I go on, and tell him I've been reading *The Fearless Miss S.* "You really had me worried there," I say. "Johnny Guitar was pretty formidable."

Owen sits back in his chair. "You don't have to humor me."

"I'm not humoring you! I thought it was—real. Even though Johnny Guitar is a pretty strange name for a character."

He smirks. "You don't have any idea why he's named that, do you?"

"Should I?"

"No. It's sort-of sweet that you don't."

I can live with sort-of sweet.

"I spent yesterday listening to Taylor Swift," I say. "And I've been hearing it in my head all day, even though I was only playing it about half the time. I suspect there are subliminal enticements embedded in the music, so your brain won't let it go. If so, they're surprisingly effective."

"Which album were you listening to?"

"All of them. Although today it's mostly been *1989.* I

don't need to be welcomed to New York . . . but damned if I didn't let her welcome me anyway!"

"I actually can't imagine you liking that song."

"I do. I mean, I give in to it. The lyrics are trite and the music is eighties pastiche and her shout-out to gays is like, *Oh thanks so much*. The whole time I'm listening to it, I'm thinking that when this girl moved to New York, she moved into a multi-bedroom apartment on the top floor of a designer building, which isn't really the universal moving-to-New-York story. I don't believe she really got to experience anything in the song herself, not in an unencumbered way. But in a sense, that makes the song even more poignant. Because she's singing about this experience she'll never have like we normal people have. It's touching that she wants to be a broke grad student so badly."

Owen nods. "I think about this a lot. I think if even a girl as rich and set as Taylor feels these emotions, doesn't that make them even more legitimate? It's like nobody gets to escape from heartbreak or doubt, and that makes heartbreak and doubt seem more . . . shared, I guess."

All of a sudden, I'm choking up.

"What?" Owen asks, looking alarmed. "What is it?"

"I don't want you to be thinking about heartbreak and doubt," I tell him. "Those should be the furthest things from your mind."

"Awwww," Owen says, reaching over and holding my hands. "I'm not saying I'm feeling them along with her. I just know they're out there. I've faced them before, and there will always be the feeling that I may face them again. That's not because of you. That's because I'm human."

I pull my hands out of his and reach over for my bag. "I have something for you," I say.

My hands are actually shaking. I know our relationship

took a step backwards the last time we were together, and now I'm afraid I'm jumping it too far forward. We've shared hundreds of small gestures in the year we've been together, but this is the first big gesture, or at least the first expensive one, and I want him to know I did it because I love him and want to make him happy, not because I'm desperate to keep him interested in an asshole like me.

On the subway ride over, I practiced all the things I'd say. Silly Taylor Swift references about him belonging with me, or me belonging with him, or how we're safe and sound. Or more earnest words about being a fool, about wanting him to know I support whatever he wants to create, in any form he wants to create it. All true. But instead of any of this, I take the printout from my bag and hand it over and say, "Here." Then I sit there without breathing as he unfolds the paper and reads it.

"No," he says. Then, "How? I mean—really? **Really?!?**"

"Really."

This time he doesn't reach for my hands. He jumps out of his chair and comes around and hugs me. Even though it's awkward with me in a chair and him standing, I hold on for a little longer than usual, and so does he.

When he's back in his chair, he asks, "But how did you get these? The concert sold out in, like, ten seconds. They're recording it for HBO!"

"I have my connections," I reply.

He will never, ever know how much I paid.

It's not like nothing's happened. It's not like we go back to where we were, not exactly. Another element has been added, and that element is The Fearless Miss S.

That night, when we get back to his apartment, he heads straight for his laptop. I don't ask him why, because now I know. He puts on headphones and starts typing. I turn on the small TV in his bedroom and watch it with the volume low.

After about forty-five minutes, he takes off the headphones and looks around, dazed.

"How's it going?" I ask him.

"Good."

I don't know if it's okay for me to ask what Miss S is up to. It's his own private world—but it's also one he makes public eventually.

I decide to try. "Can you tell me what happens next? Or should I just wait until you're done?"

He leans back in his chair and looks at me. "I don't know. I haven't really thought about it. I don't want to leave you out, but I've never shared it with anyone while I'm writing it. I'm worried, in a way."

"I promise I won't be mean," I tell him.

"No, no—it's not that. I don't think you'll be mean. But I think that I'll care too much about what you think. And I'm worried that if I share it with you first, if I let you in as I'm writing it, then I'll start writing it for you. I know that's not what you're asking for, but it's the way it would be. It's easier to think of thousands of strangers reading it."

This makes sense, and I'm still a little hurt. But being in love means living with a little hurt, so I can take it.

"New territory," The Fearless Miss S tells Abigail as they head out in a limo after the Grammys. "We're heading into new territory."

"That's a good thing, right?" Abigail asks.

The Fearless Miss S smiles, leans back in her seat, and looks out the window in a glance that sees far beyond the California they're in.

"Absolutely," she says.

This is what makes me happy.

The lobby of the United Palace, every inch covered with gold and ornament. It's like the inside of a genie's lamp, on a Liberace scale.

The excitement of everyone around me. The feeling that every single person around me feels lucky to be here, lucky to be alive.

The young teen girl wearing a homemade Fearless Miss S T-shirt, and the look on Owen's face when he sees it. The way he doesn't say a word to her. The way she still thinks of The Fearless Miss S as her own.

The way Owen can't sit still when we get to our seats in the balcony.

The moment of recognition, the moment of awe, when the lights go out.

The cheer that follows that moment, so all-consuming that we can only experience it synesthetically, as a sight and a taste and a lift and a sound.

The way my boyfriend goes "Ohmygod ohmygod ohmygod" when the girl he both doesn't know and knows so well takes the stage.

The way he turns to me—not to be worried about what I think, but to share his amazement.

Every song makes me happy. Even the sad songs. That's the trick, isn't it? To get to the place where even the sad songs can make you happy, because they make you feel so much more a part of life. They make you realize there is music in even the most difficult things.

But most of all, there is the transcendent happiness when she starts to play "Out of the Woods"—the happiness that is both joy and relief, that is clarity, that is everything we've wanted, for the three minutes and fifty-six seconds that it will last.

The happiness of singing along.

The happiness of singing along with the boy I love.

The happiness of seeing in his eyes that he is so happy, too.

TRACK THIRTEEN

As the Philadelphia Queer Youth Choir Sings Katy Perry's "Firework" . . .

Alright, choir. Let's do this.

I'm sorry—I know how much some of the others like this song, but we should be singing "Born This Way" instead.

Why did Tim have to put me next to Joe? I know conductors can be cruel, but this . . . this is too much.

Is Tyrone really ghosting me?

I mean, Tyrone understands we're in this choir together, right?

Just because there are two boys kissing in the video, it doesn't make it a gay anthem. "Born This Way" is clearly a gay anthem.

Project, Dan. Stop looking at your feet.

Joe has to stop smiling at me. I cannot even hold a thought, not to mention a song, when Joe is smiling at me.

I can see him in the audience. Right there.
And if you had told me two years ago that my
father would be sitting in the fourth row at a
queer choir concert with me onstage—I would
have laughed, and it would have been the most
pained, excruciating laugh you'd ever heard,
because it would have been the laughter of
someone who'd completely, utterly given up.
I'd thought he was going to see it coming. But
when I told him, there was genuine shock, the
kind that's so strong you can't even begin to
hide it. Loss for words, then the wrong words
rise up immediately after. He reacted like I'd
told him I was dying, when really I was telling
him I wanted to live. He didn't understand.
And then he made that foolish demand,
telling me to fight it. Telling me he'd get me
all the help I needed. As long as I fought it.
As long as I was still his daughter. Not his—
whatever the other word was. He wouldn't say
it. He wouldn't come close to giving me that.

I never, ever would have made out with Tyrone in
that supply closet if I'd known he wasn't going to
acknowledge my existence the next day.

I'm singing extra loud for you, Tyrone. Hear that?

Rakesh, this isn't a dance show. They came to hear you hit
the notes, not audition for *Drag Race*.

I waited outside overnight before Gaga played because
I wanted to be in the front when they opened the doors

to general admission. I sacrificed a night of my life and honestly I would have gladly given up a year of it, because that night was the most amazing night of my life. When she sang "Born This Way," she was singing it right to me, and I was singing along so loud, I swear she could hear it. I was elevating her and she was elevating me and there was no doubt in my mind that *this way* was the right way, that I was born to wear what I want to wear and say what I want to say and kiss who I want to kiss. She unlocked all that for me.

And all I'm saying is—Katy Perry's never done that for me.

> What do you do when your father wants you to change back into his idea of you? You hold your ground. Even if you have to move out of your house. Even if you're not welcome at Christmas. Even if it puts everyone in the middle in an awkward position. After a certain point, it was not my job to make him understand. I had to hope that in the fucked-up equation of parenthood, the coefficients of disappointment and fear would eventually be overtaken by how much he missed me and how much, essentially, he loved me, or at least saw how the other people he loved could find a way to love me without any qualifiers.

Joe's hand is inches from mine. Centimeters. This has to be what love is, to physically feel a person even though you're not actually touching.

What I hate, Tyrone, is how excited I was to see you today.

Singing is best when it testifies. Singing is best when it shines with truth and love. Singing burns brightest when you mean the words to be heard.

I want Mr. Glenn to see me now. I remember when I auditioned for him—upstart ninth grader trying to get a spot in the high school chorus. I don't know anything. When it's my turn to audition, I tell him I'm going to sing Christina Aguilera's "Beautiful." He asks me if I'm sure. I tell him I'm very sure. I've even downloaded the sheet music from the Internet. I hand it over to him and he sits down at the piano, asking me if I'm ready. I sing along to it all the time—shower, car, bedroom—and I'm sure this will be the same. Even though it's just a piano accompanying me, I try to hear all the

instruments as I tear
right into the song,
trying to hit the notes
just like Christina does.
Mr. Glenn doesn't stop
me—he plays the whole
song through. And
then when it's done, he
looks at me and says, "I
have a question." I ask
him what. And he asks,
"Why are you singing
falsetto?" I don't know
what he means, and
instead of pretending I
do, I ask him what he's
talking about. "That's
not your real voice," he
says. "You're probably a
baritone. Not a tenor."
I tell him I still don't
understand. He's patient.
He says, "Your speaking
voice is different from
your singing voice. Can't
you hear that?" And I
say, perfectly sure, "I
know, but my speaking
voice isn't my real
voice—my singing voice
is." What I don't say,
because I haven't come
close to figuring it out

yet, is that I'm not even
trying to be a tenor. I
want to be a soprano.
But maybe Mr. Glenn
gets that. Because he
doesn't laugh or tell me
I'm wrong. He thanks me
for sharing my song with
him. I don't get into the
chorus, but I get to keep
my voice. I start to figure
things out and pave over
the gravel that never
should have been in my
speaking voice, so now
it's smooth music instead
of a rough road. While I
never make it to soprano,
I'm now a damn strong
alto. If I auditioned now,
Mr. Glenn would have to
let me in.

A song can give you a place to be, a place to live for three
and a half minutes. If the song works its wonders, you don't
have to be anywhere else.

I have to stop looking at him. He must sense that I'm
looking at him. The whole audience must see it.

There was this one time after rehearsal when Joe
and I were going the same way and we had to have
talked for at least fifteen minutes after we got to the

corner where he was supposed to go his way and I was supposed to go mine, and even though we were mostly talking about the chorus and whether Fredrique deserved the "Over the Rainbow" solo and whether we were going to get to tour at all this summer, I really sensed this subtle flirtation between us, although maybe *subtle flirtation* is just the usual way gay friends talk to each other, and it's not like we ended up going in the same direction after that, because that night he was going to a birthday party, but he *did* ask me at least twice if I was going in his direction even though he knew it wasn't my usual direction, and why am I only figuring out now that I should have just made up an excuse to go in his direction and *why am I so bad at this?*

When Gaga sings, it's genuine. When Katy Perry sings, I'm not so sure. But right now, we are genuine. We mean it.

Sing it in defiance of all the people who want you to be quiet. Sing it to lift your own soul from the depths. Sing it to be the music you want in the world.

You know what, Tyrone? It's wrong to make a guy feel safe and then pull all that away without a word. I know you don't want it to happen again—I am definitely getting that message. But I'm telling you right now, I'm making it my decision: It is *never* going to happen again. And if anyone asks me why all of a sudden I'm not eager to be sitting next to you on the bus, I'm going to tell them exactly why.

"He always loves to hear you sing," Mom said. And I told her, "Yeah, but which voice is he expecting to hear?" Still, she took him to the Christmas show. Told him it was the only present she wanted that year, and he said, fine. He said it wouldn't prove anything. But as he sat there in the tenth row, thinking he was anonymous, I saw him. And when we started to sing "Silent Night," I saw him start to cry. I, who had vowed a million times over that he would never make me cry again, began to let the tears fall like they were the silent notes housed all along within the music. When Mom invited me back home after, he didn't protest, nor did he acknowledge what it meant. We've been navigating that conversation and absence of conversation ever since. Over a year . . . and he hasn't missed a show since.

Oh my god my fly is open. This whole time, my fly has been open.

I want him to notice me and I don't want him to notice me and I want him to notice me and I don't want him to notice me and I guess what I'm saying is I don't know what I want.

Who am I kidding? I WANT JOE.

Here come the fireworks. We build and build with our voices, and then we hit the heights—

I will get better at this, Tyrone. Thank you for helping me figure out that the way a guy treats you is much more important than how he makes your heart race.

I am not afraid to sing for my father here. He is not afraid to listen. I am proud of our peace because it is something I made.

Joe's hand is opening. Getting closer. He's smiling at me as he's singing. Singing to me. I'm not imagining this, am I? He wants me to take his hand, doesn't he? I must move my hand. Is this really happening?

Silly rabbit. It took you long enough to go the shortest amount of space. It took you long enough to hear me singing to you.

Holding hands with Joe. Everyone can see I'm holding hands with Joe. Or maybe nobody can see I'm holding hands with Joe. But definitely Joe can see that I am holding hands with Joe. And he is not letting go. No, neither one of us is letting go.

I don't have any friends out there in the audience. But that's because I have so many of them onstage with me. That's what I love about the choir: We are all in this together.

Bring it home. Bring it on home.

We are so much louder together than apart.
We are so much brighter together than apart.

I am a part of this. I am making this.

We are making this.

I am the sound I create. I add the sound I create.

Boom.

Boom.

Boom.

Follow the sound of my voice.

I love this song when we sing it.

This is what it feels like, to be alive. We sing to be fully alive.

TRACK FOURTEEN

The Vulnerable Hours

Later, there would be people who would try to explain it away. There was something in the light, they'd say. The sky was a color that nobody had ever seen before, a rose-tinted darkness that made the air more tender to breathe. Other people would swear that the tincture in the air wasn't light or color but scent, an uncertain distillation of the things you were afraid to admit you desired. The temperature could not be blamed, because it was so mild that nobody felt it. Not a single person in the city shivered the entire night, nor did anyone feel overburdened by heat. Minds wandered to other things.

Sarah Wilkins may have been the first to feel it. She was in her room, alone, getting ready to go out. She could hear her mother yelling at her sister in the kitchen—something about a lack of respect, probably stemming from the fact that Sarah's sister had taken to leaving without saying goodbye. Sarah drowned out the fight and focused on her face in the mirror. She tried not to feel sad about the acne on her forehead or the fact that her bangs were too long. *I just have to try to make it better,* she said to herself. And then she surprised herself by adding, *Why?* She put on her cover-up, her blush, her lipstick. She teased and gelled and pulled her bangs into shape. *It's a party,* she told herself. But the *why* still lingered.

Amanda called to say she and Ashley were two minutes away. Sarah was only going to the party because Amanda and Ashley wanted to go. The guy who was throwing it was a complete jerk, and the guy Amanda wanted to see there wasn't much better. Sarah never told her this, because what was the use? When had a friend's opinion ever undone a crush?

Even worse, Amanda's crush had a friend. Sarah had already forgotten his name—or maybe nobody had bothered to mention it to her. All that mattered was that he was going to be at Devin's party. Amanda had even told her what to wear. Ever dutiful, Sarah had put on the skirt they'd bought at Bloomingdale's over spring break. Amanda had said Sarah looked good in it, but Sarah suspected she was only saying that so she'd feel less guilty about her own purchases.

"Aren't you excited?" Amanda and Ashley asked when Sarah met them in front of her building. Sarah didn't say it, but she realized she was the opposite of excited. Then she realized she didn't even know what the opposite of excited was. She'd never allowed herself to express it, so the word had dissolved.

On the subway downtown, Amanda and Ashley gossiped about who was going to be at the party and then tried to guess what was going to happen. Sarah kept silent, not even realizing she was staring at the woman on the seat across from hers. The woman was alone, quietly reading a magazine. She looked like that was all she wanted for the moment, and she was content in having it. Sarah was surprised by how jealous she felt. She didn't know this woman; this woman was old. Why would Sarah simply assume a stranger's life was better than hers?

The boy throwing the party went to one of the private schools that didn't even bother to be named after a saint. He didn't greet them at the door. Instead the girls found the door cracked open, a bare-bones invitation to walk from the hall-way of the building into the hallway of the apartment. It was already crowded with teenagers—mostly anonymous, mostly drinking. Amanda and Ashley led the way, angling through the crowds until they found the bed with the coats on it. Then they angled again until they got to the place where the beer was being distributed. Sarah took a bottle, because it was handed to her. She said thank you, because it was the right thing to say. But she didn't take a sip, or even look around much. She noticed the copper pots hanging on the walls and wondered if they were ever used, or if they were just there for decoration. She asked Amanda, and Amanda either didn't hear or pretended not to. Instead she and Ashley took sips from their bottles and scoped out the crowd. Sarah knew Amanda and Ashley were not going to leave her; they were in this together. This had always been a comfort to her, because she feared being left behind. But now, on this strange night, she wanted just that. She wanted them to forget she was there.

Sarah was not used to making excuses, so she fell back on the most universal one: She said she had to go to the rest-room. That's how she said it—*restroom*—as if they were in a restaurant instead of some rich kid's home. Amanda and Ashley said they'd wait for her in the den; the jerk Amanda liked had last been seen heading that way, and Amanda didn't want to miss her chance.

Sarah didn't know which direction the bathroom was in, so she chose the direction opposite the one Amanda and Ashley were taking. It was still early in the evening, but already couples were making out against walls and boys were putting on their jackets to go to the roof for a smoke. Sarah wanted to put her unsipped beer bottle down, but all of the available surfaces were too close to people. She had no desire to be pulled into a conversation. She just wanted to find a room where she could close the door and lock it and be alone.

Lindsay Weiss saw Sarah walking down the hall, looking into doorways, trying to find something. Lindsay would never have been able to explain it, but immediately she recognized what Sarah was feeling. She knew it as if it was happening to her. So she cut off the boy from Regency who was attempting to flirt with her, and she caught up with Sarah just as she was about to peer into a bedroom.

"Excuse me," she said to Sarah. "You look lost."

Before, Sarah had felt stirrings, but they had been isolated stirrings. Now, having this girl come up to her and say she looked lost, the stirrings filled her with noise. Not the noise of sound, but a noise much louder than that: the noise of thought.

"Yes, I'm lost," she said. And she could have left it at that. She could have just asked where the restroom was. But something about tonight made her go further, made her more honest than necessary. There was something in this girl's eyes that already understood. So Sarah found herself adding, "I'm completely lost. I don't belong here at all."

The truth feels different from other things. The closest you can come to describing it is that it feels like taking a perfect breath.

Without having to think about it, Lindsay knew the next thing to say was, "I'm Lindsay."

And Sarah could find just enough energy to say, "I'm Sarah."

Sarah had never wondered what it would be like to tell the total truth. If asked, she would have said she had done it numerous times before. And it would have been a lie, as much to herself as to the person who had asked. Now, she understood this. Now, she wanted to try to tell the total truth.

They ended up where Sarah had been intending to go all along—the bathroom off of the parental bedroom. Mom's bathroom, clearly, with its museum of perfume bottles, its royal-majesty mirror, and its hand towels embroidered with shells. With the party raging on, it was the quietest part of the apartment. Lindsay perched on the edge of the tub while Sarah put the seat cover down and sat on the toilet.

"What is it?" Lindsay asked.

"Can I really tell you?"

Lindsay nodded.

"I don't want to be here," Sarah said. "I don't really want to be anywhere I usually go. I have no idea where I want to be instead, but I know that I can't keep going to the same places. My friends have no idea who I am, and maybe I don't know who they are, either, but they live much more on the surface than I do. Is that awful to say? I don't mean it as an insult. They're the way they are and I'm the way I am. Neither way is better or worse. It's just that my way is better for me."

Lindsay didn't pass judgment. Instead she asked, "So why did you come tonight?"

Sarah shook her head slowly. "Because I can usually trick myself into thinking I'm going to have a good time. It's like this social amnesia kicks in, and I forget how ugly I feel and how out of place I am and how miserable I'll be. It's amazing how you can convince yourself of something when you don't think you have any options."

I should be crying, Sarah thought. She was effectively erasing everything that was supposed to matter to her. What her friends thought. What the guys might think.

Lindsay heard what Sarah was saying and she knew: This was a girl who wanted to walk away. And who *would* walk away, even if it hurt. What Lindsay felt then wasn't the desire to walk away, too, but instead the desire to remain. She knew that Sarah's problems were not her own, even if she could understand where Sarah was coming from.

"I don't want to be here," Sarah said again.

And Lindsay replied, "You should never be somewhere you truly don't want to be."

"Is it that simple?" Sarah asked.

And Lindsay said yes, it was that simple.

There is such freedom in learning you can leave.

Less than a mile away, Stewart Hall was sitting with his friend Phil in Tompkins Square Park. Later, they would each wonder whether being outdoors made them more susceptible to the night. The day hadn't been at all out of the ordinary: Stewart had gotten new headphones at Best Buy while Phil had worked on an English paper and had messaged with a girl named Deborah who he'd met at camp. The conversation had been inconsequential; they often chatted about visiting each other, but they never did.

"So what's up?" Stewart asked. They'd just gotten to the park.

"Not much," Phil answered. "You?"

"Not much."

It was Stewart who'd called Phil, who'd said they should hang out. They usually met in the park, then saw who else came by.

"Not much?" Phil said.

"Yeah, not much."

Phil started thinking.

"And how are you?" he asked Stewart.

"What do you mean, how am I?"

"I mean, how are you?"

"Fine."

"Fine?"

"Yeah, fine."

"You tired?"

"Are you kidding?"

"No. You tired?"

"Hell yes, I'm tired. I'm always fucking tired."

Phil nodded. "You know what I wonder?"

"I have a feeling you're going to tell me."

"Yeah, I'm gonna tell you. I'm wondering, why are the answers to these questions always the same?"

"What questions?"

"You ask, 'What's up?' I say, 'Not much.' Then I ask, 'What's up?' and you say, 'Not much.' If anyone asks how we're feeling, or how we're doing, we say, 'Fine.' If someone asks if we're tired, we say of course we're tired. Because everyone is tired. There is not a single person we know who isn't tired. That's the only truthful answer of the three."

Normally, Stewart would just tell Phil to get his head out of his ass, but for some reason, he went along with it. He was listening, which wasn't something he always did with Phil.

"But isn't *not much* true?" he asked. "I mean, are you saying that something's up and I don't know about it?"

"I'm just saying that if nothing's up and we're feeling fine, then why are we so tired all the time? *Something's* got to be happening." Phil stood up from the bench. "We can't all be doing nothing, right?"

"I'm not saying *nothing*," Stewart pointed out. "I'm saying *not much*."

But Phil was already heading somewhere. Since the weather was so ideal, there were a lot of people in the park, even long after sunset, well into the night.

"Where are you going?" Stewart asked. Then, not getting an answer, he followed.

There were two girls from the neighborhood sitting on a bench about twenty feet away. Tamika and Danika, or something like that.

"What's up?" Phil said to them.

"Not much," they responded.

He nodded and moved on to the next bench, where a homeless guy who smelled like bad cheese was sitting.

"What's up?" Phil asked.

"Not much," the guy said.

Third bench. A poet type with a black notebook on his lap, pen poised for words that he clearly sensed were on the way.

"What's up?" Phil asked.

The poet looked up thoughtfully from his poetry daze.

"Not much," he replied. "Not much at all."

Stewart could sense his friend getting more and more frustrated. Still, he wasn't expecting what happened next.

They saw a few members of their group—Mateo, Ben, Miranda—ahead.

"Hey, man, I called you!" Mateo yelled out when he saw them coming.

"Hey!" Phil yelled back. Then, when they were closer, he asked it: "What's up?"

And Mateo said, "Not much."

Next, Phil asked Ben, and Ben said, "Not much." Then Miranda, and she said it, too.

"That's not true!" Phil yelled. "We're all so full of shit—*not much not much not much*. Mateo, *something* has to be up. Ben, I know there's something going on in that head of yours. Miranda, why don't you just come right out and say it?"

Something clicked into place then. Was it the way Phil said it? Or was it the light or the scent in the air that opened them up? Or maybe they were just tired of not really answering.

Whatever the cause, Stewart could actually see the change—the way Phil's question was suddenly a real question, not just something to say.

"You want to know what's up?" Miranda asked. "You really want to know?"

Phil nodded.

"Well, I'll tell you," she said. "I'm here with Mateo and Ben, right? But I'm also on the lookout for my brother, because he's been acting weird lately, and I think he might be coming to the park to score. I mean, we've hardly seen him in the past few weeks, and when he's home, he'll just lock his door and do whatever behind it. The other night, we were both brushing our teeth at the same time, and I tried to ask him what was going on, but he just looked at me like I was some girl renting a room from his parents, and he said nothing was going on. Nothing at all. I just thought he was being a jerk, but then when he was leaving, he tells me not to worry. And I'm thinking, *If there's nothing to worry about, then why are you telling me not to worry?* I know who he hangs out with, and they're not a problem, but suddenly I'm wondering if he's hanging out with someone else I don't know about or if he's gotten into trouble. I mean, I know he's done some shit in the past, but it's always been under control. He's got his friend Mike, who keeps him in line. But it's not like I can call Mike and ask him what's going on—Darius would knock me in the head if he knew I did that. So I'm just trying to see what I can see, you know? Darius likes to come to the park and do his thing. So maybe I'll catch him at it."

"How 'bout you?" Phil asked, turning to Mateo. "What's up?"

"I'm not over Deena," he said. "You *know* that's what's up."

"You hoping to see her?" Miranda asked.

208

"I'm always hoping to see her. Even when I'm all like, *Fuck hope*, I'm still hoping."

"And you, Ben?" Phil asked. "What's up?"

"Just had to get out of my house, man. Being there makes me feel like I'm living a murder, you know?"

Phil didn't know. None of them knew. Ben never talked about home.

Phil thought: *We talk all the time about people opening up, as if it's some kind of physical unfolding. But the only thing that can open us up to another person is words. Words on the inside, telling us to do the things we're most afraid to do. Words on the outside, sharing what's really going on.*

Sometimes all we need is a little attention to open up.

People kept knocking on the bathroom door, but Sarah and Lindsay didn't feel too guilty about staying locked inside; they knew there were at least two other bathrooms in the apartment. People could deal.

Then there came a knock that was less insistent, more of a question than a statement.

A voice followed it.

"Sarah, you in there? It's me, Ashley."

Lindsay watched Sarah, wondering what she was going to do.

Sarah didn't seem to be surprised at being found, or even that worried.

"What is it, Ashley?" she asked through the door.

"I was just looking for you. Are you okay? You've been gone for a long time."

Sarah noticed the *I*—Ashley was almost never an *I*. This had to mean that Amanda had found her guy and left Ashley to the wolves.

Sarah sighed. Had she really thought her life wouldn't be able to find her? Did she really think it would get distracted and not notice she was gone? She looked to Lindsay, silently asking if it was okay for her to open the door, to let the interloper in. Lindsay nodded; she knew from experience that even though it was important to hide away in the bathroom when you needed to, it was equally important to leave it eventually.

Ashley looked stupidly confused when the door finally opened and she found two girls inside. Had Sarah and this girl been making out? Was Sarah a *lesbian*? Ashley couldn't understand how a bathroom could be used for anything other than making out or, well, going to the bathroom. Ashley wasn't perceptive so much as receptive—she needed someone to explain things to her. And Amanda was too busy flirting with Greg to be there.

Sarah said, "Ashley, this is Lindsay. Lindsay, Ashley."

This new girl held out her hand, and Ashley wondered if she'd washed it. After either making out with Sarah or going to the bathroom. Whichever.

It looked clean and dry, so she shook it. Then she asked Sarah what she was doing.

"Just talking," Sarah said. "I needed to get away."

Get away? Ashley was confused. They'd only been here for a half hour or so. Which was long for being in the bathroom, but pretty short for being at a party.

The next possible explanation that came into her head was that Sarah had gotten her period and that Lindsay had given her a tampon. Although that didn't explain why Lindsay was in the bathroom with Sarah, or why Sarah hadn't asked Ashley or Amanda for a tampon. Not that Ashley or Amanda would have had one; this one time, Amanda's purse had fallen open when she was with a boy and the tampons had fallen in his lap and Amanda had been so mortified that she said they would just have to rely on scamming them off other girls from now on. Ashley had actually sent this story in anonymously to a teen magazine's embarrassing moments column, but they hadn't printed it.

Sarah could not for the life of her figure out what was going on in Ashley's head. More than anything, she wanted Ashley to go back to the party and leave her and Lindsay alone again. Sarah knew she should have never opened the door. Now there'd be no closing it again.

"There you are," a male voice said. A not-as-cute-as-his-clothes indie-rock boy was shouldering into the doorway, looking at Lindsay. "I totally lost you."

Lindsay was happy to see Jimm, only not right now. This girl needed her more than he did. At least until she left the party.

"Jimm, Sarah. Sarah, Jimm," Lindsay introduced. "And . . . I'm sorry, I've already forgotten your name."

"Ashley."

"Jimm, Ashley. Ashley, Jimm."

The presence of a boy made Ashley stop thinking too much, especially since he was clearly with Lindsay, and therefore Lindsay wasn't a lesbian. Not that Ashley minded lesbians. She would just be hurt if Sarah had been one all along and hadn't told her and Amanda.

On other nights, Sarah would have given in. She would have asked Ashley where Amanda was, and they would have headed to that general vicinity together, to chaperone her flirtation and provide interruption if it was needed. She would have let Amanda's guy introduce her to the guy she was supposed to fall for tonight, and maybe she would have been so bored that she would have fallen for him. Or at least pretended to, if he was pitiable enough. But not tonight.

"I'm going to go," Sarah told Ashley.

"But we just got here!" Ashley replied.

"I'm going to go," Sarah repeated, this time to Lindsay.

"You should," Lindsay told her. "Do something you want to do."

"I just want to wander," Sarah said.

"Then wander."

"C'mon, Sarah," Ashley said. And Sarah felt bad, because she knew if Amanda was in the boy zone, Ashley was going to be a barflower for the rest of the night.

"Do you want to come with me?" she asked.

Ashley shook her head. "Is it cramps?" she whispered.

Sarah decided to avoid the polite lie.

"I don't belong here," she said. "I'd rather be doing something else. So I'm going to do something else."

Ashley took it personally, even though Sarah had asked her along.

"Are you mad at me?" she asked.

And Sarah thought, *Well, I wasn't until you said that.*

Lindsay was scribbling her phone number on the back of a receipt.

"Call me when you get there," she said, passing the paper over.

"I will," Sarah said, and hugged Lindsay goodbye. Then she did the same to Ashley, who was still confused.

As Sarah pushed forward into the crowded hallways, a strange grace filled her. Instead of being sick of all the people around her, she recognized that many of them were actually having fun. This crowded, loud, playerful atmosphere was the right kind for them.

She laughed when she got to the door and realized she didn't have her coat. Then she plunged back in, seeing

Amanda out of the corner of her eye as she passed the living room. Amanda was in firm girl-grasp of her target guy's arm. Her peripheral vision was turned off, so Sarah could slide by, retrieve her coat from underneath a guy in the third stage of passing out, then head back to the door.

As soon as she was out of the apartment, she felt free.

It didn't matter that she had nowhere to go. *Nowhere to go* was the perfect destination.

While Mateo, Miranda, Ben, and Stewart talked about what was going on with them, Phil sneaked away. He wasn't done with his questions. There was still some kind of answer he was looking for, but he hadn't found it yet.

He saw two guys sitting on a bench, both about his age, probably from Stuy or Bronx Science or one of the other smart high schools. They were clearly with each other, but they weren't really talking. It reminded Phil a little of him and Stewart, how some nights they'd sit around for hours and wait for something to happen instead of making it happen themselves.

One of the guys was lost in thought, and Phil could see how that would happen on a night like tonight. The second guy looked at Phil strangely as he headed over.

"Hey," Phil said to the guy who seemed to be paying attention. "What's up?"

"We don't want any drugs," the guy replied. "Sorry."

Damn, Phil thought. *Do I look like a dealer?* He laughed. "I'm not selling drugs. Just coming by, saying what's up."

"Oh," the guy said. He didn't seem to know what to do with that. He wasn't exactly apologizing. Almost as an afterthought, he added, "Not much really going on."

The quiet guy looked up now. No longer lost in thought, because clearly there was one thought that had found him and taken hold. It was hurting him.

"What's up?" Phil asked him.

"You're not the person I should be telling," the boy replied.

"Fair enough," Phil said.

Suddenly he felt out of place, self-conscious. Why was he talking to strangers? What was he trying to find?

But there was something in that quiet boy's eyes.

"Say it," Phil told him. "Not to me. But to whoever you need to say it to."

"Thanks for your advice," the louder guy said sarcastically.

"See you," Phil said. He spotted a girl he knew, Isabel, coming into the park. He wanted to get to her before she saw the others.

"What's up?" he called out to her, leaving the two guys on their bench.

"Oh, it's all the same," she said, coming over for a hug. "You know."

"What do I know?" Phil asked. "Remind me."

"What was that about?" Simon asked. Even if he'd been sarcastic with the guy who'd come over, the sarcasm was diluted now by a simple confusion.

"He was just being friendly," Leo replied. "Remember friendly?"

They were both in a bad mood, and Simon wasn't sure why. Leo had been weird all night. Simon had been friends with him long enough to know what these moods were like, and how to get through them. But usually he also had a clue about what had caused them—Leo knowing he had to dump his boyfriend, Leo feeling he was fucking up his chances at a good school, Leo feeling overwhelmed by his parents' expectations and the feeling that the illustrations he spent all his free time on were never going to be any good. Simon knew these things because he and Leo talked about them. But tonight: nothing. At dinner, they'd volleyed between trivia and silence. Normally, Simon might not have even noticed. But tonight he did, and Leo's bad mood started to put him in his own bad mood. Maybe it would have been a good thing if the guy *had* been selling drugs. It would've been something to do.

"I love you."

Simon had been zoning out, but still he heard it. So quiet, but unmistakable. He turned to Leo.

"What?"

"Nothing."

"No. Tell me."

Leo sighed. The saddest, deepest sigh. "I said, 'I love you.'"

"To who?"

"To you."

Simon didn't know where this was coming from. "Well, I love you, too," he said.

"No, not like that, Simon. I mean, I really love you."

Simon was about to respond, but before he could, Leo went on.

"You have no idea how many times I've told you. I can't believe you finally heard. I have been saying *I love you* to you for years. *Years.* Sometimes when you're asleep on the subway and I'm sitting next to you. Sometimes if the music's really loud. Or if we're at the movies and you're not paying attention to me. I'll be watching you watching the screen, and I'll say it really softly, and I've always felt that if you were meant to hear it, then you'd hear it. I have been in love with you for years, Simon, and it's become too heavy. I can't do

215

it anymore. I know it's ridiculous and I know this is going to be a disaster, but you have to understand it's been a disaster for me to try to keep it inside, only letting it out in all of these *I love yous* that you never hear. I know you're going to be kind to me, because that's what you do. I know you're going to say that we're friends, and that it's about friendship, but you have no idea how many times I've watched you, how many times I've had fierce arguments with myself about you. I always told you the truth when you weren't listening—and now you're listening, and it scares the hell out of me. I know this will change everything, and it will probably screw it all up, but I have lived with this so long, Simon, and I just can't do it alone anymore. I have to tell someone, and that someone needs to be you. That guy—that guy asked, 'What's up?' And I realized that the answer to the question was *I love Simon*. Whether you lean over and kiss me—which I know isn't going to happen—or whether you push me away and tell me you don't want to see me again—which I'm pretty sure isn't going to happen, either—I just need something to happen. I can't keep having the same feelings over and over again in secret. Because if you hold something inside long enough, you start to hate it. And I don't want to hate you. The opposite, really. I love you, you see. I love you."

"But, Leo—" Simon began.

"No," Leo interrupted. "Please don't start with a *but. . . .*"

Sarah couldn't figure out what was happening in the city that night. As she wandered, she was witnessing the strangest things. Shopkeepers walking out of stores, leaving them unlocked, wandering off with their aprons still on. Waiters walking away with their order pads still in their waistbands, taking out cell phones and saying, "I need to see you now."

There were painful, aching fights in the streets—not between strangers, but among friends or lovers or people trying to be either, the truth suddenly so plain to see. People were clutching at photographs, searching through purses for the love notes they could never throw out. *Love* had suddenly become an active verb—prodded, confessed, kissed into words. There were no innocent bystanders, because how could you see this and not think of the person love always made you think about? Maybe you felt the absence of that person. Or, like Sarah, you felt the absence of the absence. Walking through the honest chaos, she felt moved but untouched. *I am by myself,* she thought. *I am by myself.* And that was okay. That was fine. That was what she wanted.

"What's up?" Phil asked.

"My mother is dying and I don't know what to do."

"What's up?"

"I'm a fake. And I'm not going to get away with it."

"What's up?"

"It's a beautiful night, don't you think?"

"What's up?"

"Phil, I haven't seen you in two or three months. And I'm not ready to forgive you for that."

"What's up?"

"The opposite of down?"

"What's up?"

"I'm afraid of this park. Bad things happen in this park."

"What's up?"

"I need to eat."

"What's up?"

"I feel guilty because I forget about the war."

"What's up?"

"I just want to be satisfied, and I don't know if that will ever happen."

"What's up?"

"It's getting late, isn't it? I feel like it's getting late."

But, Leo, Simon thought, *I will never love you like that.*

Sarah was not used to being up so late. The city, she felt, had entered its vulnerable hours, not quite awake and not quite asleep, not quite loud but unable to be silent. The line blurring between what was thought and what was said.

She thought briefly of Ashley and Amanda, that old life that would probably still be hers in the morning. She wondered if Lindsay was still at the party, or if she had gone home. Maybe Lindsay would be a new part of the old life. Maybe the old life could have new parts.

The streets were getting less and less crowded as people took their confessions indoors. Walking through the East Village, Sarah could see that many lights were still on, and even if they were off, that didn't necessarily mean that the people inside were asleep. Murmurs and moans, conversations and confessions in many forms seeped through the walls and into the streets. Sarah could hear some of the shouting coming from the street-level apartments: "You never loved me!" "This is what I want you to do." "You are too good for me, and I've always known it." She did not stop to listen. These things had everything to do with the night, but nothing to do with her.

When the streets had been more crowded, Sarah had been overwhelmed by the immensity of humanity, how many of us there are and how little we can affect. Now, with the streets emptying out, she was struck by a different kind of immensity—the immensity of space and building, the immensity of all that's around us. It didn't make her feel inconsequential, as it normally might have. Instead she found some comfort in the immensity. It guaranteed that she could always wander. And it also guaranteed that she'd never have to wander too far.

She followed Eighth Street until she got to the park. It, too, was emptying out. People looked exhausted from speaking, but glad about what had been said. On one bench, two guys held on to each other, one of them clasping, the other one trying to comfort. On another bench, a young woman cried silently, shaking her head in disbelief. But not everyone was sad or longing. Other couples kissed under lamplight—some extending the kiss beneath their clothing. Sarah saw one guy watching it all, looking more exhausted than most. She'd had no desire to talk to anyone for hours, ever since she'd left Lindsay. But now the impulse returned. As she walked over, he looked up at her. He didn't say anything until she'd arrived.

"What's up?" he asked.

"Not much," she said. "And everything."

Because wasn't that the truth of it? In terms of the immensities, nothing much was happening to Sarah. But on her own terms, things were.

"What's up with you?" she asked back.

It was the first time the whole night that a stranger had offered Phil this. And now that it had been asked, he realized it was what he had been waiting for. It was what he needed. And he couldn't figure out how to respond.

"I'd like to be able to give you an answer," he said. "I'd like to know."

He began to tell her everything that had happened that

night—all the people he'd asked, all the answers he'd received. Stewart and the others were long gone; he was the only one of his group left in the park. It was as if he had lost something here, and he had to find it before he could leave. But he wasn't sure what it was, or what it looked like.

"It's a strange night," Sarah said. Then she told Phil about the party, about leaving, about wandering. She told him about the vulnerable hours, about what it was like to be lit by a multitude of stars instead of a single sun.

"It's loneliness," he said. "These hours bring out the loneliness."

"I'm not sure," Sarah told him. "I used to think it was loneliness, when I thought about it at all. But maybe it's just the fear of loneliness. I think that makes us more vulnerable. But tonight I don't mind being alone. If you let go of everyone else, it's amazing what you can see."

"And who you can meet," Phil added.

Hours ago, Sarah would have thought this was a flirtation. But now it was just an observation. A late-night, early-morning observation in the middle of an empty park and a full city.

"I'm Sarah," she said, offering her hand.

"I'm Phil," he said, taking it.

"I'll be here tomorrow at sunset."

"In that case, so will I."

And with that, they parted. Because Sarah wanted her wandering to end at home. Because she wanted to start the new part of her old life. Because she realized now: If you can conquer the vulnerable hours, you can allow yourself to be yourself, to go forward. You breathe in the night air, and it sustains you.

TRACK FIFTEEN

Twelve Months

JANUARY

What a dispiriting time to start the new year. We wrap ourselves in layers upon layers, and still there's always some part
of us that's exposed. We want the feel of corduroy, of yarn,
of flannel, but all we get is ice. It's only the start of winter.
Perhaps that's the worst part: the knowledge that winter isn't
close to over, that we are going to have weeks more of this, at
a time when each week itself feels like a winter. Every now and
then, a bird will land on the fire escape, and I will think, *You
fool*. We turn on all the halogens, try to trick ourselves out
of the dimness, but it has settled in our bones. *I don't want to
wake up*, I say every morning, and you say, *Wake up*. The floor
is cold, the sky is dark. I turn on the bathroom light and don't
recognize this as the life I want. You turn on the radio—it tells
us the temperature and makes things sound even worse than
they are. *Wind chill*, we're warned. You make coffee. I drink it.
I want us to barricade ourselves inside. I don't want the world
today; what I have in this room is good enough. *Wake up*, you
say. *I can't*, I tell you. I can't. It's just too cold.

FEBRUARY

Here it is, placed perfectly beside the unlucky thirteenth. The light is staying longer, but I hardly notice, because it's still so cold. People who invest their hopes in a groundhog get what they deserve. It snows the morning of the fourteenth, and for a moment, I feel a perfect lightness. You call me from your office, ask if I'm looking out the window. The cabs are the only cars on the street, their brake lights studding the smudge-white like rubies. We consider our plans, the reservations we've made. Plans: as if we're building a house, as if we need a blueprint. Reservations: as if we've always had some hesitation, some doubt. *I have reservations about our reservations*, I say. Why spend the evening with other candlelit couples? I would rather see the snow gathering in your hair. We need to hurry, before the snowfall becomes an accumulation, before the lightness turns heavy. It is the shortest month, and we are at its pivot. There is a card in my pocket for you, but I haven't signed it yet.

MARCH

Some days you're the lion, some days you're the lamb. And likewise with me. The winter has left us tired, just as likely to bite as to comfort with woolly words. You've lost your scarf, then try to justify it by saying you don't need it any longer. Color slowly returns to the world, and then it snows again. I buy you a new scarf, because it's on sale. You swear you don't need it. I start to wonder why children are told to draw the skies as blue, when so often they are simply gray. In fact, the sky outside is the color of paper right now. *We need to go away,* you say. I reply, *Spring break, woo-hoo!* March invites sarcasm. We were never the drunk kids on the beach. We wouldn't have been able to find the party house. *I was thinking something like Paris,* you say. *Is there anything like Paris besides Paris?* I ask. This is not the right response. I make the lamb swallow the lion. *Really?* I say. *Could we?*

APRIL

So here it is at last. I walked home tonight and the clock on the bank told me at six-forty-five that it was seventy-one degrees. Since I was in a reveling mood, I reveled in the fact that I live in a neighborhood where the bank clock tells me the temperature. First real day of spring, twenty days after spring was supposed to have begun. Students blooming in Washington Square Park. Every bench taken, people lying on the don't-step-on-the-grass. In the center, the concentric circles of watching, ringed so tightly you can never gather what the crowd is looking at unless you join it. I never join it; such clusters make me think of drugs, philosophy, and Hacky Sack, and I could never manage to Hacky Sack, not once, not even on the first day of spring. So I head past the arch, past the strollers and the strollers. I head home to you, and find you've already opened the windows. I love days that are caught between heat and air-conditioning, days that provide their own utility. I know this won't last. Listen—here comes the first crack of thunder, sounding like a car falling from the sky and hitting the ground. Tomorrow's forecast calls for rain, colder, maybe nice by the weekend. I can't complain, I won't complain, but I will entreat: Shower us, April, with more days like this, so true and momentary. Winter has lasted too long. Summer comes too soon.

MAY

It's this morning, I tell you over our usual quick breakfast. We grab our cameras and head out; the closer we get, the more caps and gowns we see, until every configuration has a soon-to-be graduate at its center. The gowns are a ritual, I know, but I think they also work to remind everyone whose day it is, and why every family needs to pause for something bigger than its own disagreements. Look at all the happiness here. Later we will compare our photographs, and make up stories to go with them. This girl is the first in her family to have gone to college. This man worked the night shift so his son could major in semiotics. This couple hasn't seen each other since their divorce four years ago. Only when their daughter's back is turned do the uncertainty and anger surface, complicated by the love they have in common for the girl in the purple gown. I skipped my graduation—I was already on to the next part of my life. You go to reunions. I take pictures of you as you take pictures. You are so proud of the capped and the gowned, each and every one of them. I am stuck thinking about how we will never be young like this. Not together. We are already beyond this. We are already fending for ourselves. To these students, we are the sign of things to come.

JUNE

We are a hundred blocks away from our home, and we decide to walk. The evening feels like dawn, the last traces of sun still there as the television hour begins. The air opens itself up to music, and as we walk within it, I imagine each person we pass as a musical note, adding up to this sidewalk symphony, this combination of hot and cool and night and day that still feels new even though we've felt it hundreds of times before. You tell me how this would've been the week that you headed off to camp, when you were young. You tell me about your parents dropping you off at the bus, about how sad and scared you were at first, and then, as the years went on, how you couldn't wait to see your friends, how your parents became an afterthought, your wave to them perfunctory. We can imagine now how it must have felt for them—that tug at their hearts, and then the freedom as the bus rolled away. Eight weeks of a quiet house. Eight weeks alone together. Eight weeks of nights like this. I cannot be tired as we walk and walk and walk. I cannot be tired as I listen and listen and listen. On nights like this, you can skip over the tired part. On nights like this, you slip right into the dream.

JULY

It's time for an escape, but since everyone else is escaping, there isn't much of an escape to be had. Not from the city, not from each other. As our car trudges toward Cape Cod, you say, *I'm not really feeling the independence, are you?* It's much safer for us to drive together when it's cold out. Now it's the tale of someone who likes air-conditioning stuck with someone who likes the windows down. Our lack of velocity pushes it in your favor, but I can't help it—I roll the window down anyway and hear the traffic report coming from the car next to us, hear the woman telling her kids to stop jumping around. There isn't much hope, it seems. Our conversation has slowed to the speed of the traffic. I offer you grapes. You say you don't want any grapes. Then, six minutes later, you say you want some grapes. *Do you want me to peel them for you?* I ask, and you say, *I don't even know what that means.* I want to change the song that's playing. I don't dare look at the map and offer another route. This is the way we're going. Eventually we'll get there. The only question is whether it will be worth it, or whether it's already been ruined.

AUGUST

The only thing that can get us to leave the bedroom is when the circuit breaks, and one of us has to trudge to the fuse box to restart the apartment. It feels like someone's left the oven door open—a slow, heat-worn suicide. We are running out of ice cream, ice cubes, ice packs. The air-conditioning unit sounds like it should be powering a battleship, and for hours at a time, it will take a time-out. We can't bear the furnace of our bodies. It's as if God is mocking all of the times we liked our sex sweaty, blazing, flush. Now we're stuck in bed and neither of us wants to touch the other. Nothing personal, of course. It's just too darn hot. Days like this, it feels like everything is already over. There is no longer any reason to move, no reason to say a word. We've become plants; all we want is to be watered. When the air conditioner kicks back in, we stand in front of it. We don't touch each other; we just position ourselves there, full of such base gratitude.

SEPTEMBER

I want you to buy me school supplies. I want glue for my fingers and crayons for my back pocket and a piece of chalk so I can practice writing my name on the walls. I want to put leaves between sheets of wax paper and iron them, so they can hang on all the windows. I want my notebooks to be new again. I want that sensation of writing on the first page. I want you to tie apples to the trees so I can pick them. Then I want you to put one of the apples in a brown paper bag with a cheese sandwich and a carton of chocolate milk. I want to blow the milk with a straw until the bubbles pour out of the spout. Don't be mad at me. Please let me do this. Give me this new beginning and I will sit at the front of class. I will pay attention. I will even clean the erasers. I will pick you for my team at recess and sit with you every day at lunch. Just let me sharpen these pencils first. Let me feel, just for a moment, that the world is precise, and I have exactly what I need.

OCTOBER

I am a star of the silent screen, miming words without ever saying them. You are a ghost beneath a sheet; I can't tell your expression, if you're even bothering to haunt me. Trick or treat? In this moment, I am dressed as the Big Bad Wolf, and you are a straw wall. No—wait—you're brick. Trick or treat? We once went as peanut butter and jelly, but nobody got it—we needed two other people to be the bread. I'd been happy we'd found a costume that hadn't involved hierarchy, because who wants to hear from the lips of a lover, *I think you should be Robin*. Trick or treat? Right now you could easily be Mount Rushmore, and I am the feather duster trying to make the mountains laugh. Or no. You are a glass of lemonade, perched proudly on a summer day. And I am the fly who buzzes around it, who can't stay still. Trick or treat?

NOVEMBER

The leaves have fallen, and we need to decide if the bare trees are beautiful.

DECEMBER

Perhaps the thing we need to celebrate the most is getting through the year. Perhaps the greatest gift we can receive is to be given more, and to know that the more will be good. These are the carols I sing; these are the words I will use to garland our branches. *Come here. Come close. Be with me.* We often talk about the ups and downs, but mostly I feel the sideways slants, the near and the far. Maybe that is why what I want most this time of year is stillness, and you there with me for the quiet, breathing part. Let's turn off the lights, turn off the computer, turn off the music, keep the door closed. Let's light a single candle and walk through our lives. I want you, but more than that, I want to be with you. Up and down, sideways, near and far, a new angle every day. The year is over before we've known what to do with it. But that's okay, you see. Take my hand and let's walk blindly into another. That is what we do.

TRACK SIXTEEN

The Hold

1.

To me, Jewish isn't matzoh ball soup, it's lighting the candles. My grandmothers lighting the candles. My mother lighting the candles, ushering in the flames. My grandfather joined the New York Police Department as soon as they let Jews take the entrance exam. Jewish is changing the course of your life to prove that particular point. Jewish is being the exception to Christmas. My best friend (for a time) in high school had a Hanukkah bush. I told him, "That's a Christmas tree." He said, "No, it's a Hanukkah bush." I told him that in order to be a Hanukkah bush, it would have to be burning, exclusively fueled by a single drop of oil. Jewish is both having a Hanukkah bush *and* making fun of Hanukkah bushes. It's also spelling *Chanukah* any damn way you please. I like a C in there, but not when referencing Hanukkah bushes, because they don't exist. This is, I understand, a possibly wicked-son thing to say. Jewish is knowing once a year your family will rate your behavior and slot you into one of four sons at the Seder. I never wanted to be the one unable to speak, because he didn't have any good lines. The wise one seemed holier than thou, and while I often felt holier than thou, it was never in an actual God Loves Me More context. So basically, I campaigned for the wicked son. Let me be the doubter. Jewish is doubting, because Jewish is being screwed over by authority time and time again. (*Dayenu.*) I've never asked my brother if he wanted to be the wicked son. I feel my biggest competition was my cousins. We were all oldest sons. We all wanted to be the wicked doubter. I wonder what Rabbi Akiva would make of that. Jewish is knowing all the names but not remembering exactly who they were or what they did. (I know Elijah comes to the door. BUT WHY?) Jewish is six years of Hebrew school, six years of halfhearted attempts at learning the language and children's Shabbat services where the cantor would strum his guitar. For a while, I thought all prayers were Soft Rock. Hebrew school created an alternate universe from real school, and in this alternate universe, all the other kids were Jewish and knew the difference between a *borei pri hagafen* and a *motzi lechem min ha'aretz*. Later I'd go to camp with kids from Hebrew school and go to college with kids from Hebrew school and bump into kids from Hebrew school on the sidewalks of New York City; we don't remember the names of all of Jacob's sons, but we do remember each other. I can still read Hebrew. As long as there are vowels. As long as you don't ask me what it means. As a writer, I respect that God's name is unpronounceable. That makes sense. Jewish is giving words their worth. I don't particularly believe in God, but I believe in saying Kaddish. I believe in it because it's what my great-great-grandparents said when someone died, and it's what my parents said when my grandparents died, and one day when I die, it's what will be said for me. Jewish is choosing our traditions and choosing what they mean. I fast on Yom Kippur not because I care what God thinks of me, but because I've been offered a vocabulary for introspection and repentance, and I choose to use it, in solidarity with all the others who have used or are using it. I don't spend the day in synagogue; I spend it at my parents' house, with my family, because that time is holier to me. My parents' friends and their children come over to our house to break the fast, or we go over to one of their houses. The rabbi sometimes drops by. A nice guy, but when gay couples couldn't get married at our temple, I went out of my way to avoid talking to him. For me, Jewish has always been about acceptance and social justice and saying we are all slaves until everyone is freed. So Jewish and gay have never been incompatible. But we're liberal. Just after college I saw a documentary called *Trembling Before G-d* about gay Orthodox Jews and their struggle, and I realized My People can be as blind and intolerant as any other People. To me, Jewish is understanding this and fighting this. Jewish is *tikkun olam*, and knowing the world is broken, and wanting to fix it through love and kindness. My family taught me this. Jewish is when we gather together. It is hiding the afikomen where the youngest cousin can find it. It's the joyful cacophony of a family that can't sing well still singing the blessings. It's latkes and maror and marshmallows melted on sweet potatoes and—okay, so maybe Jewish *is* matzoh ball soup to me. I'm vegetarian, so I can't have it with chicken stock. My mom makes a separate vegetable stock for me and puts two matzoh balls in. That's Jewish, too, to me.

2.

If you were young and gay and Jewish in the early 1980s, you edified your desire however you could. Even if it involved a book called *Great Jews in Sports*.

I am sure there are kids who would have picked up *Great Jews in Sports* at the B'nai Bookmobile. But mostly it was a book given as a gift. It was a hagiography of Sandy-Koufax-Who-Wouldn't-Play-On-High-Holy-Days and Hank Greenberg and others I can't remember. And if you were young and gay and Jewish in the early 1980s, the centerfold of your attention was always Mark Spitz.

Oh, Mark Spitz.

Nine-time gold medalist at the Olympics. Perhaps the greatest Jewish sports hero of all Jewish sports heroes. Swam himself into the history books.

The iconic shot (look it up) is him wearing a number of his gold medals.

But if you're young and gay and Jewish in the early 1980s, the gold medals are mere jewelry. Because what you see isn't just a sports hero. No, what you see is a strong, sexy, confident Jewish man proudly parading in a very short, very tight swimsuit.

This goes against all the iconography you've thus far been given about what it is to be a Jewish male. This isn't Tevye. Or Billy Crystal. Or Sandy Koufax (bless him). The cultural models for your maleness: the rebbe, the comic, or the Noble Great. All worthy models. But none of them have anything to do with desire.

Mark Spitz is hot.

This is not a word you would use in six grade, or necessarily acknowledge. But you turn to this picture of him so many times the book starts to open on its own accord to his spread. The book is telling you something, and it has nothing to do with sports.

3.

When the most popular Jewish dating site decided to finally match same-sex couples, I gave it a try. This was many years ago now.

One of my first dates was with a guy named Akiva.

We were both in our twenties. Both from the New York area. Both Jewish. Both incredibly awkward on a first date.

I asked him where he'd gone to school. He mentioned a yeshiva that sounded vaguely familiar. Which made sense, because they all sounded the same to me.

He told me it had been a challenge.

I said, "Wait—you're Orthodox?"

"Was," he told me.

"So you jumped off the God bandwagon?" I joked.

And he looked at me seriously and said, "No. I just changed the road that the bandwagon was driving on."

It became one of those conversations where the other person shows you his scars, and you have to decide whether or not to tell him that, actually, they're still bleeding. He was telling me about making his own life, about making his own relationship to God, but at the same time it was obvious (to me) that he was still defining himself entirely in opposition to where he was coming from.

"It's hard," he said after he'd taken about ten minutes to tell me how okay he was. "When you're raised one way and then try to raise yourself another way. You're given this absolute and then, wham, it's no longer an absolute. All along you thought God was closed to interpretation, and then you realize it's *all* interpretation. It's like being told there's no physics or chemistry, or that the dictionary isn't real."

I had a sense that I wasn't the first person with whom he'd shared these analogies. But I nodded. I asked him what it was like growing up gay and Orthodox. This led, naturally, to us sharing our coming-out stories—in gay dating, this is what separates a frivolous first date from a substantial one, the willingness to take this particular story down from the shelf where it sits next to the moment you first knew, and your first kiss, and the first time you had sex.

So I told him, and he told me, and his story was more interesting than mine. But I might not have remembered it if, at the end, he hadn't said, "There was this one boy at my school—he was a year older than me. One of those redheaded Jews. Copper, really. I had the biggest crush on him. Only, I wasn't sure what his story was. Then—get this—one day he runs away to San Francisco! Like, completely out of the blue. Says, 'Mom, Dad, I'm gay and you're never going to accept that, so I have to get the hell out of here, goodbye.' And then he calls a few of his friends and tells them why he's leaving. Of course, the next day, it's all anyone could talk about. The school doesn't know whether to have an assembly or order vaccinations. And I have to tell you—it gave me hope. Even though I had to live through two years of hearing his name used synonymously with every gay slur you can imagine, Hebrew or English, I would daydream about him being out there in the world, and knew that while I didn't have the guts to run away, I would get there eventually."

"Which you have," I pointed out.

This got the first smile of the date. "Which I have."

Aware of a tingle spreading from my heartbeat, I asked him, "What was that boy's name?"

"Moshe. Although I think he changed it when he left."

I asked Moshe's last name. Akiva answered with a very common Jewish last name.

I asked him what town in Long Island he was from. He named the town.

It was all falling into place.

"What happened to him?" I asked. "What happened to Moshe?"

"He's doing great. My mom sees his mom every now and then, and because my mom has so few gay sons to report back about, she always makes a point of telling me he's doing great. Still in San Francisco. Going to grad school at Stanford for some science thing. I couldn't tell you if he's, like, part-nered or anything—I think his mom only tells my mom about his academic achievements. Why do you ask? Did you know him?"

"I'm not sure," I lied.

4.

We met at my cousin's Bat Mitzvah. Of course.

(To be Jewish is to know the full meaning of that *of course*.)

My cousins weren't Orthodox, but most of my uncle's business partners were. (I'd tell you his occupation, but it's such a Jewish cliché that I'd rather not.) We were sixteen years old and we were still at the kids' table. We weren't sitting next to each other, but we were the only people at the table old enough to see over the centerpiece, so we made eye contact immediately. When I wasn't trying to help one younger cousin find a Transformer under the table or another younger cousin get the exact same size slice of challah as her sister, I tried to make conversation. It was all pretty generic until we acknowledged the centerpiece itself—a blowup of the Playbill for *The Phantom of the Opera*. (Because my cousin's Bat Mitzvah theme was Broadway. *Of course.*)

Now I was intrigued. This copper-haired Orthodox boy knew his musicals. (While I avoid Jewish clichés, I clearly don't mind sharing a gay one.) Only . . . he knew most of them through cast albums taken out from the library, while

I had already seen plenty onstage. Most crucially, I had just seen *Into the Woods* for the first time—my grandparents, thinking *fairy tales = safe fun for the grandchildren!* had taken me and a couple of my cousins to see it; the rest of the children hadn't listened, but I had. And now I was switching seats with my seven-year-old cousin so I could sit next to Moshe and recount it to him, scene by scene, as the salad plates were lifted from our table and the dancing began.

I had kissed boys before. I had felt that extra electricity between me and another boy—at first not understanding what it was, then understanding exactly what it was. While I still hadn't sewn the word *gay* into my identity, I was definitely keeping the space open for it. I was not innocent to what I was feeling as I was talking to him, as I was trying to explain what happened in the woods between the Baker's Wife and the Prince. But I couldn't tell if Moshe was having the same kind of conversation I was having.

The band launched into the hora, and before I fully knew what I was doing, I was taking Moshe by the hand and pulling him to the dance floor. Even with my family and his family and everyone else around, we could hold hands this way. He smiled at me, and I read everything I wanted and needed into that smile. Once we started dancing, I wouldn't let go. As we kicked and swirled, I wouldn't let go. As my grandmother tried to cut in to dance next to me, I wouldn't let go. As my uncle tried to pull me to the center to help lift my newly adult cousin on a flimsy folding chair, I wouldn't let go. And neither would Moshe. By the end of the dance, we both knew something had happened, and neither of us said a thing about it.

The younger cousins at our table sometimes demanded my attention, but the rest of the afternoon I devoted to talking to Moshe, and he devoted it to talking to me, right until his father showed up behind his chair and told him it was time to make the drive home. Once his dad was gone, Moshe wrote his phone number on his place card and gave it to me. Then I did the same for him.

This was before cell phones. Before the Internet. This was a time when if you had a phone number, it was your family's phone number. What you said might be private, but the fact that you were talking to a boy on the phone was not.

I hatched a plan. Michael Feinstein, a singer I admired for reasons I didn't fully fathom, was about to do a limited run on Broadway. The next time I was in Manhattan, I went to the box office and purchased two tickets for the following Sunday, using the money I'd earned from working at my high school library. Then I found a pay phone and called Moshe to ask him to join me. He asked his parents if he could. They said yes. (No doubt all they had to hear was *Feinstein* to know he'd be in good hands.)

He took the train in from Long Island. I took the train in from New Jersey. We met at a kosher pizza place for lunch beforehand. I had never had kosher pizza before, and while I'm sure culinary science has improved kosher pizza significantly in the intervening years, the pizza that day tasted like someone had taken a frozen pizza out of its box and then served us the box. Worse, because we were surrounded by so many other Obvious Jews, our conversation was guarded, afraid of the very Jewish geography that had brought us together.

It was only when we got to the theater that we relaxed into being ourselves. It was a concert of jazz standards, and we were the youngest people there by a good two decades. In walking from the kosher pizza place to the Broadway theater, we had stepped from Moshe's world into my world, and my world was far more welcoming. Even if we were the only teenagers there, we were far from the only gay couple. We noticed them. We took their existence as permission to exist in the way we wanted to exist.

Where do you start? Michael Feinstein sang.

I took Moshe's hand in mine.

Isn't it romantic?

He leaned into me. We watched other men lean into one another.

How about you?

Some of the songs were new to us. But you don't have to know a song to feel it run through your nervous system. You don't have to have the words on your lips to understand their meaning.

They can't take that away from me. . . .

It was still daylight when we left the theater. We each knew the trains we were supposed to catch. As we walked to Penn Station, we talked about the show, mostly because it was too scary to talk about anything else. The distance from the Lyceum Theatre to Penn Station was not a long one. When we got to the escalator leading down to the tracks, I started to formulate a goodbye—but all that came out was how much I was enjoying myself, enjoying his company, enjoying us.

Then he surprised me. More than any boy had surprised me up to that point, and more, I would guess, than any man has surprised me since.

"Let's go," he said. And I genuinely didn't know what he meant. But then he was grabbing my hand just like I had grabbed his for the hora, and he was pulling me across the street to the Hotel Pennsylvania.

I might not have understood what was going on, but the guy behind the front desk did, and he loved it. Absolutely loved it. One of our kind, I realize now. He made sure to ask us if we were getting the room while our parents "parked the car." He didn't look at all surprised when Moshe paid in cash.

"I was planning to pay you back for my ticket," Moshe said, "and I wasn't sure how much it cost. But this is better, right?"

I nodded. This was better.

The Hotel Pennsylvania was about half a century past its prime, but we didn't care. That ramshackle room was the most magical place either of us had ever been. The minute we got inside, Moshe kissed me like a soldier who'd just come home from the war. He gave me everything in that kiss, and I tried to give him everything in return. Somewhere in the back of our minds, we knew our parents would be waiting for us at two different train stations, but that part of our minds no longer mattered to us. What mattered was the inextricable velocity drawing us toward each other. What mattered was that we were free to touch each other the way we wanted to touch, free to be touched the way we wanted to be touched. I took his sweater off, took his pants off, and only hesitated at the tallis that had been under his sweater the whole time; he folded it neatly and put it on a chair. We were the wise sons, the wicked sons, the simple sons, the sons who didn't have the words for what we were doing, but knew nonetheless that what we were doing was larger than our lives. This, to us, was sacred. We learned: For some things, enlightenment does not come from above or even from within. It comes from beside. From being beside.

We were more naked than we'd ever been, and our nakedness had a consciousness it had never had before. We didn't have sex or even come close to having sex, but what we did was still further than either of us had ever gone before. Further into who we were. Further into who we would be. When it was over, when we were lying next to each other, limbs overlapping, traffic sending its rhythm from floors below, I felt I was allowed to float above my own life, and what I found there was an astonishingly clear peace.

Moshe was right there with me. Until he stood up. Until he put his underwear back on, sat down on the bed, and began to cry.

I moved next to him. I put my arms around him, held him.

"Are you happy or sad?" I asked, because I really couldn't tell.

"Both," he said. "Both."

We got tickets to three more Sunday matinees. We told our parents we were having dinner after, which was why we got back so late.

I took him to see *Into the Woods*, and he thanked me.

He took me to see *Cats*, and I forgave him.

We found out from talking that we'd both come to a certain *awareness* when we'd seen photos of Mark Spitz. But Moshe was careful to make the distinction: It wasn't just because Spitz was sexy in a Speedo. It was his expression. He was a winner and he was embracing that. We wanted to live like that, so damn sure of ourselves.

For our fourth date, I decided we had to see *The Phantom of the Opera*, since it had, in its own way, brought us together. I waited for him at a kosher deli, which was much better than the kosher pizza place. When he didn't show, I assumed he was running late. I went to the theater, and as curtain time approached, I left his ticket for him at the box office.

Through the first act, I was much more anxious about him than I was about the falling chandelier. At intermission,

I found a pay phone and called his house. The angry way his father asked "Who is this?" tipped me off that something was going on. I hung up; it didn't sound like he was there.

I thought maybe he'd be waiting for me in front of the theater after the show was over. I thought maybe he'd meet me in the lobby of the Hotel Pennsylvania. I sat there for two hours, *Goodbye, Columbus* in my lap, unable to read or do anything else besides wait.

I took my scheduled train. When I got to the train station at home, both of my parents were waiting. As soon as they saw me, they said we needed to talk. I wondered if Moshe had called, had left a message. But it was actually his mother who'd called, asking if I knew where he was. She said he'd announced he was going to California. She didn't believe him.

"Do you believe him?" my father asked.

I nodded. And then, to my profound horror, I began to cry.

I told my parents everything. Well, not everything. Not the details. But I told them I'd been dating Moshe. I did not tell them I'd fallen in love, but I'm sure they could hear it in my voice.

This is not the coming-out story I tell on first dates.

There were a couple of phone calls after, from pay phones in California. He apologized for standing me up, and said the timing hadn't been his choice. He told me we'd catch another matinee soon, whenever he returned to New York.

The word *love* never came up, because it would only make things feel worse—at least for me. Had there been cell phones, texting, email, we probably would have kept in touch. But there weren't, so we didn't. Our time together became a good dream, possibly the best dream. I never forgot it, but I remembered it less and less, as other dreams joined in.

I've written about him hundreds of times, and I haven't written about him at all until now.

5.

I wish I'd had the experience, the wisdom then to tell him: To me, Jewish is knowing that you can't be asked to have pride in one part of your identity and then be told to have shame about another part. Whoever asks you to do that is wrong. To be proud as a Jew is to be proud of everything you are. I wish I'd seen him crying and had known to say: To be loved by God is to be loved for who you are. To love God is to place no boundaries on who you love. I didn't know this then. I do now. Whether or not I believe in the God of my ancestors, I see God in everyone.

To me, Jewish is holding on to the people you love. To me, Jewish is dancing and kissing and loving no matter who's watching and what they might say. To me, Jewish is helping the world. To me, Jewish is helping each other. To me, Jewish is me and Moshe in that hotel room. It is who we were. It is who we've become.

TRACK SEVENTEEN

How My Parents Met

It is indisputable that this story would not exist without Nancy Rosenberg. Nancy met my mom, Beth, when they went on a teen tour together one summer in high school, two New Jersey girls on a cross-country bus trip.

My dad, Allen, went to high school with Nancy in Englewood, New Jersey. They had most of their classes together. They were friends.

Both of my parents thought Nancy had a fantastic sense of humor. Sarcastic.

They also (lucky for me) trusted her judgment.

"She kept saying she had this best-friend guy she wanted to introduce me to," my mother would later tell me.

One August night, less than a month before they were all leaving for college, my mother slept over at Nancy's house (a fifty-five-minute drive away, depending on traffic) and agreed to a double date.

My father also agreed to a double date.

Beth, Allen, Nancy, and Nancy's boyfriend, Jeff, went out to the movies. The theater they went to wasn't the one the Englewood kids usually went to. It no longer exists. But the movie? The movie absolutely exists. Because for their first date, my parents went to see *A Hard Day's Night* in its opening week. (Both of them were Beatles fans.)

It went well.

When I ask them later what their first impressions were, my father says, "I thought Mom was special." And my mother says, "I really liked him. I thought he was cool. I was disappointed I hadn't met him earlier in the summer."

My mother was headed to California, to UCLA.

My father was headed to Pennsylvania, to Lafayette.

Clock ticking, they went on as many dates as they could before the summer ended. They went into Greenwich Village to see music at the Village Gate. Mom drove back up to Englewood and met my grandparents and my uncles. (My Uncle Bobby, then thirteen, shyly watched from the stairs.)

And my grandmother had baked.

"I think Alice gave us cheesecake that day," my mother says, "and that was the end."

(The cheesecake recipe is something now passed down from Levithan to Levithan. My mother would get it soon enough.)

When the time came to separate, my parents signed the backs of their class photos for each other.

My father's reads, in part: *May the future be as happy and fulfilling as our past. I know that I have already decided you're the most lovely, beautiful, and nicest person I've ever met. I'm sorry that my temporary loss will be U.C.L.A.'s gain. May our love be as everlasting as your loveliness. Thanks for the happiest three weeks of my life.*

As my mother says, "We only knew each other three weeks, and we decided."

My father's photo is signed: *Love forever.*

They went off to college on separate coasts.

"We wrote letters every day. Even him."

"Not every day."

"Almost every day. Especially in class."

"That's true. *Especially* world history."

(Sometimes my mother would send greetings to Paul Levy, who was always seated next to my father.)

Phone calls were saved for Sundays, when long distance was cheaper. They saw each other at Thanksgiving. They saw each other over Christmas break—but barely. My dad had to have an operation on a chronically dislocated shoulder, and then my mom had to go away with her family on vacation. The moment she got back, Dad and his best friend, Bobby Merker, picked her up at the airport.

"Mom had the biggest suitcase in the world," Dad remembers. "Bobby goes to pick it up and it doesn't move an inch."

"It had no wheels," Mom says, laughing.

When summer finally returned, they were together all the time. Dad worked at my grandfather's restaurant, and would choose the breakfast and lunch shifts so he could make that fifty-five-minute drive down to see Mom in Short Hills, staying with his Aunt Gladys if it got too late.

Or my mom would stay over at Nancy's, and visit Dad in Englewood. The scene at his house was welcoming, if a bit chaotic.

"I think they were a little bit awkward with me because they were used to boys," Mom says now. "Grandma Alice was marooned. These boys were not considerate or helpful. She couldn't get a word in edgewise."

My grandmother, who came from a house with three sisters, was happy to have another woman around.

My mother's parents were a little harder to win over, especially my grandfather. My father hadn't made the best first impression.

"I would wear cutoff jeans—"

"Cutoff like *cutoff*—"

"Frayed—"

"Before it was in style."

My father drove a three-on-the-column convertible Ford Falcon with a transistor radio on the dashboard that was always threatening to slide out of the window on hard turns. He wore T-shirts and three-dollar sneakers he'd buy on sale at Alexander's. The sneakers would always wear out in the little toes, so the holes in his shoes would be in conversation with the holes in his jeans.

This was not what my grandfather had pictured for his oldest daughter.

Still, they had each other and they had New York. They saw *The Fantasticks* off-Broadway and went to more concerts in the Village. Later they'd go see Broadway shows, knowing exactly which row was the start of the cheapest seats in each theater.

It was rough to return to their separate colleges for sophomore year—and ultimately my mother decided it was too rough. She wanted to be back on the East Coast. So she applied to Penn and got in—but Penn wouldn't give her credit for her UCLA courses. ("And UCLA is a good school!" my mom says now, still miffed.) So she transferred to Boston University, cutting down the distance to Lafayette from 2,700 miles to 270.

They weren't close, per se—but they were close enough.

Over the next two years, Mom would visit Lafayette on "party weekends"—the weekends when the whole campus of the then-all-boys school would become party central. Often, she'd drive down with three girls from other Boston schools who had boyfriends at Lafayette.

Or my dad would go up to Boston. To save money, he'd hitchhike from the Delaware River to Newark Airport. Then he'd take the hourly shuttle—$9.60 with his student discount.

My mother's parents were friendly to my dad, but still not crazy about what was happening.

Mom says, "I think they didn't like the fact that I was dating one person, getting serious with one person, so young. That was more their argument. Because they wouldn't dare say anything else."

Junior year, when the fraternity pins came in, one of my father's friends, the (to me) amazingly named Coates Bateman, said, "You might as well just hand it to Beth." Then Coates took it from my father's hands and handed it to Beth on his behalf. Being pinned meant you were "engaged to be engaged"—and neither of my parents hesitated to make that step.

The weekend before Thanksgiving my parents' senior year, my mom visited my dad for the Lafayette-Lehigh game. Dad had applied to law schools but hadn't heard anything yet. The future was very much up in the air.

Mom was sleeping in the fraternity house, taking a nap. Dad put the soundtrack to *The Umbrellas of Cherbourg* on the record player, woke her up, and proposed. She said yes.

Next, Dad borrowed a white shirt to ask my grandfather for his permission. He also said yes.

Later that year, when my dad got into Harvard Law School, the first person he called was my mom. When my grandmother answered the phone, he blurted out the news—and she said, "You're kidding!"

This has become one of our favorite family stories.

My parents met the August after high school and married the August after college. They stayed in Boston, where my mom taught kindergarten in South Boston and my dad went to law school. They lived at 15 Everett Street, with a folding bridge table as their dining room table and two cardboard Steuben Glass boxes as their night tables. They ate lots of hot dogs and Chunky soups, sometimes splurging at the Arby's on the corner. They had an old refrigerator with a freezer that could fit only one meal at a time. When they moved in, my dad and his friend David had to carry their king-size bed up five flights of stairs.

"It was the funniest thing I've ever seen," my mom says now.

Love forever?

Yes, in fact.

I'm writing this on the day of my parents' fiftieth wedding anniversary.

My parents' story is the love song that has played underneath my entire life. It has been the best soundtrack my brother and I could have ever asked for.

Nancy Rosenberg had no idea what she was doing, and she knew exactly what she was doing. My parents make wonderful music alone and they make wonderful music together.

Sometimes, when you're eighteen, you get it right.

Love forever.

TRACK EIGHTEEN

We

"I bet this would be a great place to pick up girls," Courtney says to me, her eyes scanning the hundreds of pussy hats pouring by Coca-Cola World on the way to the march.

"If you say so," I tell her. The only girls I ever pick up are friends like Courtney, who can bring a lesbian reality check to my flightier gay-boy fancies.

"I've already given my heart away, like, five times," Courtney tells me. "They just haven't noticed yet."

"They're distracted by your sign."

"No doubt."

There's pretty strong competition for best sign here. Since we're in Georgia, there are a lot of creative suggestions for how to put the *peach* into *impeach*. (It helps that the president's skin is the same color as a nectarine's.) There's an umbrella with an angry cat face on it that threatens *This pussy grabs back*. Another sign has Keith Haring figures spelling out MAKE AMERICA GAY AGAIN.

Courtney went full Bechdel with her poster art, cartooning famous queer women in various protest poses. Gertrude and Alice hold hands and stand their ground. Frida wears a shirt that says *I'm Kahling You Out*. Sweet Ellen pumps a fist and calls out, "*Nasty if I wanna be!*" Audre grins and holds a sign that reads *The Lorde is on our side, and that is all we need.*

Sappho gets a speech bubble and defiantly proclaims, *"I will turn your lies into fragments!"*

The problem is, it's starting to rain, and while other people laminated their signs or covered them with clear tape, Courtney's is entirely unprotected.

"Shit," she says as a few drops start to make Susan Sontag's hair streak.

I fumble open my umbrella as the spatter turns into a torrent. It's not big enough to cover us both. People duck into doorways for cover; we hug the Coca-Cola World entrance, but it only gives us a partial respite.

People continue to hurry toward the plaza outside the Center for Civil and Human Rights, where the march is set to begin. I worry if we delay too long, we'll end up missing the speeches, including John Lewis's kickoff. He's the person we all want to see.

Courtney stares down at her poster. I know she spent a lot of time making it.

"I guess I'll keep it under my coat for now," she says. She's wearing a pink jacket that will barely cover the poster board.

"Don't do that," a girl next to us says. She looks like she could be Alice Walker's teenage self, and she's put down her own tape-covered sign, which reads *We have been raised to fear the yes within ourselves—Audre Lorde.*

"I like your quote," Courtney says.

"Thanks," the girl responds as she rummages through her bag. "Ah, here." She plucks out a translucent square. "Take this."

Emergency poncho, the label reads.

"It's see-through," the girl explains. "So people can still see that kick-ass sign."

"Don't you need it?" Courtney asks.

The girl gestures to her own yellow raincoat. "I'm covered."

"But does this really count as an *emergency?*" I ask. "What if this poncho is meant to save a life?"

Courtney, who I've known for years, shoots me the look she deploys when something that falls out of my mouth gets relegated to Attempted Quip status without crossing the Effective Quip threshold.

The amusing part is that the girl I've only known for a minute or two shoots me the exact same look. Since both of them are shooting at me, they don't even notice their identicalism.

"Thank you," Courtney says, breaking away from me to look back at the girl. "I'm Courtney. This is Otis."

"With an O," I chime in. (It's just something I do.)

"I'm C.K.," the girl offers.

"Well, thank you, C.K.," Courtney says with some enjoyment.

"Hey! Courtney's initials are C.K.!" I realize aloud. "Your name doesn't happen to be Courtney Khan, does it?"

I see something shimmer across C.K.'s face, but she quickly shakes her head. "Nope. C.K. stands in for my first and middle names—don't ask, 'cause I'm not going to tell. My last name is Hamilton."

As soon as she says this, three people behind her start squeeing and saying how much they LOVE *Hamilton*. "*I am not throwing away my shot!*" they sing. Others join in.

"You must get that a lot," I say to C.K.

"You have no idea," she replies.

"Well, boys named Evan Hansen must have it worse," I point out. "They must wake up and curse Ben Platt on a daily basis."

Instead of getting a big laugh, this observation is greeted with a sheet of water that comes crashing to the ground.

"Well, that's not good," Courtney says. She unfolds the emergency poncho and attempts to put it on. The head hole is not immediately discernible from the armholes. C.K. hands her protest sign over for me to hold, then helps Courtney straighten the poncho out.

"You're an EPT, aren't you?" I ask.

Both Courtney and C.K. stare at me.

"What?" I say. "An EPT—get it? An Emergency Poncho Technician?"

They start laughing. But it's not at my joke. I can tell.

C.K. looks at Courtney. "He doesn't have a clue, does he?"

Courtney looks at me like I'm a pug. "Nope."

But . . . okay. Now they're next to each other. Getting along. So at least I've done *something* right.

"Are you here with a group?" I ask.

"I am," C.K. says. "But we seem to have scattered. I was going to try to find them."

There's a beat. I wait for Courtney to say it, since it would be better for Courtney to say it. But I also know that crushes tend to tie Courtney's tongue, so I step into the pause.

"Want to march with us for now? It would be great to have an EPT on hand. Just in case something malfunctions."

"Otis! Stop!" Courtney says. Then, quickly, she turns to C.K. and adds, "I mean, with the acronym. Not with the invitation. You should totally march with us."

"I'd love to," C.K. says, taking her sign back from me. "Shall we?"

"Into the rain!" I say.

"Into the rain!" Courtney and C.K. echo.

The rain is falling too fast to sink into the ground, so the sidewalk is a mess of puddles as we join the throng heading to the plaza. And it *is* a throng now, a convergence. It feels like people are coming from all corners of the state to be a part of this. All ages, all races, big groups and individuals walking on their own. And the weird part is, none of them seem like strangers. We all have the fact that we're here in common, and that's enough to feel a deep and inspiring kinship. It's been a rough two months since Election Day; we've had to question a lot of things we never thought we'd have to question, and the whole time, we've had to worry that we're more alone in our anger and sadness than we thought we'd be. It was a national election, but it felt so *personal*, too—profoundly personal. When the breakage of the country occurred, it felt like we'd been broken as well. Now it feels like the pieces are coming back together. On the outside and on the inside. Just from gathering together and carrying signs and walking as one.

Plus, there are the hats. I taught myself how to knit in order to create my hat and Courtney's. They didn't come out quite as well as the YouTube tutorial promised they would. They *are* pink yarn creations with two cat ears each—but these particular cats are strays that have been in a few territorial fights, leading to a certain patchiness of fur and waywardness of ear.

C.K.'s hat, though, is up to my grandmother's standards for knitwear. It's stitch-perfect, its ears poised and alert. As she and Courtney get a few steps ahead of me, I see she's even knit herself a tail, which mischievously pokes out of her yellow slicker.

I wonder if Courtney's noticed it yet. She seems more intent on focusing on every word C.K. says.

The crowd is starting to coalesce around us, so that by the time we round the corner to get to the plaza, it's a solid sea of people, and the only way to go any farther would be to bob and weave, leaving a trail of *excuse me*s in our wake.

I've made it back to Courtney and C.K.'s side, but it's as if my umbrella is really an invisibility cloak, for all I'm registered by their rapport.

". . . my father actually used the phrase *Communist hordes*, while my mother cloaked her disapproval in terms of my own safety," Courtney is saying. " 'What if there's a bomb?' she actually asked. And I couldn't help it—I said, 'Well, why don't you tell your side not to bomb us, okay?' That really pissed my dad off—he said we were just playing into the enemy's hands—and I had to ask, 'Who *exactly* are the enemies, Dad? You did get the memo that Republicans love Russians now, right? So is it ISIS? Do you think ISIS is going to target the Women's March in Atlanta?' "

"What did he say to that?" C.K. asks.

"My mother interrupted at that point, to say she only wanted me to be safe. And I said if my safety was really her number one concern, then maybe she should have voted to make sure I'd have health care after I graduated . . . and luckily that's when Otis honked and I was out of there. To give her credit, there's been some follow-through—she texts every ten minutes to make sure I'm fine."

"My mom's marching in Washington," C.K. says. "She lives up there. And I keep texting her every ten minutes to make sure she's fine."

"I think our biggest threat right now is pneumonia," I say. The wind has joined the rain, rendering my umbrella's future precarious.

"I'm sorry I don't have any more emergency ponchos," C.K. tells me.

"How about a comforter?" I ask. "Do you happen to have a waterproof comforter in there?"

It's nearly one o'clock, which is the time the rally is supposed to start. But now some people are saying it's been delayed because of the rain. I try to check the website, but my phone can't get any Internet—there are too many people using the signal at once.

"It doesn't make any sense to delay," Courtney says. "We're all here."

We hear a cheer, but it's coming from behind us, not from the plaza. We turn and see a parade of six or seven people zigzagging through the crowd. They're each holding the same sign—a photo of Carrie Fisher as Princess Leia, staring down the enemy with her hands calmly behind her neck.

We are the resistance, the caption on the posters reads in bold Barbara Kruger letters.

All the other posters—*FIGHT LIKE A GIRL, F-ck This Sh-t, Women's Rights Are Human Rights, Our Lives Begin to End the Day We Become Silent About Things That Matter*—part to let the Princesses pass.

"That's what I'm talking about," C.K. says, saluting.

"Can you feel it?" Courtney asks.

"What?"

"The Force. It's here."

It takes C.K. a second to tell that Courtney is making a joke *and* completely serious. Because while it's not the return of any Jedi, there's definitely a Force unleashed here, the same Force that rises anytime you strike back against an Empire. I think we all like to believe that Carrie Fisher would approve.

I notice that C.K. isn't making any attempt to find her friends in the crowd. Possibly because it would be futile—there are just too many of us. But possibly because she's finding Courtney's company enough.

Since I know Courtney so well, I can see what C.K.'s attention is doing to her. She hasn't expected it—she never expects it—and as a result she's not quite sure what to do with it. The two pieces are clearly clicking together, but it has yet to be determined what the full shape of the puzzle is. All that can be known for sure is the click. Courtney's been brokenhearted before, so she can't help but feel the pain of the unclicking buried inside that initial click. But she *can* choose to ignore it, if she's convinced enough.

288

All of this can be read in her face, in her posture. All of this can be read, if you know how to read her.

We're close to the MAKE AMERICA GAY AGAIN banner again, and I can't help but check out who's carrying it. One is a muscled guy in a muscle T-shirt that reads *I blocked Mike Pence on Grindr and this is his revenge*. Another is a woman who looks like she could be a teacher in any elementary school classroom in America, wearing a dress that would make Ms. Frizzle proud, covered in stars and planets.

As the rain continues and the wait goes on, there's some shifting from foot to foot and more checking of phones. Every now and then, there's a chant—"Rise up! Rise up!" and "This is what democracy looks like!"—but by and large, the feeling that pervades is . . . patience. In the context of a crowd, I find this somewhat remarkable. We, who are always in a rush, who always have more than a dozen things we need to do by the end of the day—we are okay with standing still. We are fine with talking to each other until it's time to go. It's as if the strength of the congregation has briefly turned down the volume of our obsession with time. This gives me hope; we have not only the power of our voices but the power of patience on our side.

Courtney, C.K., and I are lucky we're on the sidewalk; the people on the grass are beginning to sink into it, although they don't seem to mind too much.

When Courtney's poster folds a little under her poncho, C.K. reaches over to smooth it out.

"Thank you," Courtney says. And I notice that C.K. doesn't step back—she remains close. Courtney stays there, too. Even in the rain, even in the crowd, Courtney looks happy. And I think that this is the first time in a while that I've seen this. We've had our guard so far up about what's happening to our country that I think it's made it harder for us to let our guard down in our daily lives. Especially Courtney. I can believe in dancing my despair away, in singing loud even when your heart is dying. But not her. She won't risk coming out of her shell, because she feels she needs to be in her shell in order to survive.

She stayed over with me on election night, because as the dumbfounding results unfolded, we both knew there was no way she'd be going back home to face her parents. *This isn't happening,* we kept saying to each other, and while I found it funny that the newscasters seemed as gobsmacked as we were, Courtney couldn't find anything funny about it. Funny had moved off to another planet. Exiled.

Waking up the morning after the election was like emerging from a dark, dark room into the glare of a spotlight. It was a shock so strong that I couldn't walk steady, couldn't make out shapes or colors. My thoughts were a startled cacophony of causes and effects, and no matter how quickly I blinked, I couldn't sort them out, couldn't get my eyes to adjust. In my sadness, I reached out. In my fury and my incomprehension, I reached out. And Courtney was there, just as I'd hoped she would be.

But even as I reached out, I could feel she wasn't reaching back—not as much. She was retreating.

She might have disappeared altogether, into sleepless worry and unyielding despair. But I wouldn't let her. I forced her out to movies. I went over every Saturday night to watch *SNL.* I rallied her around this march. I certainly understood the desire to pull back into a shell, to protect yourself from all the venom that suddenly filled the air. But I also felt that as safe as a shell may be, it also prevents you from moving, from uniting, from resisting in an active way. Trump and Bannon and all the other assholes wanted us inside our shells so our voices would never reach them, would only be heard by our own ears. I just wasn't going to let them win like that. And Courtney—well, Courtney took some coaxing. But this march gave her a reason to step out of the shell.

There's a roar from the plaza—the speeches are beginning. Unfortunately, the loudspeakers sound like they're underwater; we can discern voices, but not words. We can sense we're being welcomed by speaker after speaker—that's the tone. But as ten, then fifteen minutes pass, there's a certain amount of restlessness brewing. It's still raining, but not as much. Side conversations continue.

Then, all of a sudden, there's a cheer much louder than any of the ones before. *JohnLewisJohnLewisJohnLewis*, the crowd around us buzzes. "We love you, John!" people call out. We can feel him stepping to the podium, even though we can't see it.

The loudspeakers find a divine burst of energy and lift to loudness. Or maybe it's just that all of us fall into an absolute, reverent silence. While the other speakers were clouds of voice, intimations of tone, John Lewis's words round the corners and travel the lengths of the avenues. They are faint, but they are present. They persist.

"Sometimes you have to turn things upside down to set them right side up," he tells us. His voice bears the weight of the trouble he's seen, and his words soar on the strength of the victories he's shared. "When you see something that is not right, not fair, not just, you have a moral obligation, a mission, and a mandate to say something, to do something. We cannot afford to be silent. I just want to thank you. You look so good! This is unbelievable. There's hundreds and thousands of people, I tell you! Thank you. I want to thank you for standing up, for speaking up, for getting in the way, for getting in trouble, good trouble, *necessary* trouble."

The crowd erupts into a chant of *Thank you, John! Thank*

you, John! Thank you, John! Courtney, C.K., and I all chant along.

Congressman Lewis says, "Thank *you.* Thank *you.* You're wonderful." Someone must cry out *I love you,* because he comes back with, "I love you, too. I love you so much. You will never know how much I love you."

It's almost absurd how purely this affects me. Here we are in 2017, and it's still stunning and moving to me to hear a grown man talk about love so openly, so unashamedly.

I notice a guy about my age who's leaning into an older group of protesters. They can't hear what's coming over the loudspeakers, so as Lewis's words appear, the young man repeats them to the group.

"You don't need to use social media," he tells them. "You use your feet. Use your hands." A few seconds after the rest of us, they cheer.

Courtney reaches out and takes my hand. Then she takes C.K.'s hand and holds it, too.

"I know something about marching," Congressman Lewis tells us. "I know something about marching. When I was much younger, had all of my hair, and was a few pounds lighter. I marched in Nashville . . . I marched in Washington . . . I marched from Selma to Montgomery. I'm ready to march again! And I come here to say to you—don't let anybody, *anybody* turn you around. And never, ever, *ever* give up. Never lose hope."

We cheer some more. For him. For hope.

We barely feel the rain. I only feel Courtney's hand in mine, and sense C.K.'s hand in hers.

"We're fighting for our sisters, for our mothers, for our daughters. But we're also fighting for our brothers, for our sons, for those who are not able to stand up and fight for themselves."

As I look at the multitudes around us, we are told that there are gatherings in cities across the nation just like ours, that there are over half a million people right now in Washington, DC, alone. And it's as if I can feel the alchemy of hope working, that transmutation of despair into determination.

Lewis concludes with a rousing proclamation. "I'm fired up! I'm ready to march! I have on my marching shoes! So let's do it!"

What does it feel like to hear your voice join tens of thousands of other voices in a wordless cry of pride and defiance? It feels like somehow you have attained a state of nature. It feels like your strength, which you have long limited to your body's capacity for strength, now transcends that body and takes on the shape of a storm. You do not lose yourself—even in the enormity, you still hear your own voice the loudest, and those that are close to you are still distinct. But you are yourself and something much larger than yourself, all at once.

C.K. reaches her free hand back to me, and I take it. The circuit is completed.

"This is amazing," she says. "This is everything we need."

Courtney and I agree. I am the first to let go, but the two of them remain connected. I lean over to see if the marching has begun. It's going to take a while for the movement to get to us. There are some people already hankering to go, but I figure it'll happen when it happens. There are more cheers from the front of the crowd—Congressman Lewis and the others must be on their way forward.

I look at more of the signs: *We Shall Overcomb. John Lewis Represents Me, Trump Doesn't. Build Bridges, Not Walls.* I look at more of the people carrying the signs: Teenagers with their parents. A group of older ladies who look like they just got off the tour bus on their way to see the Eiffel Tower, fanny packs prominent. Two men who can't stop kissing each other. The rain has definitely ended, so the umbrellas have been folded and the pink hats are again the most prominent marker of our spirit. *I'm Really Not Happy About This. Keep Your Tiny Hands Off Our Press. WE the People. Stronger.*

The sun comes out, and almost immediately it feels warmer. C.K. takes off her raincoat and folds it around her tail, then looks at Courtney and says, "Here, let me help you out of that." She reaches under the poncho and lifts both sides so it clears Courtney's poster, then floats above her arms. Courtney gives in to the movement, holds her head straight so C.K. can lift the poncho free. For a moment, they stand there, C.K.'s arms above them both, Courtney's arms at her side, their faces inches apart.

"Thank you," Courtney murmurs.

"Glad to be of some use," C.K. replies, crumpling the poncho down so it becomes no bigger than a small plastic bag.

They couldn't be like this in any crowd. But in this crowd, the intensity between them can emanate. Nobody else will question it or interfere with it. The moment gets to be itself.

Slowly, we begin to move. I'm not sure I've ever seen a more polite crowd. There's a lot of *you first, no YOU first*, and eventually we are moving around the Georgia Aquarium and making our way to the plaza.

C.K. reaches into her pocket and takes out her phone. I'm hoping it's because she wants to use the camera, but no— instead she's checking a text. Then another.

As much as Courtney may think she's hiding it well, I can see the concern on her face. The needle of bad luck is pressing hard against the balloon of her happiness. She was starting to think of C.K.'s time as hers, but now she's feeling like she was only borrowing it from C.K.'s *real* friends, out in the crowd.

True friend that I am, all I can think is, *Please may she not already have a girlfriend. Please may she not already have a girlfriend.*

"What's up?" I ask casually as she texts a response.

"Nothing." C.K. puts the phone back in her pocket. "Some of my friends are over there." She points to a building that has yellow construction-material walls. There have to be tens of thousands of people between here and there. "They want me to find them. But I was like, *That's just not gonna happen.*"

"It's okay if you need to go," Courtney says. Because that's what Courtney does, always providing the escape route from her own heart. I try to signal her to stop, to not give the out unless she wants it taken.

"I'm really good here," C.K. says. "Assuming you guys don't mind."

"It wouldn't be the same without you," Courtney quickly replies. And I think, *Good for you. Don't worry about where it ends up; just keep it going.*

We're coming onto the plaza outside the Center for Civil and Human Rights now, and nearing the new sculpture that lies at its heart. The crowd could easily go around it, but most of us are going through. The sky is lighter now, the weather beginning to feel like early summer, and volunteers are handing out free bottles of water for anyone who needs them. As we walk under the monument, Margaret Mead's quote plays against the glass, backed by white clouds and more than a hint of light blue sky.

NEVER DOUBT
THAT A SMALL
GROUP OF
THOUGHTFUL,
COMMITTED
CITIZENS
CAN CHANGE
THE WORLD.

It's as if Mead is speaking to us across time. I stop to take a picture, already sensing that I'm going to need to collect moments from this day to get me through the next four years.

Pockets of people cheer at Courtney's sign and C.K.'s sign. They hold them up proudly. People start to chant, "Hate does not make America great!"—louder and louder with each repetition. We get to the stairs by the side of Coca-Cola World, and as we're walking up, I turn around to see what I think will be a trail of people behind me . . . and instead find people as far as the eye can see. Pink hats and baseball caps. The full skin spectrum. *The future is STILL female* and *I'M with HER. And HER. And HER. And HER. And HER.* and *White Silence is Violence. Black Lives Matter.* and *All People Are Created Equal.* Behind me, a woman in a black windbreaker holds a portrait of Ruth Bader Ginsburg saying *I DISSENT.* We aren't just marching through the plaza—we are surrounding it.

OUR BODIES. OUR MINDS. OUR POWER.

Everyone is waiting her turn to march—and then everyone is *taking* her turn to march.

We skirt around Coca-Cola World. As we stride, the city watches over us. We find our way to Centennial Drive, which is now the main artery of the protest. We enter the bloodstream.

Courtney and C.K. are ahead of me again, are holding

hands again, and from the way they lean in to each other, I can construct the rough shape of a heart. Next to me is a twelve-year-old white girl in a white T-shirt with a similar red heart on it; she wears red lipstick and her hair looks like it was shaped by 1920s Hollywood. She isn't carrying a sign; she is enough of a sign herself, walking purposefully with her mother beside her.

I fall a little farther back. The woman beside me is carrying a Hillary sign. In front of me, there's a dark-skinned toddler on his mom's shoulders—a black-and-white striped long-sleeve T underneath his orange T. He looks fussy, so his mom turns around and walks backwards so he can face his other mom, who makes faces to cheer him up. He bursts into a cloud-break grin, facing us all now like he's conducting the crowd. Everyone around him welcomes this.

I spot a row of Porta-Potties and see a bespectacled guy with a bright pink *Radical Queer Librarians* poster. As I pass, a blond spitfire of a librarian joins him. I've noticed many librarian-related signs in the crowd today, although I can't explain why. I am happy to be librarian-adjacent.

I catch up to C.K. and Courtney, who are now talking about the largest crowds they've ever been part of . . . which turns into a conversation about the first concerts they ever went to . . . which turns into a conversation about whether an affection for the Jonas Brothers is more or less shameful than an affection for Nelly. (The answer, of course, is that neither is particularly shameful.) Courtney starts to serenade C.K. with "Burnin' Up." C.K. responds with "Just a Dream." We're passing the convention center (more librarians, cheering from the sidewalk) and getting close to the modernist monolith of the new stadium, which in its construction phase looks like something Darth Vader deemed too ugly for his own backyard.

We're heading for the elevated length of MLK Drive, and as we turn onto it, a brass band a few dozen feet ahead of us starts to play. I don't recognize the song at first, but then the tune kicks in and I realize it's "I'm Every Woman." Courtney and a few other women in the crowd start to sing along. But C.K., for the first time, looks *bashful*. I don't get it, but as the song goes on and the bashfulness persists, my gaytuition kicks in—in my case, it's most useful for making largely useless pop-culture connections.

"Holy shit!" I say to her, far too excited. "Your real name is Chaka Khan, isn't it?"

Courtney, thinking I'm making a dumb joke, groans, "*Otis.*" Then she turns to C.K. and says, "Sorry about him. He was raised by goats."

"No," C.K. says. "Actually, he's right. My mom is . . . a big fan."

"No shit!" Courtney says.

"Mmm-hmm," C.K. confirms.

"Well then, dude, you *have to* sing," Courtney says, pulling at her arm.

"After all, it's all in you," I add.

"Shut up," C.K. and Courtney say at once, then sing along as the four tubas at the center of the brass band bring the tune home.

"This is what democracy looks like!" we call out again and again as we continue down MLK. I can hear waves of cheers coming from ahead. When we get closer to the spot where the cheers are emanating from, I realize that the crowd is cheering the police officers who are watching over us. People are calling out thanks, and many of the police officers are smiling and waving back.

There are no counter-protesters in sight.

My phone vibrates and I see it's a message from my mom,

checking to see if everything is okay. As I'm texting her back, I look at Courtney and say, "Hey, text your mom." She turns to C.K. and says the same thing. C.K. then turns to the woman next to her and says, "Text your mom." The woman says it to the guy next to her. And then, all of a sudden, people are starting to chant, "Text. Your. Mom! Text. Your. Mom!" People are pulling their phones out, taking pictures, sending them. I take a video of the chant for my mom, then send it to her with the message, *You did this. We're all good.*

As we get to the edge of the Fulton County Court-house, there's an African American woman standing on a ledge above the sidewalk. She looks like she, too, could be a librarian—glasses, cool earrings, white T-shirt, black skirt. She is hoisting a sign above her head that proclaims *I AM MY ANCESTORS' WILDEST DREAMS.* We call our admiration out to her and she calls us forward.

The brass band pipes up with "This Land Is Your Land." Behind them, another sign is hoisted: *Protect each other.*

I turn around and face two women with matching *Be a Good Human* sweatshirts. Behind them, the streets are filled to the horizon line.

It is a sea of people, and I feel one of the strengths of this is that it not only joins us to the other bodies of humanity that are forming in cities and towns across the world today, but reaches back and unites us with all the other marches in history that were about justice and fairness and resistance to those who would undermine equality and opportunity. It's as if when we march today, we are retroactively marching behind John Lewis in the sixties and marching on the mall for gay rights and abortion rights in the nineties and marching to protest the war in Iraq in the new century and the brutality in Ferguson only a short time ago. All of these histories overlap in us, and they are the fuel to our fire.

We are nearing the state capitol, the end of our route. We have by now been out here for hours and our feet are starting to feel sore. But it doesn't feel like enough, not nearly enough.

The capitol is in view now. The band unexpectedly fills the air with "I'll Fly Away" and we all start to sing along. People who learned it from their parents or their grandparents. People who learned it from church. People who learned it from Alison Krauss. People who learned it from George Jones or Johnny Cash. We sing it at the capitol and then past the capitol, right up to the heavens.

As I watch, Courtney puts her arm around C.K.'s shoulders. C.K. reaches over and takes off Courtney's hat. Then she reaches to her own hat, removes it, and places it on Courtney's head. Next, she puts Courtney's on her own head. They sing the whole time.

We strangers are all smiling at one another. We are so much louder together than we are on our own. I knew I was here to protest; I knew I was here to unite. But what I didn't know was that I was here to remember why I am so in love with the world. As hard as it is, as difficult as it may be, I am deeply, unfathomably in love with the world that can have us here like this. I will always fear losing this world, but I must always keep in my heart what having it is like, and what loving it can bring. I must remember that I am not the only one who loves it. This love is shared by multitudes. It is visible in tens of thousands of different ways right now. Because when you are in love with the world, you want the world to know it.

There is a sniper on the roof of the capitol, watching over us. When we wave to him, he awkwardly waves back. John Lewis is probably on his way to a reception by now, or on his way home. This isn't a race; there is no finish line. There is simply a corner where some people are going one way and some people are going another.

I'll fly away
I'll fly away

We cheer as the band ends the song, because music is a victory, and our march is a victory, and we love each other so much at this moment, all of us in this together.

I don't want to breathe this in—breath passes through too quickly.

I don't want to simply remember it—memory starts to feel unreal.

I want this in my DNA.

I suspect it's always been in our DNA.

As we reach Capitol Avenue, we need to make way for all the marchers behind us. When we get to the corner, I will ask C.K. which direction she needs to go. When she says left, I'll say I need to go right—and then tell Courtney I'll catch up with her later, so they can continue their conversation wherever it may go. I will watch them walk away in their matching-yet-different pink hats, and then I will wander through the city as we marchers continue on, the glory remaining in our hearts. *Were you there?* we'll ask each other. *I was there,* we'll say. From this center, we will spread to the far reaches, go to our homes and to the places less welcoming to us. We will not stop being together. Our love will endure.

TRACK NINETEEN

Give Them Words

For the Freedom to Read Foundation, and all of the librarians, teachers, booksellers, writers, and others who fight for such freedom.

You are here for
the inquisitive and the ignored,
the noble and the bored,
the slouchers and the hecklers,
those caught under the spell of spelling
and those who couldn't even begin to spell
their own vulnerability.

You are here for
the loose-end, loose-change tenth grader sitting
all alone at four o'clock, staring at the screen and
scrolling, scrolling, scrolling through the world
without stopping on any of it.

You are here for
the maladjusted truant with the heart of gold she
thinks is made of coal, because every time she tries to
feel something, smoke rises.

You are here for
the girl who sees college as her only way out
the gay boy who wants to get married someday
the lonely girl whose father hits her
and her brother, who knows it's happening but
doesn't know what to do.

You give them words.

You are here for
the geeks who know more about Spider-Man than
they know about life
the gamers who, if they're not careful, will shoot their
way right into a war
the nice girls who want to scream but are afraid of
breaking something
the mean girls who hate themselves more than they
hate anyone else
the children of addicts and accountants, the
grandchildren of bigots, the great-great-grandchildren
of slaves, the great-great-great-grandchildren of chiefs
and immigrants.

You give them words.

You are here for
the boy who has never been to Russia
and the girl who has never been to Detroit
the slow and violent starvers
the bold and ignorant strivers
the boy whose boyfriend makes him feel like shit
the girl who thinks sex is safe because the boy she's
with says so

the know-it-alls who know nothing, time and time
again.

You give them words.

Like me, you have seen them
fumble in the daylight
risk the articulation
shudder away from who they are because of what
they've been told
as if the truth is an electricity that will damage them
when we know it is there to power them, empower
them,
plug them in to what the wider world has to offer.

You know that some of them struggle every morning
to rise from the weight of their own thoughts.
You know that some of them have swallowed every
name they've ever been called without being able to
digest them, so that they hardly know who they are
anymore.
You know that some of them can only feel their own
isolation, and none of the joy of the people around
them.

Words are the bridge.
Words are the balm.
Words can take us out of the hands of the people
who believe in closed borders and closed minds.
Words are the open base from which we build.

If they do not have parents and schools that will teach
them that all human beings are created equal,

you give them words to know that all human beings
are created equal.

If they do not have friends and family who will show
them that every life has a context, and every context
has a meaning,
you give them words to show them the context, to
bring out the meaning.

If they do not know who they are, you give them
words to provide the options.

If they do not know how they'll live, you give them
words to demonstrate that they are not alone in this.

You are here for
the sallow boy who remains quiet as his friends make
fun of the free lunch
the headstrong girl who will grow up to be president
or something more important, like an English teacher
the scared boy who never thought he'd be a father
the elevated girl who dreams of catching fireflies
because she read about them in a book that was born
two hundred years before she was.

You are here for
the girl with the mockingjay tattoo
the boy who needs to laugh at Captain Underpants
because there are holes in his own
the girl who learned to speak out from reading about a
girl who spoke
the boy who no longer wants to be phony and the boy
who's caught him in the rye.

You give them words.

By learning the ways other people have told stories,
we learn to tell our own.
By telling our own,
we become free.

Yes, free.

The girls with their reverent dog-eared pages.
The boys who need to keep that book with that title
under their beds.
The girls who don't need God as long as they have
Margaret.
The boys who know what a real monster looks like,
because Walter told them so.

You may know me
I am the boy who walked over to the library every day
after school
as my mom went back to school for her degree.
I am the boy who worked for five dollars an hour in
the high school library
pressing magnetic strips against the spines
making sure the microfilm was in order
and using my employee discounts
to build a library of my own.

I met more gay teens in books than I ever did in high
school.
I traveled so much farther in books than I ever did in
high school.
I understood more about the colorful chaos and the

delicate despair of the world from books than I ever
would have figured out on my own.

I am the boy who never imagined words I use
could make strangers feel less strange and less
estranged.
I am the boy whose kind parents were the kind of
parents
who let him meet as much of the world as he could
find on a page,
because there was nothing on a page
that couldn't be found somewhere in the world, in
some way.

You gave me words.

Which is how I know you are here for:
The child who grows up in a house that values noise
over conversation.
The child who has been taught to disregard science
and reason.
The child who has been given shame instead of pride.
The child who was born into the wrong body and has
been told it can never change.
The child whose beliefs are never believed.

Like them, I thank you.
I thank you in all those moments that feel thankless.
I thank you in all those moments when you feel you
will not win.
I thank you because person by person, word by word
into life after life,
you do win.

You have not chosen this path because it is easy or luxurious.
You have chosen this path because it matters.

It matters to us all.
The loudmouths and the deeply shaken.
The survivors and the ones who need to be prepared for the tragedy that hasn't happened yet.
The marginalized and the ones who need to know what the margins look like, since they cannot see them from the tower.
The rebels and the choir girls and the rebel choir girls.
The heartbroken and the innocently mistaken.
The reluctant and the avid and everyone in between.

We thank you.
Thank you for leading us to the truth.
Thank you for fighting when you need to fight.
Thank you for encouraging when you aren't obligated to encourage.
Thank you for believing in us.
Thank you for believing we matter.
Thank you for this freedom.
And most of all, thank you for giving us words.

Liner Notes

Many of these stories first appeared in other anthologies. I would like to thank all the editors of those books, because it is highly unlikely any of the stories would exist without their interest and guidance.

"Quiz Bowl Antichrist" first appeared in the anthology *Geektastic*, edited by Holly Black and Cecil Castellucci.

"The Good Girls" first appeared, in slightly different form, in the anthology *Girls Who Like Boys Who Like Boys*, edited by Melissa de la Cruz and Tom Dolby.

"The Quarterback and the Cheerleader" first appeared in the tenth-anniversary edition of *Boy Meets Boy*.

"Your Temporary Santa" first appeared in the anthology *My True Love Gave to Me*, edited by Stephanie Perkins.

"A Better Writer" first appeared, in altered form and with a different title, in the anthology *Crush*, edited by Andrea N. Richesin.

"A Brief History of First Kisses" first appeared in the anthology *First Kiss (Then Tell)*, edited by Cylin Busby.

"As the Philadelphia Queer Youth Choir Sings Katy Perry's

'Firework' . . ." first appeared in the anthology *Proud,* compiled by Juno Dawson and edited by Rachel Bodeen.

"The Vulnerable Hours" first appeared in the anthology *Up All Night,* edited by Laura Geringer.

"The Hold" first appeared in the anthology *It's a Whole Spiel,* edited by Katherine Locke and Laura Silverman.

"We" first appeared, in altered form, in the anthology *Hope Nation,* edited by Rose Brock.

"Give Them Words" was written for the Freedom to Read Foundation's forty-fifth anniversary. For more about the Freedom to Read Foundation and all the amazing work it does, go to ftrf.org.

Many of the stories not listed above started as ones I wrote for my friends for Valentine's Day, a tradition that began my junior year of high school and continues to this day, many years after. The friends who've received these stories are far too numerous to mention here, but I thank them all for their friendship and encouragement.

Usually in my books' acknowledgments, I thank the friends who've sat across from me as I wrote them . . . but the stories in here span a decade, so once again it's impossible for me to list everyone. I would, however, like to thank Lawrence Uhling for helping me get all the stories together and Billy Merrell for always being there for me and my stories.

To reiterate the dedication and Track Seventeen—I love and thank my parents very much, for everything.

Thanks as well to everyone at Random House, the Clegg Agency, and my foreign publishers, for all their support. And thanks once again to my longtime editor, Nancy Hinkel. Let the centuries fall where they may; I'm happy to have decades with you.